The Turning Point

ALSO BY MARIE MEYER

Can't Go Back
Across the Distance

The Turning Point

MARIE MEYER

FOREVER
YOURS

New York   Boston

Copyright © 2016 by Marie Meyer
Excerpt from *Across the Distance* copyright © 2015 by Marie Meyer
Cover design by Brian Lemus
Cover copyright © 2016 by Hachette Book Group, Inc.

Forever Yours
Hachette Book Group
1290 Avenue of the Americas
New York, NY 10104

hachettebookgroup.com
twitter.com/foreverromance

First ebook and print on demand edition: January 2016

Forever Yours is an imprint of Grand Central Publishing.
The Forever Yours name and logo are trademarks of Hachette Book Group, Inc.

The publisher is not responsible for websites (or their content) that are not owned by the publisher.

The Hachette Speakers Bureau provides a wide range of authors for speaking events. To find out more, go to www.hachettespeakersbureau.com or call (866) 376-6591.

ISBN 978-1-4555-9098-8

For Tex. Our vacation's all planned!

The Turning Point

Chapter One

I smoothed my fingers over the gold lettering of the college's emblem etched on my diploma cover. Even though it was empty, and my actual diploma would arrive in the mail in a couple of weeks, I reveled in the fact that I was a college graduate. All my hard work and sacrifices had paid off, and in a few short weeks, I'd start med school. Everything I'd planned was falling into place.

Smiling, I looked out the backseat window of Mom's Murano. After the pomp and circumstance of the morning, Mom, Nonna, and I were en route to our favorite restaurant, a little Italian bistro down the street from Mom's gelato shop, ready to celebrate my graduation.

As we traveled down the highway, trees blurred into a wall of green on the side of the road, while Mom and Nonna chatted away in the front seat, caught in a heated discussion over Nonna's newest guilty pleasure television show, *Dating Naked*. Where Nonna thought the show was hysterical, Mom was completely disgusted by the thought of a seventy-one-year-old woman finding it enjoyable.

And the fact that Mom got her panties in a twist over it only made Nonna love it even more. They lived to antagonize one another.

"Andrea, there is nothing wrong with watching fine young men parade around in their birthday suits," Nonna scolded. "Right, Sophia?"

Mom glanced at me in the rearview mirror. "She's got a point, Mom."

"Yeah, if you're Sophia's age." Mom gestured to me in the backseat. "She's supposed to like it."

"Oh, nonsense!" Nonna waved Mom's comment away. "The day I give up admiring the male physique is the day you better call the funeral director, because I'm probably dead."

"Mom!" my mother shouted.

"You're missing out on some tasty television, Andrea." Nonna tsked and shook her head.

"Whatever. Any fun plans tonight, Sophia?" Mom asked, changing the subject. "Parties?"

I thought back to the girl in front of me in the procession line. She'd been on the phone, planning some epic party. I hadn't gotten an invite. And why should I? In the last four years, I'd passed on a social life—friends, clubs, parties, boyfriends, anything that could be considered a distraction. I studied, worked hard, and got into medical school. That had been the plan all along. I had goals, and I was determined not to let anything get in the way.

Yet, as much as I wanted to ignore the small pinch in my chest, I couldn't help remembering when I used to be the girl planning the parties. When my life wasn't just textbooks and late-night study sessions, but soccer games and parties, boys, laughter, and fun.

Then Penley died and my priorities changed.

Losing my cousin, best friend, and teammate to an undetected heart condition my senior year of high school put things into perspective faster than a striker firing on a goalkeeper. Who knew that hypertrophic cardiomyopathy—the leading cause of cardiac death in young athletes—would become an integral part of my lexicon and the reason I planned to dedicate my life to pediatric cardiology. I'd never felt so powerless. I didn't understand. Why hadn't the doctors known her heart was weak? Would she still be alive if we hadn't gone out drinking the night before? One minute we were running down the soccer field together; then the next she wasn't, because her heart quit beating. If I could save just one child from Penley's fate, then her death wouldn't have been in vain. I missed her every single day.

"Nope." I answered Mom's question.

"Aw, Soph," she sighed, sneaking a peek at me in the mirror again.

"It's fine, Mom." I averted my gaze. My partying days were a thing of the past.

"I worry about you," she mumbled. "You work so hard…put so much time and effort into school, planning your future, but at what cost, Sophia?"

Here we go again. Why did she have to do this today? Rain on my parade. Make me think of Penley more than I already was.

"Enough, Andrea," Nonna scolded. "This is Sophia's day. Leave her be."

"It's okay, Nonna." I didn't like when they argued, especially about me. "Mom"—I sat up straight and wiped my sweaty palms on my thighs—"I'm doing what I want. What makes me happy."

Mom forced a smile. "Okay," she agreed with a heavy dose of exasperation. "As long as you're happy." She flipped on the turn signal and merged onto the off-ramp. As the car slowed, she turned left.

"I am. And where are we going? The restaurant is in the other direction." I pointed to the right.

"We need to make a stop first." Mom glanced at Nonna and smiled.

With the look she gave Nonna, I knew they were up to something. "What stop?"

Nonna turned around and smirked in my direction. "Oh, sit back and enjoy the ride, *Principessa*."

Sit back and enjoy the ride? Did they know me at all? I hated surprises. "Tell me what's going on. Please?"

"Chill out, Sophia, we're almost there." Mom turned again, this time into a new car lot.

"Mom?"

"What?" She pulled the car into a parking space near the entrance and killed the engine.

Nonna bounced in her seat, clearly overcome with excitement. "Everybody out!" She pulled the latch on the door and jumped out of the car. At seventy-one, she was quite agile.

I knew full well what was going on. Mom had been hinting about me needing a new car for the better part of a year. "What did you two do?" A smile pulled at the corners of my lips.

"Ladies," a salesman crooned, coming out to meet us. "Everything is ready and waiting. Follow me."

Mom and Nonna giggled like schoolgirls, looping their arms through mine. I shook my head. They had no shame.

We walked to the back of the building and came up right behind the salesman as he stopped.

"Here she is." He sidestepped, bringing his hand up in a sweeping motion, showcasing a sleek, black car bearing a bright red ribbon on top. I'd always thought giant bows were reserved for car commercials, not real life. But here I was staring at one. I gaped.

A key fob dangled from the man's pointer finger. "She's all yours," he said with a toothy grin.

"Well, go on, *Principessa*." Nonna wiggled her bony elbow into my side, forcing me from of my stupor.

"How... You can't," I sputtered. "This is way too much." The car was a brand-new Acura TLX; there was no freaking way either one of them could afford something like this.

"You can't drive that piece of shit clunker on your first day of medical school," Mom added. "You need something befitting a future doctor."

Tentatively, I stepped closer to the car, afraid it would disappear into a cloud of mist if I touched it. The sales guy dropped the key fob into my left hand as I ran a finger over the shiny door latch. It was gorgeous. I loved the elegant, sleek design.

Pulling open the door, I climbed inside. Bombarded by the musky scents of new car and leather, I drew in a deep breath, then exhaled slowly. The black leather interior held the heat of the day, warming the skin on the backs of my legs.

"Mom. Nonna." Gripping the steering wheel, I eyed each of them. "This is..." The car was too much, but seeing the immeasurable amounts of pride and happiness on their faces, I knew this was what they wanted.

"Happy graduation, *Patatina*." Mom's voice wobbled as she latched on to Nonna's arm.

"We're so proud of you, Soph," Nonna added.

I exited the car, my arms opened wide. "Thank you." I wrapped them in a hug, squeezing as tightly as I could. I loved them so much. Things hadn't been easy after Dad walked out on us, but Mom and Nonna were two of the strongest women I knew. I could only hope to be like them one day.

"As much as I love this mushy stuff, we've got reservations at Charlie's." Nonna patted my back, a cue to let go. "And I'm famished."

Taking a step back, Mom quickly swiped at her eyes. Like me, she wasn't a crier, and if I called her on it, she'd deny it, saying her contacts were giving her fits.

"I'm riding with Soph," Nonna announced, clapping Mom on the back.

Mom gave Nonna a sidelong glance. "I kind of figured."

"It's been a pleasure doing business with you, sir." Nonna shook the salesman's hand and skipped—yes, literally skipped—around to the passenger side door.

"Nice doing business with you, ladies. Enjoy."

"Thank you," I said, climbing behind the wheel.

Mom started toward the front of the building, calling over her shoulder, "I'll see you guys at the restaurant."

"Well, start her up," Nonna instructed.

With a huge smile on my face, I pushed the button to start the engine, and my brand-new car purred to life. "Thank you, Nonna." I stared at the white-haired woman next to me.

"Anything for my *principessa*." She patted her arthritic hand on my knee. "Now, let's go. I'm hungry."

"Yes, ma'am." I grinned, shifting into reverse. Looking over my shoulder, I eased my new car from the parking space just as I remembered the giant ribbon on the roof. "Oh"—my foot came down on the brake, the car jolting to a halt—"the ribbon." I shifted my gaze upward where the shiny material was threaded through the interior.

"What about it?"

I raised an eyebrow, giving Nonna a dubious stare. "I can't drive down the street with it on the roof." I reached up, my fingers settling on the Velcro holding the ends together.

"Don't you dare," Nonna said, her hand covering mine. "You leave that ribbon up there. This is your day, *Principessa*. You get to flaunt the hell out of it."

"Nonna!" I lowered my hands and laughed.

"I mean it. My granddaughter is a big deal and everyone needs to know this."

I shook my head. "I love you, Nonna."

"I love you, too. Now, can we go eat, please?"

"Yes." I smiled, easing off the brake.

Pulling out of the parking lot, we headed north, toward Charlie's, with a big-ass red ribbon atop my car and Mom following behind.

* * *

"When does your med school summer session begin?" Mom asked, finishing her stuffed shells.

"In a few weeks. I thought I'd help out at the shop until then."

Mom smiled, yet it didn't touch her eyes. "That'd be great, Soph, but wouldn't you rather do something fun with your few weeks of freedom? I remember being twenty-two; the gelato shop was the last place I wanted to be."

I picked the last toasted ravioli from my plate and took a bite.

Chewing slowly, I did my best to avoid my mother's pitiful stare. I knew where she was coming from. Being proud Italian Americans, Mom and her brother—my uncle David—took over the gelato shop when Pappous passed away. Nonna didn't want to sell, so Mom and Uncle David inherited the business. I always wondered what Mom would have rather done with her life if she hadn't been forced to take over the business. Her life hadn't gone the way she'd planned or hoped, that was for sure.

"How about dessert?" Nonna asked enthusiastically. "This is a special day—we need to sweeten up this conversation. Far too depressing for my delicate ears." Nonna frowned and pressed her hands to her ears.

"Anything but ice cream." Mom cringed.

Nonna nodded. "Deal. Tiramisu?"

"Yes, please," I sighed. I loved Nonna dearly; she *always* had my back. I knew Mom meant well; she didn't want me to look back on my life and regret the choices I'd made. She just had a difficult time understanding that my choices were what I wanted.

After we finished our dinners, the waiter brought three plates of tiramisu. No matter how much we loved each other, dessert was the one thing we refused to share.

With a forkful of liquor-drenched ladyfingers at the ready, Mom spoke before she took her bite. "Your dad called again." She stuck the fork in her mouth, awaiting my response.

Why? Why wouldn't he leave me alone? I had no desire to call him back. NONE. With the exception of a prompt check each month and birthday and Christmas gifts each year—which conveniently happened on the same day—I hadn't seen him since he left when I was seven. Why was he calling now?

"You should call him, Soph. See what he wants."

"Why? As far as I'm concerned, I don't have a dad." I swirled my fork in the glob of whipped cream on my plate.

"I know, Soph. But it's the sixth time he's called in two weeks. Whatever it is, it must be important for him to call so much."

"Nope. No thanks. Not going to happen." I scooped a large bite of custard and shoved it into my mouth. Nothing cured that sinking feeling in the pit of my stomach like food.

Mom sighed. "It's up to you. But I have a feeling he's not going to give up."

I put my hand in front of my mouth and mumbled around the food there, "You talk to him, then."

"I've tried. He won't."

"You know, if you talk to him this time, see what he wants, maybe you won't have to interact with him any longer," Nonna piped up.

I shook my head. "He left us. He walked out and never came back. He doesn't have the right to demand my time and attention."

Mom's features softened. She understood how much it hurt me when my dad left. I was a daddy's girl. Some of my earliest memories were centered around my dad. I remembered getting all dressed up for the Girl Scouts Daddy–Daughter Date Night when I was seven years old, just a couple months before he walked out on me.

Dad wore a dark suit and looked so handsome with his black hair slicked back. He gave me a wrist corsage with pink and purple carnations that matched the color of my dress. Mom put a little makeup on my cheeks and lips, curled my hair, and sprayed some of her expensive perfume on my wrists. I felt like a princess.

The whole evening, Dad danced with me. I'd stood on his toes and looked up at his face and smiled. He beamed. His eyes were shiny, his hands firm, holding on to me for dear life as he whirled me around the elementary school's gym floor.

Or at least that's what I remembered. My seven-year-old brain had no idea that he'd planned on leaving me. When he left, I was devastated. I'd called him countless times during the day, every day. He never called back. He never visited.

Just two gifts a year and a sizeable child-support check once a month, that's what I got. Not what I wanted…or needed.

I wanted my daddy. The guy who taught me to dance.

Tears stung my eyes. It still irked me that after all this time he could still reduce me to tears. I hated him. I swiped at my eyes and stared at my empty plate. I didn't remember finishing my dessert, and I wanted more. Emotional eating, it was the best.

"I'll talk to him. See if I can't get him to tell me what he wants." Mom reached for my hand and squeezed.

"Thanks," I muttered.

"But, honey, just so you know, I saw him at graduation this morning."

Ice ran through my veins. "What?"

"Yeah. He came."

"How did he know?"

The skin around Mom's eyes crinkled slightly as she narrowed her lids. She sucked in a breath. "I may have let your graduation date slip."

I shook my head. "Why would you do that? He had no right to be there." Dammit. All the joy and excitement of this morning had been sucked out of me. I felt shriveled and empty, dried up. *Thanks, Dad, for ruining my graduation day, too.*

"Honey," Mom cooed.

"No, Mom. This is ridiculous. Why are you always giving in to him after what he did? I've never understood why you weren't angry with him."

"Soph, life's too short to hold grudges. I need to do what makes me happy. Harboring all that anger and animosity was just too tiring. I'm not that kind of person."

Well, I was. I had no intention of ever forgiving that man. "Whatever." I dropped my fork onto my plate, wishing I had another piece of tiramisu.

"So." Nonna's spirited voice brought Mom and I back to the present. "What's on the docket for tonight? It's your graduation day; we need to do something."

I admired Nonna for trying to redeem my special day, but the damage had been done. All I wanted to do was crawl into bed and hide under the blanket. No, scratch that. I wanted to do something crazy, irresponsible, and dangerous.

Live life like I used to.

I was sick and tired of my daddy issues clouding the sunny moments in my life. A small part of me wished that girl had invited me to her party. Maybe getting drunk would erase the pain and hurt I felt as a result of my dad's choices.

That man may have helped give me life, but I refused to let him steal it away from me.

Chapter Two

Life carried on as usual. Helping Mom at the shop didn't require the use of my degree in biochemistry and molecular biophysics, but serving up scoops of gelato was exhausting in its own right. My feet hurt from standing all day and my hands were chapped from frequent washings and the freezer. I'd forgotten how hard Mom worked to keep my grandfather's dream alive. All I wanted to do was curl up in bed and fall into a steamy romance novel.

Pulling into the driveway, I waited for the garage door to open, then guided my new car into my space next to Mom's. I killed the engine, grabbed my purse off the passenger seat, and climbed out of the car.

Shuffling to the door, I went inside. The heavy scent of freshly brewed coffee lingered in the kitchen, and Mom was sitting at the kitchen table, sipping something from a coffee mug. "Hey, Mom, you're up late." I tossed my keys into the catchall dish on the counter.

"How were things at the shop?" She set her mug down on the table.

"Fine. Pretty steady all day. Had a late group come in." I walked toward the table and rubbed her shoulders. "What's with the coffee? Pulling an all-nighter?" Usually she abandoned caffeinated beverages before five, claiming they interfered with her much needed beauty rest.

Mom put her hand on top of mine and stared up at me. The look on her face scared me. No smile, no comforting reassurances. Immediately, my mind went to Nonna. Something was wrong with Nonna. I felt sick.

Nonna had been in and out of the hospital over the last year. Her balance wasn't good; she fell a lot. Couple that with the heavy dose of blood thinners she took and she'd bleed out in record time.

"Mom, what is it?"

She pulled on my hand. "Sit down, hon."

I walked around her chair and sat down beside her. "Please tell me it isn't Nonna."

"Oh no, Nonna's fine." Mom patted my knee.

Tension fell off me in waves. I felt lighter. Slumping back in the chair, I blew out a breath. As long as Nonna was fine, I could handle whatever was bothering Mom.

"Dad called again."

Dammit. "I thought you told him I wasn't interested in hearing what he has to say."

"I know you don't want to hear this, but you need to talk to him."

I shook my head. "No. I'm done with this conversation." I went to stand, but Mom forced me to stay seated, clamping her hand down on my leg.

Even at twenty-two, I felt like I was four years old again when under my mother's stern glare. "Sophia, he's not going to stop calling until you talk to him. It's important."

What the hell? Hurt and anger pooled in my stomach like acid and burned its way from my core and into my esophagus. Sufficiently riled up now, I couldn't keep my hands from joining in on the conversation, flailing them wildly. "Nothing that man has to say to me could be important."

Mom gave me a pointed stare. "Go. Hear him out, then make the decision to never see him again." She leaned forward and put her hand on my cheek. "Baby, you need to do this."

"Why—"

She shook her head. "No, let me finish." Dropping her hand to my lap, she latched on to my fingers. "I worry about you, sweetie. Trust me, once I made peace with Dad leaving, once I forgave him, I was freed. Your hatred of him scares me. I'm scared for you. I want you to have peace. This anger you carry around, it'll never allow you to have room to love life or, God forbid, love someone else."

Mom's words made me ache. "I can't."

"Talk to him, baby. Please?" Mom's voice was tainted with desperation.

Emotions boiled at the surface; I was ready to burst. I didn't know if I wanted to cry, scream, or run away and hide. How was I supposed to put fifteen years of no contact behind me and pretend everything was fine? "It's not just that I don't want to, Mom. I don't know if I can."

Mom nodded. "I get it. I felt the same way. For years, I made it my personal mission to convince myself I hated your father. But you know why I couldn't?"

"Uh-uh."

Mom sat back in her chair. "I was tired and it hurt too much. Hatred is a heavy, ugly thing, and it will only drag you down. I had to change for me." She patted her chest, right over her heart. "Do it for you, Soph. You'll feel so much better."

I shook my head. With a defeated sigh, I muttered, "Fine." Neither of them was going to let this go until I caved. I hated when life didn't go the way I'd planned, and talking to my dad was most certainly not in my plan, ever.

Mom stood up and came to stand behind me. She wrapped her arms around my shoulders and propped her chin atop my head. "Thank you," she whispered.

I stood, forcing Mom to release her hold on me. "I'm going to bed." I didn't return her affections, and I could see the sadness in the slump of her shoulders.

"Night, Soph," she said in that brave mom voice that made my stomach churn with guilt. I wasn't mad at her, but since she was here, she was the one who got to feel my pain.

I left the kitchen, walking through the living room on my way down the hall to my bedroom. Closing myself inside, I went to my dresser and opened my laptop. Once I logged in, Spotify launched immediately. I clicked on Ed Sheeran's latest album and let his soulful music fill the void.

I flopped onto my bed and threw my arm over my eyes, listening to Ed's words. His voice soothed over me, extinguishing some of the fire in my veins, but I was surprised to hear some of Mom's sentiments reflected in the song's lyrics.

Now Ed and Mom were ganging up on me.

Sure, I loved Mom and Nonna, but they were all I needed. Dad and Penley showed me a side of love that I wanted no part of. It hurt too much. I'd live behind my carefully constructed wall and find solace in the clinical, textbook world of science and medicine, knowing my heart was safest there.

* * *

Lying awake all night did not make getting up any easier. Usually, I was a morning person, ready to accomplish my tasks for the day. Not today. I wondered if Mom magically forgot our conversation from last night. That thought sent a rush of hope through me.

Untangling my legs from the blanket, I kicked them off and crawled out of bed. My bedside clock read 5:30 a.m. Despite the hour, someone was banging around in the kitchen. Probably Nonna. She was an early riser like me. Not Mom, though. She'd sleep until noon if she could get away with it.

Pulling open my bedroom door, a loud crash carried down the hall, and I flinched. With a slight jog, I ran toward the kitchen to check on whoever was in there. When I rounded the corner, Nonna was crouched on the floor, shoving a dozen pots and pans back into the cabinet. For a moment, I paused. There was something so serene about Nonna, angelic.

Her long white hair was piled high on her head in a messy bun. I'd never had the privilege of seeing Nonna when her hair was dark like mine, but Mom always told me I was the spitting image of a younger Nonna. I loved her so much. I could only hope to be as beautiful as her when I reached my seventies.

"Nonna, what are you doing?" I scolded lovingly, shuffling into the kitchen. I knelt down beside her, helping her with the rest of the mess.

"You're up early." She pushed a frying pan into the cabinet.

"Couldn't sleep. Here, let me do this." I lifted the saucepan from her fingers and put it back in its place before I took her hands and helped her stand.

I crouched back down, holding my weight on the balls of my feet. Shoving the last few skillets into the cabinet, I slammed the door closed and stood.

Nonna leaned against the counter, staring at me. "I need a skillet." She flashed a quick smile and waited.

I cocked my head, giving her a sidelong glance. Bending back down, I pulled out one of the skillets I'd haphazardly shoved inside. "Here." I held it up to her.

"Thanks, sweetie." Nonna grasped the pan's handle and stepped over to the stove. "Eggs?"

I was hungry but also feeling a little nauseous at the prospect of my day's plans. "Sure." I'd force something down. Maybe if I threw up, I'd get out of calling that man.

Nonna prepped the skillet for her world-famous "dunkin' eggs." Well, maybe not *world famous*, but she made over-easy eggs better than anyone, so in my book, they were famous.

While Nonna busied herself at the stove, I went to work on the coffee and toast. Mindlessly, I filled the Keurig's water tank and loaded a coffee pod. I stuck my cup under the spout and pressed the large cup button. The machine whirred to life and filled the kitchen with the strong scent of arabica beans, easily masking the smell of fried eggs.

"I'll take one of those, too," Nonna said, flipping an egg in the pan.

I pulled my coffee cup free and started the second one without comment. While the spout shot out dark black coffee, I put my back to the counter, crossed my arms, and waited. My eyes slid closed. I absorbed the comforting sound of the Keurig, along with the pleasant aroma the kitchen was bathed in.

"You're quiet this morning," Nonna said, breaking through my attempt at finding Zen in the white noise of the coffee machine.

My eyelids pulled open and Nonna stood before me, a plate of pristine dunkin' eggs held out for the taking.

I shook my head, trying to clear away the fog. "Sorry, I zoned out for a minute." I reached for the plate. "Thanks."

"Want to talk about what's eating you?" Nonna grabbed another plate and shoveled the spatula into the pan, serving up a round egg for herself.

"Where's Mom?" I asked, sitting down at the table.

Nonna shrugged. "Getting ready for work?" She joined me at the table, reaching for the saltshaker.

As I poured a copious amount of creamer into my coffee cup, I watched Nonna coat her eggs in a generous layer of salt. "Want some eggs with your salt?"

"Want some coffee with your creamer?" she countered, gesturing to my heavy hand as well. Then she flashed me a quick smile and continued salting. "I fully intend to enjoy my golden years."

I took a bite of eggs and washed them down with my coffee-flavored cream. "Do you know what too much of that stuff does to your blood pressure?"

"Don't you go all doctor on me, missy." Nonna pointed her fork in my direction. "I may be proud as hell of you, but that college degree of yours is not going to stand between me and my food."

I saluted her with my fork. "Yes, ma'am." With Nonna, you had to know what battles to pick. I was not about to stand in front of a proud Italian woman and her food.

For a few quiet bites, Nonna and I enjoyed our breakfast. Then she put her fork down and gave me a questioning look. "Did you make toast?"

"Oh, goodness! I forgot!" I dropped my fork. It clattered onto the plate, and I slid my chair back on the linoleum, screeching loudly.

"Soph, sit down. It's okay. I'm nearly finished anyway." She waved me to sit.

I plopped back into my chair and scooted toward the table. "Sorry, Nonna." The talk with Mom last night had me off my game. It wasn't like me to forget.

"Don't worry about." Nonna patted my arm. "Nothing to get your panties in a twist about." She smiled widely.

Nonna was beautiful. Her thick, long silver-white hair curled gently at the ends just enough to make the prettiest of women jealous, despite their age. It framed her heart-shaped face perfectly, giving depth to her olive complexion. But of Nonna's features, it was her eyes that spoke the loudest (which was amazing, because Nonna was loud by nature). Her emerald eyes held so many stories.

Pushing away from the table, Nonna grabbed my empty plate along with hers. "What's eating you, *Principessa*?" She walked our plates to the sink, rinsed them off, and added them to the dirty lot in the dishwasher.

I watched, unable to do much else. A sick feeling pooled low in my belly like it had right before I took the MCAT. The only difference was that I *wanted* to take the MCAT. I didn't want to see my dad.

Ugh. I hate this.

"My dad keeps calling. Mom wants me to go see him."

Nonna shut the dishwasher and turned around. "Hmm."

Hmm? That's all the sage wisdom she could come up with?

"Can I show you something?" Nonna asked finally.

"What?"

She started toward the living room, calling over her shoulder, "You coming?"

Feeling like my veins pumped lead instead of blood, I sluggishly got to my feet and trailed in her wake. Down the hall, Nonna turned left, into her bedroom. I followed right behind and saw her standing on her tiptoes in front of the closet.

"Nonna, what are you doing?"

She craned her neck to look over her shoulder. "Don't just stand there—get over here and help me."

Nonna's neatly made bed took up most of her small room. I skirted around it, running my fingers over the sateen burgundy bedspread. Standing shoulder to shoulder with Nonna, I reached up and helped her pull down the spiral-bound notebook she was fingering. Of course, the one she wanted had to be at the bottom of a large stack of other, larger notebooks.

"Just hold the top ones back while…uhh…," she grunted. "While I yank."

Her small fingers hooked inside each end of the wire spiral. Not much taller than Nonna, I had to stand on my tiptoes, too. I put both my palms against the teetering stack, keeping them still while Nonna pulled the one she wanted free.

"Almost…got…it…," she groaned. "Uhh." She blew out a breath and dropped back to the flats of her feet with the notebook in hand. "Got it."

I gave the disheveled notebook tower a shove to realign it and took a step backward. "Whatever it is you want to show me, it must be good."

Nonna patted the bed, beckoning me to sit beside her. "I haven't looked at these for the better part of twenty years."

With her knobby, arthritic fingers, she flipped the cover over, revealing yellowing paper marked with black lines. "What's that?" I asked, inching my butt closer to her. I stared at the paper…the sketches.

"Back in the day I used to be a pretty decent artist. Before this, of course." She held out her hand. "Damn arthritis."

"May I see?" I touched the side of the sketchbook and she passed it in my direction.

On the page before me was a beautifully rendered charcoal sketch of my mother, a much younger version. I wanted to touch the lines that made up her face but feared I'd mar them, so I refrained. I admired with only my eyes. "Nonna, this is exquisite." I looked up and met her eyes.

"Your mamma was one of my favorite subjects, but not my ultimate favorite." She rested her hand on mine, gently brushing my fingers away from the side of the notebook. "Let me show you."

With the book still perched on my lap, she paged through a few other drawings, mostly still-life sketches of flowers, until she stopped at an illustration of my mom and dad cradling a swaddled baby.

Nonna touched the delicate lines of the infant. "This one's my favorite."

My eyes traced the precise delineations that intertwined to create a masterpiece of my once-intact family. "I never knew you drew." I was in awe of my grandmother's talent. I glanced up from the portrait. "How did I not know this?"

"I gave it up a long time ago, *Principessa*." Nonna looked lovingly upon her creation. With a shaky hand, she touched the paper again. "Did your mom ever tell you about the day you were born?" Lifting her verdant eyes to me, she awaited my answer.

I shook my head. "Uh-uh. Mom doesn't talk much about when Dad was around."

"You're right. Your mamma has a tough skin, but that doesn't mean there aren't deep scars. Let me tell you what I know."

"The day you decided to make your appearance, you were two days late." She winked. "It seems like you've spent your whole life trying to make up for the two days you lost."

I shrugged my shoulder and nodded. "I could have used those forty-eight hours." My lips curved up at the corners and Nonna pressed her hand over mine and squeezed.

"Your mamma and daddy were so excited. When labor finally started, Andrea called me, flustered out of her mind. I told her to take a deep breath and get her butt to the hospital." Nonna chuckled at the memory. "When I walked into the hospital room, your dad was right at your mom's side. I'll never forget it." Nonna smiled thoughtfully. "He had his forehead pressed to her temple, whispering assurances into her ear, helping her through a contraction. When it was over, he swept his hand across her forehead and tucked a sweaty piece of hair behind her ear."

Nonna's features were soft as she recounted her story, her eyes focused on something that happened twenty-two years ago.

"I'd always liked your dad." Nonna looked me in the eyes. No, more like pierced me with emerald daggers. "But it was in that moment I knew how much Gio loved my Andrea…and you. I could see it in his eyes. I could feel it pouring out of him. It warmed the room."

At first, there was a pinch in my chest as Nonna spoke of my dad. But hearing how much he loved Mom…and me, the pinch intensified. It felt more like a screwdriver being wedged between my ribs. If he loved us half as much as Nonna said he did, why wasn't he still here?

I loved Nonna, but she watched too many soap operas, read too many romance novels, and subsequently turned my birth into both. I didn't interrupt, but I may have rolled my eyes at her last comment.

"Yeah, you roll those eyes, girlie. I speak only the truth. You were being a stubborn little thing and refused to come out. Put your mamma through her paces."

"Mmm-hmm." I nodded. "Sounds like me."

"Every time your mamma pushed, your heart rate would drop. Scared everyone to death. That's when they prepped Andrea for surgery, an emergency C-section. I thought your daddy was going to have a heart attack, he was so worried."

"Nonna, does this story have a point?" Since when had she turned into the leader of the Giovanni Belmonte fan club?

She waved her hand. A trait I'd gotten from her, talking with my hands. "It does, and I'll get there. Anyway, when you were born, there were more complications. You weren't breathing on your own."

The screwdriver burrowed deeper, twisting on its way in. "Mom never told me that."

"Ah, well, it's all water under the bridge now, *Principessa*. You've been breathing just fine for quite some time." Nonna gave a thin-lipped smile and continued. "They had to send you to a hospital that was equipped with a neonatal facility. Your mamma couldn't go, so your daddy went with you."

I felt the onset of tears, but I held my breath, keeping them at bay. I was *not* going to cry.

"Even before your mamma got to hold you, you had already bonded with your daddy. About two weeks after you were born, you were finally well enough to come home. That was the day I drew this." She tapped the notebook on my lap. "Andrea and Gio were on the couch and you were bundled tightly in the blanket my mom hand knitted for you. Gio brought you to his face and just cooed." Nonna's voice rose as she relived the memory. Her eyes sparkled like lit Christmas trees, her smile shining through. "That picture is seared into my brain. I could develop dementia and still remember that scene."

"Nonna, you shouldn't joke like that." Sometimes she had no tact.

"Oh, nonsense." She flailed her hand again. "That night, I went to my room and drew this portrait from memory. He loves you, Sophia. You should talk to him." Nonna wrapped her arm around my shoulder and drew me to her side.

"This drawing is lovely, Nonna. But, sadly, my last memory of *him*"—I spat the word—"is him leaving. I have no desire to speak to him."

"I have no desire to see the gynecologist, dear, but that doesn't mean I shouldn't."

I rolled my eyes again. "Nonna," I groaned.

"You can do what you want; you're a big girl. But my two cents, go see him and then you can be done with him." She nodded once, took the notebook from my lap, and slapped it closed. "Want to use my phone?" she offered.

I shook my head. "No, I'll use mine."

She winked at me. "Good, because I just remembered I need to make an appointment at the gynecologist."

"Nonna!" I screeched. I got up from the bed and went to the door, ready to leave before she divulged any other medical information. I may be going to med school, but I did not need to know anything else about my grandmother's yearly exam.

"See, now we both have to make uncomfortable appointments. Misery loves company, *Principessa*."

"I have one word for you, Nonna: HIPA. Just remember HIPA."

She waved me off. "Oh, you and your fancy medical words."

I smiled and turned on my heel, walking out of her room. I admired her ability to lay the guilt on thick, her sketch giving me the courage I needed to make a very difficult phone call.

Chapter Three

If I'd thought talking to my dad on the phone was hard, getting my butt out the door to drive to his place was nearly impossible. All morning I procrastinated like it was an Olympic sport, which was totally not like me. But today, it was my favorite pastime.

Any little thing I could find to take up time, I did. Instead of a quick shower, I opted for an hour-long bath, taking my time to read the latest romance novel I'd downloaded. The blazing hot water did wonders for my nerves and the steamy romance transported me to a fantasy world that was much more pleasurable than reality.

By the time I was a shriveled prune and nearly halfway through my book, I finished up my bath, taking extra care in washing and conditioning my hair. I was a shoo-in for the procrastination gold medal.

As I brushed the tangles out of my long, dark hair, there was a knock on the door. "Soph, you about finished in there? I've got to get to the shop."

"Yeah, Mom." I pulled the door open. "Sorry."

She checked her watch. "What time are you meeting your dad?"

I shrugged, playing dumb. "Don't remember." Innocently, I went about brushing my already tangle-free hair.

Mom cocked her head and put both hands on her hips. Over the years, she'd gotten really good at that "Mom" glare. "Soph?"

Inwardly, I cringed as she held the "o" in my name a little longer than was necessary, and then her voice did that weird pitch change thing at the end, getting higher before she pinched off the "f" sound. I was six years old again. Moms wielded some magical power in their voices that made their grown children feel three feet tall and mildly ashamed.

Wide eyed, I answered as I bent over to fish the blow-dryer from the cabinet below the basin. "What?"

"I know what you're doing. Just get it over with."

I stood back up, plugged in the dryer, and flipped it on high. "What?" I said again, louder.

Staring at Mom's reflection in the mirror, she shook her head, lips moving.

"I can't hear you," I shouted. This time I really couldn't.

Mom put her hand on the dryer and forced me to lower it. Next to my ear, she said loudly, "I need to brush my teeth."

"Oh, right." I stepped to the side, closer to the bathtub, so she could do her business at the sink.

"Thank you," she mouthed.

I smiled and continued working the hot air from the blow-dryer across my head. For once, I was thankful for my thick hair and its unwillingness to dry quickly.

Mom spat into the sink, met my eyes in the mirror, and said, "Hurry it up, Sophia. Don't make him wait all day."

I pretended to ignore her. Who cared if I made him wait all damn day? As she left the bathroom, I gave her a tiny smile and a nod, still running the noisy dryer.

* * *

Yep, I definitely won the gold medal. By the time I pulled out of the garage, it had taken me four hours to get ready. That was a new record by far. But now was the moment of truth.

I pulled up to the front of Gio Belmonte's palatial home, a mansion compared to the shotgun-style house I'd grown up in.

I killed the engine and let my head rest against the back of the seat. "Come on, Sophia, you can do this." I hadn't seen my dad in fifteen years, and it was by the grace of God that I'd never run into him considering we lived a town apart. I doubted I'd even recognize him if I did run into him. My only memories were that of a seven-year-old child. Surely he looked different…older.

Sitting up straight, I stared out the passenger side window. The orange tile shingles appeared to shimmer in the steamy afternoon sun. The lawn was well kept, along with the two nicely trimmed bushes in front of each window.

God, I don't want to do this. I knew I sounded like a petulant toddler, but I couldn't help it. I'd made my peace with him being gone. Why did he have to open old wounds? He'd made a clean break. Why come back now?

Only one way to find out, Soph. Mom's voice sounded louder in my head than my whiny one.

"You're twenty-two freaking years old, Sophia. Act like a damn grown woman and get in there," I mumbled, pulling the latch on the door. I put one heeled shoe on the ground and got out of the car. With my purse in hand, I smoothed out the black pencil skirt and black and white striped shirt I wore and stepped around the car and up the brick-paved walkway.

I pushed the doorbell and listened to the chime play "Für Elise." A moment later the door peeled back and an attractive brunette smiled back at me. Her dark blue eyes were kind.

"Sophia?" she asked.

I nodded, clearing my throat. "Yes."

"I'm so glad to meet you. Your dad talks about you often. I'm Lydia."

Does he, now? I wonder what it is he has to say, considering he knows NOTHING about me. And who was this woman? Lydia? Mom never said anything about another woman.

"Thank you." Despite all the negative comments running through my head, I managed to find an untapped well of polite words still lingering deep inside me. I smiled, hoping it looked sincere, because it certainly didn't feel that way.

"Come in." The woman pulled the door open wider and stepped to the side, allowing me access to the gorgeous foyer.

The floor of the entryway was composed of small pieces of mosaic glass tiles. Each tile fit together to create a beautiful yellow sun outlined with deep ocean blues. My admiration of the floor wasn't lost on Lydia, who was closing the door behind me.

"It's stunning, isn't it?" she said adoringly.

I brought my eyes up and nodded. "I've never seen anything like it."

"This house has a rich history. Your father would love to tell you about it, I'm sure." She walked a few steps past me and motioned with her arm. "He's waiting for you in the library."

I followed her down the hall, taking in the abstract artwork adorning the walls as I went. "This place has a library?" My voice echoed down the marble hallway.

It was official. Gio Belmonte was *not* the guy I remembered. That guy had been a figment of a child's overactive imagination. My dad still lived in our tiny shotgun house, drank a beer at dinner, and stole kisses from my mom when he thought I wasn't looking.

"Right this way." Lydia stopped at the entrance of what I assumed was the library. Like Vanna White, she showcased the doorway with a flourish of her arms and hands.

I stepped up to the door and peered inside, suddenly very nervous to see him. "Thanks."

"I'll leave you two alone."

No sooner had I turned around to beg her to stay than she retreated down the hall. Her dark hair bounced with each click of her heels on the white and black checkered tile floor as she disappeared around the corner.

I wrinkled my nose and gave a silent growl, balling my hands into fists at my sides.

"Sophia?" A distant, deep male voice called from the other room. "Come on in." The voice came closer.

I took a deep breath and put one foot in front of the other, crossing the threshold. The checkered floor carried from the hall into the room. Instead of walls there were bookcases stretching from floor to ceiling. As a bibliophile, I'd died and gone to heaven. I could spend hours in this room soaking in all the titles that lined the shelves. My eyes roamed to the ceiling as I stepped backward, taking in the stacks. *Wow*.

"Sophia." That voice brought my admiration of the library to an end, like a needle scratching across a vinyl record. I wasn't a bibliophile here to admire books; I was an abandoned daughter. And this wasn't heaven; it was hell. Who knew the two places could simultaneously take up the same space.

My eyes followed the sound of his voice until I saw a man in an electric wheelchair coming toward me. *A wheelchair? When did that happen?*

"Sophia, thank you for coming," he said, smiling broadly.

It had been years since I'd seen him, and he looked nothing like the man I remembered. He was a stranger. But even more off-putting was that I looked like him. I had Mom's eyes, but there was no denying that I was Gio's daughter. The shape of his face, the slant of his nose, we even had the same plump cheeks when we smiled.

"Can I get you anything?" he asked. It was in that moment that I realized I had yet to speak.

"Um…uh…" Apparently I'd forgotten how to speak. "No." I shook my head. "No, thank you."

"Come, sit down." He motioned toward the sofa in the middle of the room with his head. Pressing the button on the arm of his wheelchair, he moved in that direction, too.

I followed, albeit completely ill at ease with the whole situation.

He parked his chair at the end of the sofa and patted the cushion, an invitation for me to sit.

Reluctantly, I accepted, though opting for the middle cushion. I needed space.

"How are you, Soph?" he asked, folding his hands in his lap.

"It's Sophia," I corrected. *Soph* was what Mom and Nonna called me. It was too intimate. He didn't get to call me that.

He nodded. "Sophia."

For a moment, we both sat quietly. As much fun as it was listening to the both of us breathing, this was not how I planned to spend a Wednesday afternoon. I could be helping Mom at the shop or studying for school, which began in a week and a half. Geez, getting a root canal would have been more preferable.

"Mom said it was imperative that you speak with me?" I wasn't here for small talk, so he'd better get to the point.

"Right." He cleared his throat. "I did need to speak with you. For a couple of reasons. I'm sure you're busy, so I'll be brief."

"Thank you." It was about time he cut the crap and stopped pretending we were best buds.

"I wanted to tell you how proud I am of you. I was glad your mom told me about graduation."

I sat, emotionless. If he was waiting for me to thank him for making time for me, he was going to be waiting a long time.

Rubbing his palms against the tops of his thighs, he sighed. "Anyway…"

Was he uncomfortable, too? Hmm…

He lifted his right hand and grabbed a large manila envelope from the little table beside him. "I got you something. A graduation present." He held the paper out to me.

I shook my head. I didn't want his gifts.

"Sophia, please take it. I want to do this for you." He stretched his arm closer.

Slowly, I reached for the envelope, half expecting it to bite my fingers off. Once it was within my grasp, I laid it in my lap, not bothering to look inside; it was going in the trash the minute I got home.

Gio's eyes fell to my lap for a moment before he brought them back to my face. The smile was gone from his eyes this time. I think he was finally catching on to the fact that I wasn't going to accept his gift. He pressed his lips into a thin smile. "It's a trip to Italy," he said nonchalantly.

I looked at the unassuming package. A trip to Italy? Who gives a complete stranger a trip to Italy?

"My parents never moved to the States. It wasn't until college that I moved here. We have a lot of family heritage over there, Sophia. I wanted to give you the opportunity to get to know that part of you. I also thought it'd be nice if you met your *nonno*. He's never left Battipaglia. He grew up there, as did I."

"Is your mother still there?" I asked. He hadn't mentioned her.

His shoulders slumped, and I noticed his hands twitching slightly in his lap. Parkinson's disease maybe? My mind flipped through different neurological and muscular disorders that caused muscle spasms.

"She passed away several years ago. I wish she'd had the chance to meet you. She would have loved you."

Yeah, hindsight is twenty-twenty, isn't it? But I kept my snarky bitterness to myself. I didn't need to be hateful at the expense of my dead grandmother. "I'm sorry."

"That's actually the other thing I wanted to talk to you about."

"My grandmother?" I asked, confused.

"She's part of it. Did your mother ever mention why I left?" His black eyes bore into me.

I shook my head. "Mom doesn't talk about you."

"Nor should she." His expression was somber. "I'm not making excuses for my actions, Sophia, but there was a reason why I left you and your mother."

"And it has to do with my grandmother? What? She didn't approve of you having a family, so you left?" I realized I was raising my voice, but I couldn't help it. I didn't want to hear his reasons. In my opinion, there wasn't a reason good enough to warrant abandoning your wife and young daughter…a daughter who thought the world of her dad, no less.

Gio raised his hand. "No, no, it was nothing like that. Even though your grandparents never had the chance to meet you, they were very proud."

Years of hurt and anger pooled in my veins. It took every ounce of self-restraint I had not to get up and leave his cold, impersonal mansion. I glanced at my watch, wanting him to just say what he needed, because this was turning into a colossal waste of time.

Looking at Gio again, I noticed his gaze drop to my wrist, too. "I'm sure you're busy." All the softness and warmth in his tone disappeared. I guessed he realized that I wasn't interested in a stroll down memory lane or a chance at rekindling a daddy/daughter relationship.

"I'm dying," he said matter-of-factly. "I have the same illness that my mother passed away from."

"I'm sorry to hear that." And I was. No matter how much I disliked the man—no, I hated him—I didn't wish illness or an untimely death upon him.

"There's no easy way to say this, Sophia, but what I have is genetic."

Genetic? What was he saying? My mind cataloged all the genetic disorders I'd studied over the last four years of school. "And what is it? What's your diagnosis?"

He took a deep breath and exhaled the words. "I have Huntington's disease."

Like the roar of a train barreling straight at a car stuck on the tracks, my dad's words hit me with the same amount of force. His words reverberated in my head like the sound of metal on metal. Sparks flew and incinerated any hope I had of becoming a doctor. The moment Huntington's was out of his mouth, I was already reciting symptoms.

A genetic dominant disorder that gradually kills nerve cells in the brain. Individuals with Huntington's experienced loss of coordination, uncontrolled muscle spasms, declined cognitive function, impaired walking and speech…the list went on and on, until eventually, you died.

All I needed was one dominant allele, and I could kiss my future good-bye. By the time I finished my fellowship, I could be presenting with early symptoms. Cardiac surgeons needed steady hands. I stared at my hands…hands I wouldn't have control over. I stared at Gio. He couldn't be much over fifty and he was already confined to a wheelchair.

Where does that leave me?

Goose bumps rose on my skin, along with a thin layer of sweat. I shivered. Swallowing, my throat felt like sandpaper. It closed off, refusing to allow any more oxygen into my lungs. The walls closed in.

When my dad walked out on me fifteen years ago, he changed the course of my life…how I viewed life and love. Now, with a four-word sentence, he derailed my life's goals, everything I'd worked so hard for.

By nature I wasn't a gambler. I didn't like taking chances. Too many horrible things happened in my life as a result of having no control, and now, here I was spinning the roulette wheel. Did I have the gene or not? A fifty-fifty chance stood between life and a horrible death.

"I think you should get tested, Sophia. That way you can know for sure," Gio said casually, like he hadn't just shot my future to hell. "I can give you the number of a genetic counselor and I have the finest doctor money can buy."

Genetic counselor? Doctor? Tested? The train cars kept piling up, slamming into one another. I had to get out of this house. I needed air.

"I have to go." I stood abruptly, shouldered my purse, and stalked to the door.

"Sophia," Gio called after me. "Wait!" he shouted.

The second I was out of the library, the air was lighter, and I could breathe a little easier.

"Sophia?" A female voice sounded from behind me. "Are you alright?" Lydia, the woman my dad was living with, came up and put her hand on my back. "You don't look well. Can I get you some water?"

I shook my head. "No. I just need to leave. I've got to go." I shrugged her hand off my back and worked my way down the hall, toward the front door.

Without glancing back, I ran down the hall, pulled the door open, and stepped into the blazing sunshine. The illusion of a happy summer day was on full display. Trees swayed in the breeze, a couple of bees buzzed from rose to rose, and the sound of children's laughter floated from the houses down the street. But despite my best effort to focus on those joyful sounds, I couldn't escape the screeching brakes of my train-wrecked future.

Chapter Four

I slammed the car door shut and gripped the steering wheel hard, before I let my head fall there as well. My lungs heaved and my throat burned like it'd been rubbed raw with sandpaper.

The air around me grew hot quickly, but my shock-addled system wouldn't allow me to move. My fight-or-flight response lasted long enough to get me out of the house, but now I was frozen, despite the rising temperatures.

Still slumped over the steering wheel, I felt a drop of sweat roll down the middle of my back. I thought about opening the window when I heard a tap on the glass.

A muffled voice called my name. "Sophia."

My head weighed a thousand pounds. Slowly, I lifted my forehead, my eyes focusing on the person standing outside my car.

Lydia. What did she want?

She tapped on the window again. "Can you roll down the window?"

I started the car. A blast of torrid heat blew from the vents. I reached for the thermostat and turned down the blower before depressing the window control.

With a gentle hum, the window retreated into the door. Lydia smiled and passed the envelope to me. "You forgot this."

My fingers wrapped around the paper. "Thanks," I replied hoarsely. I met Lydia's kind eyes. She was very pretty...and young. I'd guess late twenties, not much older than me. I found it odd she was with Gio and not someone more...vibrant, youthful. *Someone who wasn't dying of a genetic disorder that could be passed on to her future offspring.*

"Why are you with him?" I asked. It wasn't any of my business, but I was beyond caring about appropriate lines of questioning.

Lydia tilted her head and her eyebrows pulled in when she squinted. "What do you mean?"

Brushing my hair behind my ears, I sat up straighter. "Why are you with Gio?" I said louder. Did she need a more detailed question? *Why are you sleeping with a man who's dying?*

Then the lightbulb came on. Understanding dawned across her face and she shook her head, smiling. "Oh no." She waved her hands, as if to clear away my awkward question. "I'm your father's nurse. I do live here, but there is no romantic involvement between Mr. Belmonte and me." She paused for a moment, then gave an unnerved chuckle.

"Oh." I glanced at the envelope, tossing it onto the passenger seat before looking back at Lydia. "I'm sorry, I jumped to conclusions."

She pressed her lips into a smile and waved again. "No apology needed."

"I should go," I said, suddenly very tired. I'd survived the earlier train wreck, but now I was spent. I needed to sleep for a day…or ten.

Pressing on the window button, the glass moved back into position. "Sophia," Lydia added before the window was completely up.

"Yeah?"

"This isn't my place, but I spend a lot of time with your dad. I've heard so many stories. I don't know if he told you, but the reason he left was so you and your mother wouldn't see him like that." She nodded in the direction of the house.

I looked back at the house. Minutes ticked by before I turned back to where Lydia stood. "Cowardly. If you ask me."

Lydia opened her mouth to say something else—probably to defend my father's actions—but I finished putting up the window, sufficiently ending our conversation. I was through with excuses.

* * *

I drove without a destination in mind, my car leading me to Wash U's campus. School had always been a safe haven. When I quit playing soccer, getting lost in schoolwork centered me and brought me peace. In a week and a half, I'd return to my classroom sanctuaries. Lord knew I needed the distraction of lectures, tests, and homework now.

I got out of the car and walked down the quiet sidewalk, finding an empty bench outside the medical library. The wind did little to cool the hot, muggy air. My clothes stuck to my moist skin. I'd chosen the most uncomfortable day to sit outside, but what options did I have? There was no way I was ready to face Mom and Nonna. *Did they know about Gio?* Heaven help them if they did and neglected to tell me I'd just wasted the last four years of my life killing myself to get into med school.

The hush of distant voices floated on the hot breeze, but I couldn't see anyone. Campus was otherwise deserted. Gio's voice echoed in my head: *I have Huntington's disease.* Each word was a nail in the coffin of my career.

What was I going to do? If I went through with the test, I'd have a concrete answer, one way or the other. *But do I want to know if I have it? Do I want to know if I'm dying?*

I glanced behind me. Regal and commanding, one of my favorite places on campus, the medical library stood proudly. I'd spent so many hours tucked inside its inviting walls, studying…preparing. For what?

My stomach cramped and my lungs tightened. Tears welled inside me, begging to be released. But I refused to free them. I didn't cry. That wasn't me. Crying was a form of letting go, not being in control. I was always in control of everything: my emotions, my grades, my life…my future.

Everything…up until now.

This was the turning point. I needed to gain control of this situation. "What are you going to do, Sophia?" I asked myself. It was okay to talk out loud since no one was around to hear. At least that was how I justified it.

The wind rustled the trees and whipped my hair into my face. I listened for an answer, but nothing came. For the first time in my life, I didn't have a plan.

* * *

When Mom came into the kitchen from the garage, I was ready to pounce. I jumped to my feet the second she opened the door and threw her keys in the catchall.

"Oh, hey, Soph. How'd everything go?" she asked, pulling her long black hair into a messy bun.

"Not good." I didn't mince words.

She'd stopped in her path toward the counter and glanced over her shoulder. "Not good? What happened?"

"Tell me you didn't know. All I need for you to say is you didn't know."

Mom swirled to face me head-on now. "What on earth are you talking about?"

"Mom, he's dying."

Her jaw dropped as my words registered in her brain. I breathed a sigh of relief at her reaction. Had she known, she wouldn't have looked the way she did.

"Come again?" Mom walked to the table and pulled out a chair.

Following behind, I joined her at the table. "He has a genetic disorder called Huntington's disease. It's rare."

"Oh, goodness." The color drained from her cheeks. "I knew he was in a wheelchair and had hired a full-time nurse, but I had no idea his condition was life-threatening." Mom's eyes met mine. "I'm sorry you had to go there alone today." She patted my leg.

"Mom," I choked. "There's more."

"What?" Concern clouded her milk-chocolate eyes, turning them the color of coal.

I scooped her hands into mine. "His mom died from the same disorder. It's genetic." I hoped she understood what that meant without me having to explain. I didn't think I'd get through the explanation without my emotions getting the better of me.

"Genetic," she whispered. Then realization cleared away the confusion from her eyes. I'd never noticed how expressive Mom's eyes were. "And what is it that he has again?"

"Huntington's disease. It's a neurodegenerative genetic disorder."

Again with Mom's expressive eyes, they widened. "What does that mean?" She squeezed my hands.

"There's a fifty-fifty chance I could have the same disorder. It's passed from parent to child. I'm assuming by your reaction that no one on your side of the family has it." I spoke as if I were talking about someone else…how a doctor would talk to a patient. If I kept it clinical, practiced my doctor-speak, then the words couldn't hurt me. I wouldn't cry.

Mom shook her head.

"Dad's mom died from HD. Dad got the gene from her, which means there's a possibility that I could have gotten the gene from him."

Mom's eyes were glassy, filled to the brim with unshed tears. "What do we need to do?" she asked, almost inaudibly.

I shook my head. "There is nothing we can do. If I have it, I have it. There's no cure."

Swallowing, Mom searched my face. "Soph," she breathed, standing up. As she rose, she pulled my arms up, forcing me to stand as well. Pulling me into her arms, she held me as tightly as she could. "I had no idea."

I closed my eyes, taking in her comforting scent. Mom always smelled like clean clothes, honey, with the lingering smell of cream carried from the shop.

"Mom," I mumbled into the crook of her arm. "Don't say anything to Nonna, please."

She rocked me for a few more seconds and then pulled away so she could see me fully. "But we don't know for sure you have it, right?"

I nodded. "I would need to be tested. If I have two recessive genes, I'm in the clear."

"Well." She smiled. "Then I need to dry up these tears. Not worth getting worked up about until we have a definitive answer." She sniffled and wiped her eyes with the back of her hand.

"I don't know if I want to know, Mom." I took a step backward, resting my hand on the back of the chair.

"Why not?"

"If I get the test and it comes back that I do have HD, then everything I've worked so hard for will have been for nothing. I can kiss practicing medicine good-bye."

"That's not true," Mom argued. She walked around the counter and headed toward the cabinets. Pulling one open, she took out a glass. "You don't have to have perfect genes to be a doctor."

I rolled my eyes. "Mom, they don't let people with degenerative muscular disorders operate on patients. Not to mention, when HD progresses, patients also lose significant cognitive function as well. It's life-changing, debilitating, and awful."

She turned the water on and filled her glass. Taking a sip, she turned around. "Oh."

"Yeah. HD is one of the ticking time bombs of the genetic lottery. It sucks." My throat closed again. *I will not cry,* I yelled internally.

"So, you don't want to know?" she asked cautiously.

I shrugged, shaking my head. "I don't know." Plopping into the chair again, I pulled my legs to my chest and rested my head on my knees. "How old is Dad?"

She thought for a moment. "Fifty-three."

"He's lost the use of his legs and has involuntary muscle spasms," I said, going over the symptoms I saw Gio present with during our short visit, like he was the crystal ball to my future. I shifted my gaze to Mom. "He's not that old."

She walked in my direction, coming to stand behind me. Even with the chair between us, she bent low and wrapped her body over mine, like she could protect me from anything with just her body. I wished that were true.

With her mouth at my ear, she whispered, "We'll figure it out together, *Patatina*."

Her words were only marginally comforting, because I could hear her own uncertainty in the statement. And as much as I wanted to believe her, there was no "together." This was something I'd have to carry alone.

Chapter Five

"Soph!"

I rolled over in my bed when I heard my name called from down the hall. Sunlight peeked around the edges of my blackout shades, demanding that I get out of bed.

"Sophia!" This time my name was followed by an insistent knock at my door.

"What is it, Mom?" I answered, throwing my blanket to the side. Glancing at the clock, I saw that it wasn't quite 7:00 a.m. Was I supposed to work the morning shift today? Was that why she was after me to get up?

"May I come in?" she asked.

I padded over to the door and pulled it open. "Yeah?"

"What's this?" She held a yellow envelope between us.

Dammit. Italy. I'd meant to throw that away. "It's nothing." I went to take it from her hand, but she pulled it away.

"Like hell it's nothing." She lifted the flap, a big grin on her face.

Her eyes scanned the travel documents inside. "It's a six-week trip to freaking Italy. Did your dad give you this?"

"Yeah. And I'm not going."

Her eyes flicked back to my face. "Not going? What? Are you crazy?"

"No." This time I did manage to snatch the papers from her. "Did you forget about a little thing called med school? It starts in eleven days. I don't have time to go to Italy. This is yet another example that proves my father knows nothing about me."

Mom shook her head. "Screw med school."

"What?"

"You heard me." Her eyes were like laser beams boring into me. "There is no reason why you can't start school in the fall, like a normal twentysomething. For crying out loud, Sophia, all you do is study and work. Go! Get a life. Live a little," Mom shouted.

I shuffled backward. "I have a life," I mumbled. Her words stung.

"No, you don't. Honestly, Soph, sometimes I think a part of you died with Penley."

Ouch. That didn't just sting; it burned soul deep. The truth hurt.

"Before we lost Penley, you used to smile and laugh all the time. You enjoyed playing soccer, going shopping and to the movies, all the things high school kids do. When she died, you gave all that up and threw yourself into school like a madwoman. What happened to that fun-loving girl?"

I chewed the inside of my lip, waiting for this lecture to end while I toed the carpet, avoiding Mom's scrutinizing gaze.

"Sophia, I don't pull rank on you often, but I'm going to this time. You're going to Italy. You're going to be a twenty-two-year-old girl for once and have fun."

I looked up from the floor, my mouth hanging open. "Mom," I whined. "I've got school."

"To hell with school. You can start in the fall." She crossed her arms, daring me to defy her edict.

"Like you said, I'm twenty-two. Old enough to do what I want. I'm not going to Italy."

"When I was your age, I was newly married and you came around shortly after. I love you, Soph. You are the best thing that's ever happened to me. I wouldn't change one minute of my twenties. But once you get a job and start a family, you won't get opportunities like this." She pointed to the envelope in my hands. "Your dad has given you an amazing gift. Before life gets in the way, you need to do this. You'll regret it when you're older. If I have to pack your suitcase and drag you to the airport kicking and screaming, I will." Mom grinned and then winked.

"I need the distraction of school right now, Mom," I growled through clenched teeth.

"*Patatina*." Her tone softened, as did the fire in her eyes. "I'm afraid school has become an addiction for you. Let's consider this an intervention. According to your itinerary, your flight leaves in eleven days. We'll do some shopping, get your travel papers in order, and in no time, you'll be basking in the Italian sunshine. I assure you, it's much better than Missouri sunshine."

I deflated, shoulders slumped. "Mom, don't do this, please. I need school right now."

"I don't know what bigger distraction you can ask for than a vacation to Italy. It's exactly what you need. Think of it as a big history project. You can research our family heritage."

"You sound like him. He wants me to visit his dad."

"I knew I always liked your father." She winked again. Her lack of hatred toward him was irritating.

"Don't you carry even a little seed of hatred for him for leaving us?" I fell back into bed.

"Like I already said, what good did hating him do me? He wasn't here; my hatred wasn't spilling over to him. He wasn't feeling any of my pain. I carried it alone. I felt it alone. Anger's heavy, and in the end I was just hurting myself." A humorless chuckle escaped her lips.

Mom leaned on the door frame and Nonna came up behind her. "What's the ruckus, you two?"

"Sorry, Mamma, I didn't mean to wake you. *Principessa*"—Mom glared in my direction—"was flexing her royal-pain-in-the-ass muscles. I had to put my foot down and squash the attitude."

"Oh, nonsense." Nonna waved. "My Sophia isn't a pain in the ass."

Mom harrumphed, turning her dark stare in Nonna's direction. "Are we talking about the same girl?"

Here was my chance. I could play this little game, too, and bring Nonna over to my side. "Nonna," I pouted. She'd never been able to resist my pout. "Mom's making me go on vacation."

"Where are you sending the poor girl? Antarctica?" Nonna put in a soft jab to her daughter's shoulder.

"Her father has arranged a six-week Italian getaway. You'd think he'd booked her a one-way trip to hell, the way she's acting."

"*Italia*," Nonna said prayerfully. Her homeland. "When does she leave, Andrea? I'll help her pack."

"Nonna!" I whined. "You're supposed to be on my side."

"When someone gives you Italy, you say *grazie* and get your butt on the plane."

"Thank you, Mamma." My mother bowed her head to my grand-mother.

"Fine. Whatever. I'll go." I was beat down and tired. I groaned and hid under my covers.

"I knew you'd see reason. I'm headed to the shop, Soph. Won't be home until later. Oh, and call the university and get school arranged for the fall."

"Yeah, yeah," I grumbled. After this vacation, I seriously needed to consider getting my own place.

I lay under the blanket until I couldn't hear them talking any-more. When I knew it was safe, I tossed the cover off and sat up. "So much for my freaking plans." I slapped my hands down on top of the blanket and traced one of the rainbow-colored double helices with my index finger.

"Dad drops an atom bomb on my future, I have to postpone med school, and now I'm going to Italy." *Can this summer get any worse?*

Chapter Six

Once Mom put her foot down about summer classes, I was left with one week to pull myself together for Italy. Mom and Nonna had been...well, what's the Italian word for "unbearable"? If I never saw the inside of another mall for as long as I lived, it would be too soon. I still hadn't figured out why I needed three swimsuits, but Mom was certain that I did. And when she was certain, there's no arguing with her.

I tossed the black and hot pink bottoms to the bikini Mom said "I just had to have" into my suitcase with its matching black polka-dot top. There was no way in hell I planned on wearing it—it barely covered anything—but Mom insisted that I take it. Eyeing the scraps of fabric, I crinkled my nose in disgust. "You'll go to Italy, but I'm never taking you out."

"Sophia, hurry up! If we don't leave now, you'll never make your flight," Mom shouted from the living room.

I went to my door and pulled it open. "I'm—" I started to yell, but I quickly snapped my mouth shut when I saw Mom standing in the doorway. "Oh, hey. I'm just about ready." I turned and walked back to my bed, where my suitcase lay.

"Need any help?"

I yanked the zipper closed, grasped the handle, and lifted the bulky luggage from the bed. "Nope," I replied, turning around to face her.

She beamed. If St. Louis's power grid ran on sheer joy, Mom's radiant smile would light the city up for months. "I sure hope you cheer up, Soph. You're going to Italy, not the dentist."

I allowed a small portion of her radiance to soak into me, forcing my lips into a thin smile. "You're right."

She put her hands on my shoulders. "You are going to have the time of your life. I just know it." With a little shake, she pulled me into her arms and hugged me tightly.

"Thanks, Mom."

With one last squeeze, Mom pulled away, looked me in the eye, and said, "Get your things, let's go."

I regarded her with a nod. I sucked in a deep breath and exhaled, "I'm going to Italy."

"Ahhh! You're going to Italy!" she cheered, lifting my messenger bag off the bed and walking toward the hallway.

I was right behind her. This was indeed the vacation of a lifetime. Once I started med school in the fall, I wouldn't be able to drop everything and leave the country on a whim. This was my chance to be young and carefree, as Mom had put it. But as I followed her down the hall, I couldn't help but hear a dirge in the back of my head. Despite my father's grandiose gesture, this trip felt tainted. It was almost as if he were telling me, "Here, have this trip, enjoy life to its fullest, because it won't last, sweetheart."

* * *

"Air France Flight 1178 to Naples, Italy, is now boarding," a breathy-voiced attendant with a thick French accent announced over the PA.

I sighed and clicked off my e-reader, feeling sorry for the characters and the precarious situation I'd left them in. I was eager to get on the plane and pick up where I'd left off. Stowing my e-reader in my bag, I retrieved my passport and ticket, ready for the final leg of my trip. In two hours and fifteen minutes, I'd be in Naples, Italy, and the first thing I planned to do was sleep.

With my travel documents in hand, I stood and joined the line, inching my way closer to the Jetway. When I reached the front, I passed my papers to the attendant.

"*Merci*. Enjoy the flight," she said, handing back my passport.

"Thank you," I replied, and headed toward the plane.

Taking my seat by the window, I brought my e-reader back out and pushed my bag under the seat in front of me. I stared out the window. Paris. It was sad that all I got to see of the City of Lights was from the vantage point of an airport. I'd always wanted to go to Paris. *Would I ever have the chance…the ability?* I hoped the answer to that was yes.

"*Scusi,*" a gravelly voice called from the aisle.

I turned my head to see a tiny, feeble old man. He had a small satchel clutched in his hand that looked like it weighed more than he did.

"Oh, let me help you with that." I pushed my e-reader into the seat pocket and turned, grabbing the strap of his bag. He let go with a look of relief.

I pushed his bag beneath the seat and he sat down, wheezing. Between labored breaths, he said, *"Grazie."*

I smiled. "My pleasure," I replied, hoping he understood English.

"Sono Aldo." He extended his wrinkled hand to me.

With a gentle shake, I introduced myself. "Sophia. Nice to meet you."

"Sì, very nice."

I brought my hand back to my lap and Aldo laid his head back on the seat, closing his eyes. His breathing was still shallow and wheezy. I wondered how old he was.

Not wanting to disturb him, I clicked my e-reader free on and waited for my library to populate. I listened as the flight attendants began their preflight safety demonstration, first in French, then in English.

"You like to read?" Aldo asked, turning his head in my direction.

I looked at him and nodded. "Yeah."

"What you read?"

"Oh, anything really." I smiled. "But right now I'm hooked on romance novels."

Aldo gave a throaty laugh, which segued into a cough. "My Elenora liked those, too."

"So does my nonna," I added.

His face brightened. "Ah, nonna. You're Italian?"

"Sì." I nodded, happy to try out my limited Italian. Mom and Nonna hardly ever spoke in Italian, so I never picked it up. Honestly, I didn't think Mom knew Italian all that well either. When Nonna and Pappous moved to the United States, before they had Mom, they embraced American culture with open arms.

"You visit family?"

The plane's engines kicked into high gear. "Ladies and gentlemen, we have been cleared for takeoff," the flight attendant announced.

I glanced out the window as we taxied to the runway; then I looked at Aldo, answering his question. "Sort of. I plan to visit my grandfather while I'm on vacation."

"Oh, that is nice. I'm sure he's very excited."

To avoid being an obnoxious seatmate, I left out the part about never having met my grandfather and that I have no idea whether he's excited or not. That was probably more information than Aldo wanted to know, so I went with the safe answer. "Yeah."

I returned my attention to my book and Aldo closed his eyes. We settled in just as the plane tore down the runway. The landing gear lifted. In two hours, I'd be in Italy.

* * *

As the plane began its descent, Aldo continued his story.

"And then I saw her, my Elenora," he said wistfully. He brought his hand up and swiped it gently in front of him, as if he were brushing his hand across Elenora's cheek.

"Did she see you?" I asked, enthralled. His real-life love story was so much better than the story on my e-reader. I was such a sucker for old-fashioned love stories. My heart clenched, waiting for him to continue.

A smile grew on his weathered face. "*Sì.*" He nodded. "But not at first. She was across the crowded hospital room, tending to the soldiers who had more life-threatening injuries."

"I bet she was so scared, not knowing what had happened to you."

The plane dipped and my stomach sank. "Whoa," I said, grabbing on to the armrest.

Aldo waved off the turbulence. "It's nothing. Just a little bump. Don't worry about bumps." He chuckled and patted my hand.

The plane rocked again, this time with a noticeable altitude change. "Just a little bump?" I threw Aldo a glance and leaned back in my seat, holding on for dear life.

"*Sì, sì!*" he laughed.

"I'm glad you find this funny," I said through clenched teeth.

"First time you fly?"

I shook my head. "No. Just not a fan of bumps." I smiled at him.

"Elenora never liked to fly."

"Will you finish your story?" I had to hear the end before we went our separate ways.

"Oh yes, of course." He pointed a crooked, bony finger in my direction. "Take your mind off the bumps."

"Yes, please."

Aldo's black eyes twinkled as he traveled back to the day he and his lover had been reunited. The way he spoke of Elenora, with such reverence, it pierced my heart. I hoped that one day, someone would think of me with that kind of love and admiration. But then I wondered if I was doomed to live vicariously through other people's stories. Would I get a happily-ever-after?

"A nurse I did not know attended my injuries. While she patched me, I watched my Elenora move about the room. She fixed broken soldiers, too. Time"—he shook his head—"not a friend. I worried she'd moved on. I'd seen battle…I knew fear. But seeing her, a greater fear lodged in my gut." Aldo clenched his fist and shook it at his belly. "After being gone longer than a year…I couldn't bear it if she wouldn't have me."

The plane sank again; then I felt the rumble of the landing gear coming down. The flight attendant came over the speakers, first speaking landing instructions in French and then English. "We have begun preparations for landing. Please put your seat and tray tables in their upright positions. Seat belts must remain fastened until the aircraft has arrived at the gate. All luggage and loose items must be stowed securely. Thank you for flying with us today. Welcome to Naples, Italy."

The intercom clicked off, but Aldo remained silent. "Did she see you?" I asked, yearning to know the answer. He'd built up the climax to their reunion so well.

A loud rumble of laughter shook his shoulders. "I shoved the fear aside and found courage buried beneath. With my wounds bandaged, I got up and walked toward her, desperate to be at her side. The love of a woman is a powerful thing. It can cure or destroy a man."

A loud *whoosh* filled the cabin and the wheels of the landing gear touched the runway. The plane bounced.

"Elenora looked up from her patient, and her eyes, like sparkling green gems, landed on me. She gasped like she'd seen a ghost."

I held my breath.

"Then she stood, slowly, and I quickened my pace."

Energy from the speeding plane pressed Aldo and me to the backs of our seats.

"Then, once she realized I was not a ghost, she flew down the aisle and crashed into my waiting, open arms," he said on a sigh, just as the plane came to a halt on the runway, inertia throwing our bodies forward with a jolt.

"So she waited," I said breathlessly, consumed by his story.

With a little nod, he confirmed. "She waited. And now she waits again." Aldo looked up and made the sign of the cross. "One day we will have another reunion."

My heart sank. "Aldo, I'm so sorry."

"*Ciancia.* Nonsense." He waved off my apology. "When she got sick, I prayed for her. She was in a lot of pain, so I prayed for God to take her quickly. He answered my prayer and my Elenora did not suffer. She lived a long life. We were happy. No regrets. I'd do it all over again in a heartbeat, as long as Elenora was by my side. Her smile brought the sun up each day." He smiled at the memory.

Tears pooled in my eyes, listening to him speak about *his Elenora.* "Thank you, Aldo," I said, trying hard not to blink. *Stupid tears.* I hated to cry.

"Sophia, it was a pleasure to sit next to you." Aldo extended his right hand for me to shake.

I placed my hand in his wrinkled palm and he gave it two gentle pumps before he pulled me closer, placing a kiss on each of my cheeks. *"Godetevi Napoli, mia cara."*

When he pulled away, I shook my head. "I'm sorry. My Italian is atrocious."

"Enjoy Naples, dear," he repeated in English.

I stared into his glassy, dark eyes. The things those eyes had seen. I wanted to hear more of his stories, and I secretly wished he were the grandfather I was supposed to meet.

Would it be rude of me to invite myself to his house for the next six weeks?

I heard Mom in the back of my mind. *Yes, Sophia, it would be rude. Go live your own stories!*

"*Grazie*, Aldo."

"It was a pleasure, *cara*. Napoli is my home. No place finer in all of Italy. You have a good time."

Aldo stood and reached for his bag on the floor, groaning.

"No, let me." Since I was in my seat, I had better access to the luggage.

"*Grazie*," he said as I handed him his bag.

Aldo smiled and stepped into the aisle. "*Arrivederci*, Sophia. It was nice to meet you."

I smiled. "Likewise. *Arrivederci*, Aldo."

"And remember, do not worry about the bumps."

"Right." I pointed at him. "I'll remember."

I watched Aldo hobble up the aisle as I gathered my bags. Italy was definitely a bump in my summer plans, but I'd get over it and maybe even allow myself to enjoy a break from my hectic life. But my dad's news? That was a speeding train, hitting a speed bump and crashing into a brick wall at full steam. *What would Aldo say about that?*

Chapter Seven

After retrieving my luggage from the baggage claim, I passed through customs without incident and stepped outside into the stifling Italian air. Similar to St. Louis, Italy dealt with heat and humidity, too. At least I wouldn't have to adjust to the climate.

Glancing at the itinerary my dad printed for me, I saw that my hotel was a fifteen-minute taxi ride from the airport; the hard part would be flagging one down. I had no clue how to hail a taxi in America, let alone Italy, but I was about to learn. It couldn't be that hard, right? I passed the freaking MCAT; I could hail a damn taxi.

Retracting the handle on my suitcase, I rolled farther out into the sunshine. Bringing the papers in my left hand up to my forehead, I used them as a shield against the blazing sun while I took in the bustling airport.

Several taxis were lined up in front. A few feet away, a handsome man in a well-tailored suit approached a waiting cab with a raised hand. He and the driver exchanged a few words and the Suit opened the door and climbed inside. A second later, a woman with a baby did the same thing. If nothing else, my science degree taught me how to be observant.

Pulling my suitcase behind me, I navigated the noisy throng and headed to where the Suit and Mom had just been. With my hand raised, I walked toward the waiting taxis.

"Taxi?" I hollered, unsure of what I was supposed to say.

"*Sí*. Where to?" the driver asked in a heavy accent. I was thankful he spoke English, though.

"Uh, I have it right here." I glanced at the papers. "The Hotel Suite Esedra. Um…Via A. Cantani, 12," I stumbled over the address.

"Get in. Get in," the driver yelled, gesturing wildly with his hands.

I fumbled with the door, pulling it open quickly, then stuffed my suitcase inside, climbing in after. The second I shut the door, the driver pulled away from the curb and shot into traffic.

Outside I watched Naples pass by in a blur as the taxi weaved around the road. Scooters and smart cars whizzed by, cutting other motorists off without a second thought. There were so many people. I'd lived in St. Louis my whole life, thinking it was a big city. I was so wrong.

My eyes stayed glued to the window, marveling at the driver's ability to navigate the congested streets with relative ease. Only when my phone rang did I pull my eyes from the chaos outside.

Mom's picture filled the screen, her name printed at the top. Dad had added an international calling plan to my cell phone package, so I had no qualms about accepting Mom's call. He'd made it quite clear that this trip was on his dime. I pressed Ac-cept. "Hi, Mom!"

"Soph! Did you make it? Where are you?" she asked enthusiastically, but mixed with a hint of worry.

"I did. I'm in a taxi now, on my way to the hotel. You should see this place, Mom. It's crazy."

Mom laughed brightly. "I have seen it, *Patatina*. Crazy, huh?"

"You can say that again," I said.

"Have a good time, Soph, and be careful. Lots of pickpockets."

"Thanks, Mom. I will."

The taxi pulled onto a narrow street, and the driver threw the car into park in front of a yellow-sided building. HOTEL SUITE ESEDRA was spelled out in big gray letters.

"Mom, I've got to go. I'm at the hotel."

"Okay. Be safe. Love you, Soph."

"Love you, too. Bye." I shouldered the phone and rooted around in my purse for my wallet.

"Talk to you soon," Mom said, and then the line went quiet. I dropped the phone into my purse and pulled out some money.

Handing the euros to the driver, I threw the strap of my bag across my body and grabbed my suitcase, tossing the door open. "Thank you," I said, climbing out of the cab.

I freed my luggage and closed the door just as the driver sped off. *Whoa!* My hair fluttered in its wake. *This place is unreal.*

I shrugged off the impatient cabby and wheeled my belongings into the hotel, feeling proud of myself. I could mark one thing off my bucket list: hail a taxi. Check.

I got checked in and found my room, ready to collapse into bed. After traveling for almost a day, I didn't have anything left. Italy wasn't going anywhere, and I knew I'd enjoy it more after a long night's rest.

* * *

Tourists crowded the ancient streets of Pompeii, but it didn't detract from the awe and majesty the ruins inspired. The undulating stones that made up the main street weren't easy to navigate, but it didn't matter; Pompeii was breathtaking. The highlight of my Italian getaway for sure, even though I'd only begun my excursion.

I lifted the flap of my messenger bag and stored my bottle of water, then pulled out one of the many guidebooks I'd acquired before my trip. Even though Mom wouldn't let me plan my trip down to the last detail, saying I needed to leave a little room for spontaneity, there was no way I'd planned to tour Italy blindly.

Stepping carefully across the chariot-rutted stones, I navigated the haunting streets. The crumbling stone walls still held echoes of the people who once inhabited the city. Even after almost two thousand years, their cries could still be heard, carried on the breeze that ruffled my hair.

A chill went down my spine as I trailed along the busy street on my way to the Forum. I decided to begin my visit with the architecture as opposed to the famous plaster casts. Despite how long ago all those people lived, I wasn't ready to cry just yet. The immortalized dwellings alone held countless untold stories, even without the people frozen for all of time in their death throes.

As I navigated tourists, languages from every corner of the world touched my ears as people marveled and took in the town's epicenter.

Standing in the middle of the square, I stared the ancient Roman columns. Looking upward, I shielded my eyes from the blazing sun.

Hundreds of people milled about, soaking up Pompeii from all angles.

Mount Vesuvius loomed in the distance. It had been a normal day for the Romans milling about. Then, out of nowhere, a bomb was dropped on them. Their hopes and dreams, their futures, everything was reduced to ash. In some minuscule way, I understood. My dad's words rumbled in the back of my head like an earthquake threatening to shatter my future.

Enough, Sophia. You're in freaking Italy. You're here to have a good time, not a pity party.

Italy. I still couldn't believe I was here, that I'd even entertained the notion of tossing this trip in the trash. Yes, I still felt my father was a coward for walking out on Mom and me, but after thinking about what Lydia had told me, why he left, I understood him better. The motivation behind his actions made sense, even though it still hurt. And buying me a trip to Italy didn't make up for all the years he'd missed when I was a kid, but I'd be lying if I didn't think this was an outstanding graduation present. Still, in the back of my mind, not knowing if my father's fate was my own, I needed to live my life as if it was. I needed to seize every opportunity afforded to me. In fifteen…twenty years, I may not be able to climb the steps in front of me or even navigate the uneven stone roads that connected the past with the present.

I drew in a deep breath, filling my lungs with the scents of sunshine and antiquity. I held it in, committing it to memory before I made my way to the end of the Forum, toward the Temple of Jupiter.

Closing my eyes, I allowed the history surrounding me to seep into my bones and become a part of me. I took a couple of tentative steps backward, raising my face skyward, feeling the warmth of the sun on my cheeks, the breeze in my hair. Of the five senses, the eyes seemed to get all the glory. But with them still closed, my nose, skin, and ears rose to the occasion, soaking up Italy.

I stepped to my left, eyes still closed, head still turned toward the sun like a flower, when I crashed into a freaking wall. Hard.

"Fuck!" yelled a deep, male voice.

Oh, God! Not a wall…a person.

My eyes snapped open and I whirled around. "Oh my gosh! I'm so sorry!" I slapped both hands across my mouth before I vomited a thousand more apologies. Sprawled in front of me on the ground was an incredibly tall, sun-kissed, blond-haired guy. His belongings—a map, water bottle, and cell phone—lay scattered around him, and his sunglasses sat crooked on his nose.

"What the hell?" he cursed again. Pushing himself up, he adjusted his sunglasses.

The way his biceps strained beneath his white polo shirt left me speechless. I shook my head. I wasn't one to ogle, but I couldn't help it with him. This guy had an incredible body. There weren't men like him back home.

I stared as he collected his things. I should have helped, but I was still in shock—not to mention mortified—that I'd literally knocked him on his ass. Given my height compared to his, I didn't think it was possible for me to knock *him* over. A smile crept to my lips, the prelude to a giggle fit I felt bubbling inside my chest, a defense mechanism to hide my embarrassment. I bit my tongue and held my breath to keep from laughing in his face. That would be rude.

Once he had his belongings gathered, he hopped to his feet with ease. I craned my neck upward. *Damn, he's tall.* Taller than I'd thought.

"Thanks for the help," he grumbled, clearly irritated. His American accent was helpful in providing some personal information.

I shook my head. "I'm so sorry."

He brushed the dust off his butt. "Yeah, you mentioned that." Then, like clouds parting to reveal the sun, his anger disappeared as his lips broke into a stunning smile.

His straight, white teeth gleamed in the angled morning sun. Against his tan skin, they shone even brighter. *Megawatt* didn't even begin to cover it. *God bless his parents and their dedication to orthodontia.*

He held out his hand. "Lucas."

I put my palm to his, and he closed his fingers tightly. My heart gave a quick thump as our fingers made contact.

In books, I'd always read about people experiencing a spark or an electric current, indicative of an instant attraction. I wasn't going to lie to myself and say I wasn't attracted to him, because I definitely was. But there was no shock or jolt. Nothing like that. When my hand pressed against his, it was more than a momentary spark. I felt anchored…connected…not alone.

Our hands formed the source of the circuit, while our bodies directed the pulse of energy through our systems. Without our connection, the voltage would die.

And just like I'd imagined, he pulled his hand back and the power went out, like someone had thrown the breaker in a fuse box.

He lifted his sunglasses to the top of his head. Small creases pinched the skin around his eyes, and he pierced me with a cerulean gaze. His gorgeous blue eyes were hypnotizing. Cocking his head to the right, he studied me for a brief moment, then asked, "What did you say your name was?"

"Uh…" The sun bleached everything, making even the most vivid colors hard to distinguish, but his eyes were otherworldly, a deep, ocean blue that rivaled the Bay of Naples. I still stared…I couldn't help it. With eyes like that, he must get that reaction all the time.

"Forget your name?" he asked, raising an eyebrow.

"Uh…" I giggled at my own stupidity. *Yes, I'm a college graduate. I'm capable of holding a conversation. What was my problem?* "Sorry, no." I cleared my throat. "My name's Sophia."

"You're an American?"

"Yes" I confirmed with a nod. "And you?"

He folded his map and stuffed it in his back pocket. "Born and raised."

"Leave it to me to knock over a fellow countryman in a sea of foreigners."

"I won't deny your talent." He smiled broadly, his white teeth on full display yet again. But this time, I was drawn to the deep-set dimple on his left cheek.

It was completely out of character for me, but I wanted more than anything to run my fingers over his cheeks. To feel the golden smattering of stubble on his face and to have his chin scratch against my fingertips like fine sand. Bliss. Of all the people there was to knock over, why him? He was too gorgeous for words, and by the way mine disappeared in his presence, it wasn't just an opinion but a fact.

My cheeks overheated, and it wasn't the sun causing the spike in my temperature: Embarrassment coupled with his insane good looks was enough to leave me blubbering like an idiot. I squinted, raising my arm to shield the sun from my hot face.

"I'm sorry I knocked you over." Hiding my awkwardness behind a casual comment, I shuffled my feet. *"Buon viaggio."* I hitched my messenger bag securely on my shoulder, waved, and began walking away.

Did I just say "have a nice trip" after tripping over him? What was wrong with me?

"Sophia, wait," he called.

My heart hammered hard against my chest at the sound of my name wrapped in his voice. *God, what was wrong with me?* I stopped and looked over my shoulder. With two confident strides, he stood next to me again. I turned to face him. There was a considerable height difference between us, and by his cocky grin, he seemed to like the angle.

"Yeah?" My voice wobbled. It had been ages since I'd had a legitimate conversation with a guy. After the miserably awkward month when I'd dated Scotty Hendrickson in high school, and the bumbling five minutes in the backseat of his mom's car on the night of our junior prom, I'd sworn off dating altogether. Then senior year happened. After Pen died, I'd had no desire to be around anyone, let alone a guy. School provided an easy way to hide from male attention, sexual or otherwise. Once I quit soccer, I wasn't Sophia, the cool kickass athlete anymore. Nobody wanted to hook up with Sophia the book nerd, which was fine with me.

If I were smart, I'd stick to my old ways. I had no business talking to him, not after what I'd learned of my possible future...or lack thereof.

Lucas scanned the crowd, first left, then right, before refocusing his vivid blue eyes on me. "You alone?" he asked, cocking his eyebrow.

Okay. How am I supposed to answer this? It could be a completely innocent question, and he may just want to know if I'm traveling alone. But the warning bells inside my head chimed quietly: *What if he's a criminal...a murderer...a sex slave broker?* I'd seen *Taken*; I knew how these gorgeous people preyed upon unsuspecting American girls, especially those traveling alone.

"I'm sorry, that was a dumb question." He waved his hand. "I just wanted to know if you wanted to get some coffee or something. There's a café just a short walk from the ruins." He pointed in that direction.

I fidgeted with the map in my hands, pressing the corner down one way and then unfolding it to press it down the opposite direction. *Play it cool, Soph. Decline his offer and leave.*

"Thanks, but I can't. It was nice to meet you, Lucas."

His lips pressed into a tight smile, hiding his dimple. "Can I at least get your number? If you want to ditch the group you're traveling with, you could give me a call."

I bit my bottom lip, cringing slightly. I had to give him credit; he didn't give up easily. "I'm not sure that's a good idea." *Trust me, Lucas, I am not the girl for you....No future here, walk on by.*

"Right," he drawled. "Can't blame a guy for trying." He winked. "It was nice meeting you, Sophia."

"Yeah, nice to meet you." I smiled back.

There was a sparkle in his eyes as I turned to leave, for good this time. Bumping into Lucas put me off my schedule, not that the permanent inhabitants of Pompeii cared much; they weren't going anywhere, but strangely, I didn't care that I was off schedule either...I was actually enjoying myself.

Chapter Eight

The sun grew hotter as the day went on, but I was determined to see all the major tourist attractions Pompeii had to offer. The next stop on my self-guided tour was the House of the Vettii. I paused my podcasted tour before I went inside the house and searched for the bottle of water in my bag. After taking a few long swigs, I stowed it and made my way inside, pressing PLAY on my phone. The tour guides picked up where they'd left off, directing me into the home of two freedmen who once lived here, Aulus Vettius Restitutus and Aulus Vettius Conviva. With all the ancient knowledge I'd already gained in my first couple of hours spent on the streets of Pompeii, I was turning into a history buff instead of a science geek.

With my left earbud fit snuggly into my ear, I listened as the tour guides directed my attention to the right side of the vestibule upon entering the Vettii home. There, halfway up the wall on the right side, in all its grandeur, was the fresco of Priapus. According to my guides, this painting wasn't meant to be distasteful, even though the man depicted in the artwork was weighing his massive erection against a bag of money on a balance scale. According to historians, the fresco was meant to symbolize the wealth and strength of the homeowners, the Vettii brothers.

As I continued to listen to my guides, keeping my eyes on Priapus and his prodigious phallus, I felt a tickle at my right ear. "Impressive, isn't it?"

"Ahh!" I shouted, turning around and leaping backward at the same time. I slapped my hands over my mouth, realizing how loudly I'd shouted. The guy I'd bumped into in the Forum this morning stood behind me, grinning like an ass. Lucas.

He chuckled. "I didn't mean to startle you."

Lowering my hands to my chest in an attempt to slow my thumping heart and find the ability to breathe again, I sighed. "Yes, you did." He was such a liar.

"Okay, maybe I did. Payback for this morning." He laughed again, showcasing that striking dimple in his left cheek. "Fancy meeting you here."

"Yes, fancy that." I took another deep breath and paused my podcast. I pulled the earbud from my left ear, keeping my attention focused on him.

Lucas tucked a hand in his pocket and smirked. "So, you *are* alone."

What was it with this guy? "Why are you so concerned about my potential lack of travel companions?" I still didn't want to clue him in on my solo status, even though he looked completely harmless. I couldn't let my guard down.

"Like I said before, I'd love to get something to eat. We can talk. I'm headed to Herculaneum next. I'm here alone." He gestured to the empty space around him. "We could buddy up. Keep each other company. You could give me your number."

I eyed him warily. The little voice I heard this morning still echoed in the back of my head—the one that suggested he may be a criminal—but the sound was fading the more I stared into his extraordinarily blue eyes. "Where are you from?" I asked, like that made a difference. It wasn't like sex slave traders didn't live and work in the United States, too.

"San Diego, California." He held his hand out for me to shake. "Lucas Walsh."

Hesitantly, I reached for his hand. The moment our palms touched, he latched his fingers around mine, like he had this morning. My heart threatened to jump into my throat. Our connection had been restored. The power came back on and my body hummed with energy.

Pumping my arm up and down, he smiled confidently. "Nice to meet you, Linebacker. See, now we're friends. Now you can have lunch with me."

I raised an eyebrow and lowered my hand from his. "Linebacker?"

In my soccer-playing days, I'd been a fierce defender, known to plow through an advance made by the opposing team, but I was highly certain that didn't qualify me for linebacker status. "Are you insulting my size? Sure, I may not be petite at five-seven, but I don't think I look like a football player," I teased, keeping a straight face. It was time to have a little fun with him and his cocky self-assurance.

A look of horror wiped the smug, handsome grin off his face. "No! God, I'm so sorry!" He clutched both of my hands, my phone and earbuds, too, between his long fingers. "This morning, when you bumped into me...I just...I..."

It was my turn to laugh. *God, it feels good to laugh.* Since my heart-to-heart with dear old Dad, I hadn't laughed at anything. "I'm joking!" I said through a fit of giggles.

He smiled and let go of my hands, shoving his into his pockets. "Well, I can see I've screwed this up." He took his right hand from his pocket and ran it through his sun-bleached blond hair.

"Ah, come on. What happened to Mr. Confident?" I teased.

With a closed mouth, he flashed a nanosecond grin. "Insulting the girl you want to take to lunch isn't my best move."

He was so cute with his hunched shoulders and brooding pout. "Ah, come on, don't be like that. I was only joking. I like the nickname." I was such a liar.

Cocking his head to the side, he peered at me from beneath heavy lids. I could see his ego inflating like a balloon as the hunch in his stance disappeared. "Good. Then it's a date."

My head tilted, mirroring his. "I don't recall agreeing to that."

"Technicality."

"You don't give up, do you?"

"Not when it's important."

Important? Having lunch with me is important? Okay? That was random.

I stared at him for a beat. He seemed genuine. I wasn't picking up on any malicious vibes. I chewed the inside of my cheek, contemplating my next move. I hated deviating from my itinerary, but what harm could come from having lunch with a fellow American? It might even be nice to share what Italy has to offer with another person.

"Okay," I sighed.

"I knew you'd cave."

"But," I shouted over his gloat, "before I go with you, you have to answer some questions."

"Shoot." He nailed me with his striking eyes, and I felt it in my core. With him staring at me, it was a miracle I could form a coherent thought.

"What's your full name, date of birth, and your most favorite place to eat?"

He gave a puzzled look but obliged. "Lucas Tyler Walsh, June twenty-fourth, 1991, favorite place to eat...here or back home? Obviously the answers aren't the same."

"Both," I countered.

"Here: Jacks N Joe. Hometown: Hash House A Go Go."

"Those don't sound like real restaurants..." My voice trailed off. He was messing with me.

"Oh, honey. I assure you they are." Lucas folded his arms across his chest and smirked, stepping closer to me, allowing an elderly couple to skirt around us to get a look at the well-endowed fresco behind me. "Although, I'm curious as to what job I'm applying for? I didn't realize an interview was required to be your lunch date."

"I'm covering my bases. If you turn out to be a kidnapper whose sole purpose is to sell me into a sex trafficking ring, I want you to know that my family back home has your full name, DOB, and the restaurants you frequent most often."

"Want my social, too?" he offered arrogantly.

I raised an eyebrow. "You just hand that information out freely? You're an identity thief's wet dream."

"We're a fine pair, then, a sex trafficker and an identity thief. This lunch date has potential." He wiggled his eyebrows suggestively and laughed. It was a delightful sound that coaxed a smile to my lips instantly.

"What?" I quibbled, still smiling. "I'm a female, traveling alone. I've got to be cautious."

"Ha!" Lucas unfolded his arms quickly and pointed at me. "I knew you were alone."

I sucked in a breath. "Ahh! I hadn't meant to say that." *Dammit!*

"Well, rest assured, Sophia, I am not in the sex slave business." He raised his hands, palms up, a sign of surrender. "Unless of course the girl *wants* to be my sex slave. I wouldn't argue with that." A wicked smile turned up the corners of his mouth.

My mouth dropped open. Self-assured or not, I couldn't believe he said that.

"Joking." He jabbed my shoulder. "In all honesty, it would be nice to have a conversation where I don't have to translate every other word that comes out of my companion's mouth. Lunch and good *English* conversation. That's it. And your number."

I hesitated, still not sure this was such a good idea. He looked harmless enough, but… "Okay," I answered warily. "And you're not getting my number."

"We'll see." He winked again and my stomach twisted into a pretzel. Damn that wink. Damn that dimple. What the hell was my problem? I felt like my inexperience with guys was scrolling across my forehead like a stock ticker on Wall Street: *Sophia hasn't been out with a guy since high school.* Then there was his comment about his willing sex slave. Mental images of a naked Lucas ordering a scantily clad version of me to perform various sex acts. I felt my cheeks warm to a brilliant pink, well on their way to red, as the veins and capillaries in my face dilated.

Brushing my hands over my cheeks, I tried to regain my composure, but Lucas and his tall and well-defined body didn't make that very easy.

Lucas gestured toward the atrium. "Check out the rest of the house?"

A weird mix of excitement and trepidation coursed through my system. "Sure," I answered cautiously.

No, he's a stranger...and what is this feeling in the pit of my stomach? I am not allowed to be excited by this prospect...by him.

Yet, I ignored the warning from my rational side and we walked into the atrium together.

Chapter Nine

I stepped back onto the Viocolo dei Vettii with Lucas right behind me. The street was drenched in sunlight and it took my eyes a second to adjust to the glare. Shielding my eyes with my hand, I glanced left, then right. I prided myself on my sense of direction, but I'd been turned around all day. The ruins were not easy to navigate. Fumbling with my messenger bag, I pulled my map free.

"Well, that was interesting," Lucas said, resting his right hand on the small of my back. He pressed close to me and leaned over my shoulder, getting a look at the map in my hands. My cheeks felt hot, and I was certain it didn't have anything to do with the sun blazing in the sky.

Throughout the Vettii house, Lucas found small ways to touch me. I didn't know quite what to make of it. Was he overly friendly? Forward? Whatever it was, I wasn't complaining. He could keep his hand on my back and his body hovering close to mine as long as he wanted. Lucas's touch made me feel…*things*.

He cleared his throat and pointed at the map with his right hand, which he'd moved from my back to rest it on my right shoulder.

Oh, sweet Jesus, he smells good…a weird, intoxicating blend of citrus and mint, coupled with a heady masculine scent.

"Where are we headed next?" he asked, his breath tickling my ear.

His proximity made it difficult to formulate a coherent thought. "Umm…I think if we follow this street down, we'll get to—"

"The Lupanare Grande." He jabbed his index finger on the light blue triangle near the center of town, cutting off my sentence.

I peered over my left shoulder to get a look at his face. "Wolves?"

A devilish smile turned up his lips and he winked. Grabbing my hand, he spun me around quickly and pulled me down the uneven street.

Jogging to match his pace, I called after him, "Geez, where's the fire?" My shoe caught on one of the stones and I nearly face-planted.

"Your Latin's not too shabby, Sophia," he said.

Out of breath, I glared at him. "I'm a med student. Latin's kind of a thing in medicine. And you're an expert on dead languages how?"

Again, he looked my direction and smiled, his dimple on full display. *Ugh, that dimple is going to be the death of me.*

"I took four years of Spanish in high school. Latin, Spanish, Italian, Portuguese, they're all similar. Although, I do enjoy the nuances of learning a new language. I'm a geek in more ways than one."

"How are you a geek?" I raised my eyebrows and gave him a sidelong glance. His definition of geek was clearly very different from mine. He did not fit the stereotypical definition of geek. No thick-rimmed, Coke-bottle glasses, no pocket protector or high-waist jeans. As a matter of fact, he looked like he could grace the cover of any of my favorite romance novels.

He mimicked my smart-ass stare. "I design video games for a living. It doesn't get much geekier than that."

Yep, again, not what I expected. "You don't live in your mom's basement, do you?"

The dimple faded away as his smile disappeared, like I'd flipped a light switch off. His expression darkened. "Uh...no." He shook his head. "Right now, my current address is Napoli, Italy."

He let go of my hand and pushed it into his pocket. His playful demeanor vanished, replaced with an awkward heaviness. I didn't like that my comment was responsible for turning out his light, making his smile disappear.

"I'm sorry, that was supposed to be a joke."

"Hey," he chuckled, bumping his elbow against my shoulder, "no worries." Displaying that gorgeous dimple of his again, the heaviness lifted.

Our earlier hustle to get to the Lupanare Grande was replaced by a slow, steady walk down the ancient street.

"So, you're from California?" I asked, fidgeting with the map. I was glad to have something to do with my hands, a way to expend my nervous energy.

He nodded. "I am."

"What brought you to Italy?"

"Shit happened back home. I needed a break." He shrugged. "Italy seemed like a good idea." Glancing down at me, he smirked. "What about you? What's your story?"

"I don't really have a story." Not one worth sharing anyway.

"Oh, come on. No offense, but you don't seem like the 'backpack across Europe' type. What's the deal?"

Oh, just living the dream while I still can. You see, I may have a de-

generative genetic disorder, Huntington's disease. Sexy, huh? But that wasn't something I needed to unload on a complete stranger.

I nudged his arm this time, making a show of looking at his back. "I don't see you sporting a backpack, either."

"Touché. Nope, not a backpack kind of guy."

"Hmm, that's what I thought."

There was a lull in our conversation. I sneaked a peek at him as we walked down the uneven street. He wore a distant, far-off mask, like he was remembering something sad. Then, out of the blue, he bristled and shrugged, like he was throwing an unpleasant memory off his back. "What about you?" he said, turning his head to look at me. "Do you live in your mom's basement?"

For a brief second, I saw a glimpse of heartbreak. Whatever brought him to Italy must have been painful. There was a pang of sorrow in my heart. I didn't know this guy, but my heart wanted to open and carry some of the burden he buried deep inside. I didn't like seeing him sad.

"No." I pressed my lips into a tight smile, trying to keep from laughing. *Laughter is the best medicine, right? If I can make him laugh, will it take away some of the pain I just saw on his face?* "I live on the main floor."

And there it was—the light switch flipped back on and his features brightened. "The main floor, huh?" He withdrew his hands from his pockets and reformed our connection, squeezing our joined palms for added measure.

Was it supposed to feel this nice, holding the hand of a man I'd just meet? I probably should have been more cautious, but something about the way Lucas touched me said that I could trust him. "Right between Mom's room on the left and Nonna's on the right."

He cocked an eyebrow but kept the lighthearted smile. "So, why is it okay for a twentysomething woman to live with her mother, but the second a twentysomething man says he lives with Mom, it's frowned upon?"

That was a good question and a total double standard. I didn't have an answer, so I shrugged.

"We'll have to figure that one out later." Lucas came to a halt and looked upward. "This is it, I think."

Following his gaze, I took in the large, oddly shaped building. It was a two-story structure whose smaller bottom half supported the larger top portion. "So what does this place have to do with wolves?"

Lucas looked back to me. "Not wolves…she-wolves."

"She-wolves?"

"It's a brothel."

"Oh." Turning my eyes back to the building, I slowly raised my head toward the sky.

"Let's go inside." Still holding hands, we walked to the end of the line of people waiting to enter the brothel.

The line moved quickly and as we approached the entrance, Lucas dropped my hand in favor of clutching my waist.

Umm…I'm entering a brothel with a hot stranger and he's got his hands on me. Yeah, this happens in real life…this isn't weird or anything. My pulse sped up and I feared my heart would beat right out of my chest as we stepped over the threshold.

Inside, the hallway was illuminated by track lighting, drawing the eye upward. Several lights were focused on ancient frescoes, a veritable menu of sex acts Roman prostitutes offered their clients.

My cheeks flushed hot. The naughty pictures and Lucas's hands were too much. In my mind, I knew how ridiculous this situation was. *I'm mean, who picks up a stranger in a foreign country and touches her like this?* But, dammit, my body's reaction to him, his intoxicating scent of sunshine and man, and the way he hovered behind me, one would think I'd never been in the presence of a person with the XY chromosome. *Pull yourself together, Soph.*

I needed something to take my mind off the way his incredibly large hands circled around my middle. With a deep breath, I reached into my bag, dug deep inside, unzipped the small pouch at the bottom, and withdrew my phone. I took Mom's abundant warnings about Naples and pickpockets to heart. Before I left home, I made sure my bag was as thief-proof as possible. So far, I hadn't had any trouble. I prayed my good fortune continued.

Lucas's fingertips pressed into the sides of my abdomen, guiding me to the right. My breath caught and a shiver ran through my body.

Oh, good Lord, I do pray my good fortune continues.

Lucas and I shuffled along, like all the tourists crowding into the small space. Maybe putting his hands on me was nothing more than a way to accommodate what little room we had in the ruin, or a way to make sure we stayed together. *Yeah, that's got to be it.*

My heart sank at the despairing thought, because as much as I didn't want to like his hands there, as much as I shouldn't like his hands there...I really *really* did.

Shoving down my disappointment, I focused my attention on the paintings, the different sex acts: doggie style, girl on top, cunnilingus, each rendering more explicit than the next.

"The Romans were a bunch of horndogs, huh?" Lucas whispered in my ear.

I shuddered. His words and breath wielded an unspeakable amount of power over my body and rational thoughts. Or maybe it was his voice combined with the explicit paintings I was looking at. Whatever it was, my pulse was racing like I'd just passed the halfway point in a marathon. *Give me my 13.1 sticker now!*

My throat was dry, yet I scratched out a weak response. "Apparently."

Like the other tourists, I aligned my phone's camera, centering a shot of a fresco depicting a kneeling man holding on to a woman's butt, her legs draped over his shoulders, and snapped the picture. Dirty paintings weren't something I usually took pictures of, but this was history, so it's okay…at least that's what I told myself.

Lucas and I moved to the next painting, and I clicked another photo. Everyone around us had cameras out, snapping away. All except Lucas. As a matter of fact, I hadn't seen him take one picture. *Who comes to Pompeii and doesn't take pictures?* I glanced over my shoulder and smirked. "Don't want to remember any of this for later?" I joked, finding my voice.

Even in the dim light I saw Lucas's brilliant blue eyes flash. He tapped the side of his head with his index finger. "It's all up here."

I shook my head, smiling, and went back to my picture taking.

We were inching along through the crowd when Lucas pulled me to the side. "Check this out." He ducked into a tiny room, and I followed him inside. There was nothing but a stone bed built into the back wall. Actually, the entire main floor was occupied with several rooms identical to this one.

Lucas moved about the meager room, lightly running his index finger over some of the Latin graffiti etched into the wall. "Cozy," he said facetiously.

I sat down on the bed and held my phone out. "Will you take my picture?"

He smiled, dimple and all, and I could have melted into a puddle right then. Taking the phone from my hands, his fingers brushed over mine.

Crossing my legs, I folded my hands in my lap, tilted my head slightly, and smiled, ready for him to snap a quick picture so we could move on. I did not like being on display. I felt very exposed, like he could see all my secrets as he centered me in the camera's frame.

Lucas held the phone in front of his face. Lines of concentration creased his forehead. He tilted his head to the left, then to the right, and moved the phone from side to side.

A dull ache bloomed in my cheeks, and I muttered through my forced smile, "Take the dang picture already."

"You're in a brothel, Linebacker. You can't sit on that bed and pretend you're at a Southern cotillion." Lucas motioned with his hand. "Give me something. Ham it up a bit."

"Uh-uh." I shook my head. "There are too many people around. Just take the picture so we can move on."

He peered over the phone, grinning smugly. "Prop your feet up and toss your head back."

"Ugh!" I groaned, standing up. One stomp in his direction and I held my hand out for my phone. "I'll take a selfie."

"Better yet, let's take a selfie together." He did that eyebrow-wiggle thing again.

"Fine." I turned and walked back to the bed with Lucas at my side. "You are really annoying. You know that, right?"

He nodded enthusiastically, proud to have earned that distinction.

We sat down and he put his arm around me, holding the phone

out with the other arm. Moving his hand, he centered our faces in the screen. I plastered on a white, toothy grin, my ordinary "say cheese" smile. But when Lucas smiled, there was nothing ordinary about it. He had the most beautifully shaped lips. They turned up at the edges, framed by subtle laugh lines that sang of a past full of laughter and happiness. Right now, that laughter manifested as light shining from his wide, playful eyes. I could stare at him all day long.

"Nope." He dropped his hand. "This won't do."

"What? That would have been a great picture." I looked at him. "Who are you, Annie Leibovitz or something? I'm beginning to understand why you don't take pictures."

"Here." He scooted closer and hooked his arm around my waist and lifted me onto his lap, our faces an inch apart. My heart lurched. I looked into his eyes, falling into their endless blues. His gaze crashed over me like a heavy ocean wave while at the same time I was flying in a clear, cloudless sky.

It was only when he licked his lips, drawing my attention to his mouth, that I was able to stop staring at his eyes.

My arms had nowhere to go but to circle around his neck. "What are you doing?" I whispered.

He inhaled my whisper with his open mouth, pulling my expelled breath into his lungs. "Making this picture better," he intoned, his voice deep, an edge to his words.

Without breaking eye contact, he situated me on his lap and held the phone out again.

Click.

"See," he uttered, lowering his hand. "Infinitely better." His words made the wisps of hair against my neck flutter, and I shuddered.

My jaw dropped. *Holy. Freaking. Hell. Who is this guy?*

The temperature in the stone room skyrocketed. Each breath I inhaled burned a trail to my lungs and tugged low in my belly. I couldn't think. Clearing my throat, I placed my hands on his hard shoulders and pushed back, sliding off his lap.

Lucas's eyes widened and he stood quickly, taking a large stride toward the wall, becoming very interested in the graffiti once again.

"Everything okay?" I asked.

"Um, yeah." He looked over his shoulder and smiled. "I'm good." There was a pinch in his voice.

"Thanks for taking the picture," I said, joining him at the graffiti wall. I held out my hand, palm up. "May I have my phone?"

He plopped it into my hand. I tapped on the photo album icon, eager to see how it turned out. I sucked in a breath. "Holy wow."

"Let's see," Lucas said, bending low to rest his chin on my shoulder. I had to take another deep breath to keep focused on the picture and not the heat radiating off of him.

The picture captured our profiles. The contrast between us was striking; his golden California-boy features lit up his half of the photo, where my dark Italian features left my portion in shadow. My round face stood out against the sharp angles of his chiseled jawline. His long, tapered nose barely touched the tip of mine.

Then there were our eyes. The connection I felt when we met this morning wasn't just a feeling anymore…I could *see* it. A taut cord anchored our gazes. We were the only two people in the world in this picture. My heart thumped hard against my chest, like it wanted to beat but couldn't. Something tight had a hold of it, squeezing.

"I like it," he whispered at my ear. The stubble on his face scratched against my cheek and all my thoughts disappeared. I breathed him in, letting his nearness consume my senses. Chills cascaded down my back like a waterfall.

"Me too."

"Ready?" Lucas threaded his fingers with mine and squeezed my hand.

I nodded, still dazed by everything I was feeling. "Yeah." I clicked my phone off and the screen went black.

Together, we left the tiny cell and joined the noisy throng of tourists in the hallway. I was hit with a wave of sadness that Lucas and I weren't the only two people in the world anymore.

We made a sharp left turn and were through the brothel and back out on the sun-drenched street.

I squinted against the brightness, still unable to get the image of our profiles out of my head. Stranger or not, the picture of him and me had just become my favorite picture, ever.

For a few minutes I had felt like the carefree, fun-loving me from years ago. The "me" before Penley's death…the "me" that didn't know about Huntington's disease.

* * *

Lucas and I strolled down the street. We were close enough that my shoulder would brush against his arm. Pheromones mixed with the beauty and majesty of Pompeii were a potent combination, enough to get my heart pumping and my thoughts racing.

I didn't bother with the map. I didn't care where we were headed; I was just happy to be in his company. He was the very best kind of distraction, taking my mind off of things that were well out of my control. For the first time, I was actually excited not to have a plan.

The streets were flooded with tourists, even more so than they had been that morning. Lucas glanced at his watch and then nudged me with his shoulder. "You hungry?"

"Yeah, a little."

"A little? I'm starving."

I scanned our surroundings. "I think there's a place to eat around here somewhere."

"Nah." He swung our entwined hands. "I heard it's shitty and overpriced. There are a few places to eat not far from here, just outside the ruin. We could walk there, get a bite to eat, and then take the train to Herculaneum?"

I nodded. "That sounds like a great plan. But there's one more thing I'd like to see before we leave, if you don't mind. I'd understand if you didn't want to wait. We can go our separate ways; I won't be offended."

Lucas drew his eyebrows down, squinting. "Is that a kind way of saying you want to get rid of me?"

"No, not at all." I let go of his hand and waved away his concern. "I just don't want to keep you if you have other places to be."

Lucas put his lips at my ear and said, "The only place I have to be is right here."

Oh, sweet Jesus, Mother Mary, and the Pope, did my heart just do a backflip?

"What did you want to see?" he asked.

"Huh?" I looked at him and shook my head. "What?" The part of my brain responsible for speech and cognition had been overridden by the part of my brain that wanted to curl up in his arms and get lost in his eyes and…touch my lips to his.

"What did you want to see?" he repeated. "You feeling all right?" He brushed his knuckles over my cheeks. "Your face is really flushed."

"Yeah. Fine. I'm great!" I spluttered. I took a half step back, needing more space to think.

Dear Lord, what is wrong with me? I'm usually so…collected. I took pride in not being ruled by my emotions and hormones. I thought rationally, sought out all possible answers, took all variables into account. I lived and thrived on having a plan, a backup plan, and a plan for the backup. But, goodness gracious, when his breath blew across my skin, the dormant nerve cells in my body fired at will, and I morphed into a bumbling idiot.

Breathe, Sophia. Do something. Don't just stand there. And for the love of God, DO NOT look into his eyes!

Glancing at my feet, I flipped the cover of my bag over and pulled out a bottle of water. I unscrewed the cap and drank deeply. Swallowing, I tested the waters and looked Lucas in the eyes, forcing myself to breathe.

See, you can look at the charming, handsome man without hyperventilating.

"Sophia?" he said, concern coloring his voice. Two vertical creases formed between his eyebrows as his eyes pulled tight. "Talk to me. What's wrong?"

I shook my head and took another swig of water. I wiped my mouth with the back of my hand. "Nothing. I'm good." I held up my hand between us. "I was going to say I wanted to see the Garden of Fugitives."

His jaw ticked and then he broke into a grin, his dimple deepening. I had to fight the urge to run my finger over it.

"Got your map? Let's find it."

"Oh yeah." I slipped my water bottle back into my bag and took out my crinkled map. "Here."

Lucas and I examined the map carefully; then I spotted what we were looking for. I pointed down the street we were headed. "The Garden of Fugitives. That way."

"Good eye," Lucas said, nudging my shoulder. "And it's near an exit, too. Perfect."

* * *

Stopped in their tracks by something much larger than them, thirteen people with lives, hopes, dreams, and plans never got to see the light of another day in AD 79.

Tears sprang to my eyes and threatened to spill over. I hadn't expected the plaster casts to affect me this way. There were two casts in particular that tore at my heart. To the left of the enclosure was a person frozen in time, trying to crawl his way somewhere safe, or maybe to a loved one. In the strain of his muscles, I could feel his distress, his urgency to move, and a fresh wave of sadness overtook me, knowing he didn't make it to where he'd intended. Of all the ruins in Pompeii, the casts told the real story.

When I laid eyes on the tiny cast of a child, I wondered what was going through his mind. How did parents sooth their children, knowing this was the end? They'd never get to see them grow up. Their babies were going to die in the most horrific way possible. How helpless and terrified they must have felt.

Even in the ninety-degree heat, chills ran through me, prickling my skin. I wiped my eyes with the back of my hand and sniffled.

Lucas pressed his hand to the small of my back and rubbed light counterclockwise circles. Even though I knew nothing about him, I was glad to share this experience with him. His presence, his touch, brought me an unexpected peace I wouldn't have felt had I come here alone.

"It's ironic, but these casts are what breathe life into this place. They make it real," Lucas said somberly.

Sniffling again, I nodded in agreement. "Yeah."

"Going about their business one minute and reduced to this the next."

I shivered. Flashes of my dad in his wheelchair came to mind. I'd been going about my business too; then my genes—like a volcano—threatened to blow apart my whole future.

I sucked up my tears and whipped around. An emotional breakdown was the last thing I wanted Lucas to see. "Time for lunch," I blurted out.

"You're ready to go?" A look of confusion passed over his face.

"Yep." I drew in a quick breath. The air was dusty and hot. It tickled my throat, trailing a subtle burn to my lungs. I'd had enough of ancient sadness. I'd had enough sadness of any kind. I needed to get my mind off of hopeless futures.

"You're sure?"

With a deliberate nod, I sighed. "More than you know."

Chapter Ten

For all Pompeii had to offer, I was not in the right frame of mind to enjoy the beauty and majesty of the ancient city. Maybe the plaster casts hadn't been a good idea. I should have stuck to Pompeii's sexy side; at least that hadn't reminded me of death and what awaited me at home.

When I looked at the casts, all I saw was hopelessness, ruin. The frozen statues, with their animated arms, legs, and faces, would haunt me forever. Passing through the exit, it was nice to step back into the twenty-first century and put their ghosts behind me. I knew I was in Italy to do touristy things, but Herculaneum didn't sound appealing anymore—just another serving of anguish and desperation.

I needed fun. Anything to take my mind off of impending death.

"You're quiet." With his hands shoved in his pockets, Lucas kicked at a pebble, sending it skidding down the ornate sidewalk.

I shook off my dreary thoughts. "Sorry. The casts just got to me more than I thought they would. Had you seen them before?"

"Nope."

"You're a man of few words, aren't you?" Every question I asked this guy, he answered in vague, one-word responses.

"Didn't realize that question required a monologue for an answer."

"Tell me something about you no one else knows." I ignored his smart-ass comment and forced the issue. I wanted to know something personal, be in on one of his secrets.

Tourists and locals filled the busy commercial area, drowning our silence. After we'd put another city block behind us, I wondered if he'd heard me. Glancing at him, I noticed he watched his feet as he walked. I was just about to repeat my question when he said, "Mr. Waddles."

"Uh, what?"

"Something no one knows about me." He took his eyes from the ground and stared me down. "And if you tell anyone, I'll deny I ever told you."

I laughed. I couldn't help it. "What is a Mr. Waddles?"

"Mr. Waddles is my favorite stuffed animal."

"Oh, really? Do you two cuddle at night?" I teased. A gorgeous, grown man with a favorite stuffed animal? That was precious.

When he smirked, I noticed it pulled up higher on the left side. Maybe that was what made his dimple so pronounced. Whatever the reason, his crooked mouth and dimple made for a swoon-worthy smile.

"Right now, Mr. Waddles is holding down the fort in San Diego, hanging out in the back of my closet."

"And what is the story behin—"

"Uh-uh." Lucas shook his head, interrupting. "I answered your question. You're the only one on this planet who knows I still have Mr. Waddles."

I gave him a big, toothy smile. It did feel nice to be privy to one of his guarded secrets. "Wow. I'm honored. One day, maybe I'll even get to meet Mr. Waddles."

Lucas's eyes flashed. "Maybe," he drawled. "Now it's your turn," he said, pointing.

"Am I answering the same question? Something no one else knows?"

He nodded. "Go for it."

I thought about it. He'd offered a silly story, which I could have guessed was more significant than he let on, based on the way he turned the question back on me so quickly. I was confident Mr. Waddles's real story would come to light at some point. But what was I going to tell him?

Mom and Nonna knew a lot about me—I usually told them everything—but I was careful to keep them in the dark when it came to my first three years of high school. Being a freshman on the varsity soccer team, I learned real quick what it meant to be "popular." So had Penley. We partied with the best of them. Was it cheating if I told Lucas something that only Penley knew? She wasn't going to rat me out.

"I lost my virginity in the backseat of Scotty Hendrickson's mom's Trailblazer on the night of my junior prom."

Yep. Take that, Lucas Walsh. I just one-upped your Mr. Waddles.

Lucas raised an eyebrow. "Really?"

"Yeah, not my finest moment." I cringed. "Where are we eating, by the way?"

Both of us came to a stop on the sidewalk and took in our surroundings. "How about McDonald's?" Lucas pointed straight ahead. "It's always a trip to see what passes as McDonald's in a foreign country."

"I'm game." My stomach rumbled at the thought of greasy fries and chicken nuggets.

We beat a path to the Golden Arches. Lucas grabbed the door handle and pulled it open, ushering me inside.

Branding at its finest. Even clear across the Atlantic Ocean, McDonald's still looked and smelled like McDonald's. I reveled in its familiarity. But there were some differences; the menu had many of the standard American favorites, accompanied with some not-so-American choices. The McLobster for one. That did not sound appetizing at all. Seafood was gross even in the finest of restaurants. No way would I order it at a McDonald's. *Ewww!*

"What are you having?" Lucas asked, surveying the menu overhead.

My usual came to mind. "McNugget Happy Meal with a Coke."

He turned his head in my direction, cocking that eyebrow again. "A Happy Meal? Aren't you a little old for those?"

"Says the guy with a Mr. Waddles."

He pointed again. "See, this is why Mr. Waddles stays in the closet."

I pouted. "Poor Mr. Waddles, he gets no respect."

Lucas shook his head. "Yeah, yeah."

"Buon pomeriggio," the cashier greeted us. "What will you have?"

Lucas looked to me and nodded, like a true gentleman, allowing me to order first. "Chicken McNugget Happy Meal with a Coke, *per favore.*" Yeah, look at me whipping out the Italian pleasantries like a native. My cool factor just went up ten meters.

The cashier typed in my order and asked, "Is the toy for a boy or girl?"

Ah, the sole reason I always ordered Happy Meals. The toy.

Growing up, I had quite the collection of Happy Meal toys, much to my mother's and Nonna's chagrin. But, really, they only had themselves to blame; they were the ones buying them for me.

I glanced around, looking for the toy display; I had to make a well-informed decision. Behind me, it seemed my choices were Transformers or Littlest Pet Shop. "Boy," I answered. Definitely the Transformer; those things were so cool.

"And you, *signore*?"

The cashier's attention shifted to Lucas, as did mine. But he wasn't looking at her; he was looking at me. I couldn't read the expression in his wide eyes, but they were dazzling nonetheless.

"Lucas, she's ready for your order." I motioned to the lady behind the counter.

Shrugging, he snapped out of whatever trance he'd been in. "Oh, right. Umm"—he stared at the menu—"Big Mac, fries, and a Coke."

"*Grazi*," she said.

I reached for my bag, but Lucas put his arm on mine and shook his head. "Whoa there, Linebacker. I asked you to lunch, remember?"

I pulled my lips in a fraction of an inch and nodded. "So that's what it's going to be, then? Linebacker?"

Lucas paid the cashier and grabbed the tray when our order was ready. Carrying it to an empty booth near the entrance, we sat down by a window. "It got you to say yes." He winked.

"Is this a real date, then?" It had been years since I'd been on a date. I wasn't sure I remembered how to *date*. We'd had an easy camaraderie all day long; I feared putting a formal label on it would mess that up.

He stopped fiddling with the items on the tray and looked at me, his eyes smoldering. "Do you want it to be?"

When he unleashed the full force of his eyes, God help the person in their line of sight. I gaped like a fish out of water. "Uh…what do you want it to be?"

"A real date." He nodded and went back to the tray. Picking up my Happy Meal box, he held it between his fingers before passing it over. "Cute."

Reaching across the table, I lifted the yellow sports car–shaped box from his hand. "Yeah, it is cute." But compared to Lucas's boyish charm, there was no comparison. A thrill of excitement sent tingles through my body…a real date.

Smiling, I pulled apart Bumblebee's flaps and got a whiff of homey-greasy-American-goodness. Here I was, my first day in Italy, sitting in a McDonald's, on a date. I barely recognized myself. And for once, it felt nice not to be me.

I took a bite of my chicken nugget. I hadn't been hungry at Pompeii, but now I was famished. My stomach was ready to wage a civil war in retaliation to my neglect.

Lucas tore into his burger. "You know," he said, mumbling around the food in his mouth, "I'm not one to eat Mickey D's at home. Give me breakfast food or a burrito any day. But this"—he pointed to his burger—"is divine."

I took another bite and agreed. "It really is."

Lucas and I sat quietly for a minute, enjoying our lunches. Taking a sip of soda, he washed down a few fries and smiled at me. "I'm feeling this relationship is a bit one-sided."

"How so?"

"You know my birthday, where I'm from, and my favorite places to eat. The only thing I know about you is that you're American, you're traveling alone, and you got busy in the back of an SUV."

I shrugged and popped a fry in my mouth. "Seems pretty balanced to me. Three facts for three facts."

He wagged a finger. "Nope, I've offered a fourth. Mr. Waddles?"

Crap! He had me there.

"Where are you from, Sophia?"

"St. Louis. I just graduated from Washington University. I'm starting med school in the fall."

"Wow, a doctor. I'm impressed."

I nodded. I used to be impressed by that distinction, too, but it sort of felt like a lie now. I may not have the opportunity to become a doctor. And then what? The prospect of becoming a doctor had consumed my life for so long, there was nothing else I was good at. It was the only thing I knew. A sinkhole opened up in the pit of my stomach, and I was standing at the edge, peering into the scary, black depths. "Technically, I should be there right now, but my dad sprang this trip on me at the last minute and my mom insisted that I go. I withdrew from summer classes, rearranged my fall schedule, and here I am."

"Remind me to thank your parents." Lucas grinned and wiped his mouth with a napkin.

My lips pressed into a thin smile and my cheeks warmed. He was such a flirt. "What about you? What's your story?"

His smile faded slightly as he mulled over my question. "Not really that interesting."

"Oh, and mine was? Come on."

He shrugged. "I was in my second year of grad school but decided to take a break to focus on my design company."

"That's right, you said you design video games?"

"I do. Me and my friend, Dean. We've been designing video

games for the better part of three years. Our senior year of college, we struck gold when our indie zombie survival game, *Undead Resurrection*, hit it big. That was the beginning of WalStock Software Design. Since then, we've turned out a new game each year and have a pretty clutch fan base."

"Sheesh, you're like a legitimate grown-up. I'm impressed."

"Ha. Yeah, right," he said with a quick roll of his eyes. "I also like sleeping till noon, spending my days at the beach, surfing, and loading up on energy drinks. A right grown-up there," he said with a heavy dose of sarcasm.

"At least you've got stuff figured out…know where your life is headed." My shoulders slumped.

"What are you talking about? Med school isn't like falling down a damn rabbit hole. Takes a dedicated, no-nonsense adult to make it through that." He tossed the napkin on the table and sat back in his seat.

"I guess." I shook off the chill of uncertainty the best I could. "It's just, I've had some stuff happen over the last few weeks. Has me questioning whether med school is a good choice."

"Fucking life," Lucas sighed.

Stepping out into the world was scary. Even more so now that I didn't know what my world would look like in fifteen, twenty years. All my careful plans scattered like dandelion seeds in the wake of my dad's pronouncement.

I hated uncertainty. With a passion. Control was a basic life need, like water, air, and shelter. I envied Lucas. He had control of his life. It had direction and purpose, and he seemed happy. I used to have that kind of security. I wanted it back.

"Yeah, fucking life."

Chapter Eleven

I don't know about you, but my feet are killing me," Lucas said, falling into the train's seat.

I sat beside him and nodded in agreement. The blisters on my feet had blisters, courtesy of the stone-paved streets. I also discovered my legs had muscles I didn't know existed (and I knew of a lot of muscles).

"I can't remember the last time I walked that much." Sighing, I closed my eyes. Tired didn't even begin to cover how I felt. I couldn't wait to get back to the hotel, take a shower, and collapse into bed.

"This was supposed to be my last day in Naples, but I don't have the energy to pack up and leave tonight." Lucas exhaled loudly and stretched his long legs out, propping them on the empty chair in front of him.

"You're leaving?" My heart dropped into my stomach. I didn't have a reason to be upset by this turn of events; we'd only spent five hours together. Albeit, the most enjoyable five hours I'd spent in the company of another person since Penley had died, but who was counting? "Where are you going?"

The rickety train groaned and creaked as it pulled out of the station and picked up speed. We'd be back in the heart of Naples in no time. I wished I had superpowers, a way to stop time.

God, did I.

"Sorrento…Amalfi…maybe Capri? I don't know, haven't decided yet." He reclined his head, closing his eyes.

"What's that like? Not knowing what you're going to do next. Without plans, I'd go crazy." Singular focus was the only way I survived. But I admired his carefree spirit and wished I had the guts to go where the wind blew me.

Lucas shrugged. "Hmm. I've learned from experience that plans can go south in the blink of an eye. At least this way, if I don't have a plan, I have no expectations. I won't be let down."

"What happened? What plans went south?"

The train made a sharp curve to the left and the momentum forced me into Lucas's side. He rolled his head to the left and looked down at me, grinning. Without a second thought, he raised his arm and draped it over my shoulders. Tucked beside him, my heart tried to beat against the viselike grip wrapped around it.

"See, I'd wanted to put my arm around you since we got on the train but kept talking myself out of it. My expectations were disappointing me, but fate stepped in and handed me the perfect opportunity." He flexed his arm, squeezing me close.

My whole body stiffened, afraid if I moved, he'd pull his arm away. That was the last thing I wanted. I pulled in a long, steadying breath. He smelled like the outdoors—sunshine and wind…and something else…something masculine and uniquely him. Whatever it was, it was both intoxicating and comforting. All my earlier worries of him being a criminal disappeared.

"What about you? What are your plans?"

Shifting in the hard seat, I sat up straighter, clearing my throat. "I got here two days ago. I plan on staying in Naples this week. After that I plan to visit Sorrento, Salerno, Capri, and I have to make it to Battipaglia at some point, too."

"A full itinerary. Do me a favor, though. Leave a little wiggle room in your plans for fate to step in."

I cracked a smile. "Will do. I'm kind of flying by the seat of my pants on this trip anyway. I'm just certain of the places I want to check off my tourist list."

"Battipaglia is on your list?" Lucas asked. "Not exactly a tourist hot spot."

"My grandfather lives there."

"Oh." Lucas sat up.

"My father's dad. I've never met him and my dad wants me to pay him a visit."

"You actually have family here. That's cool."

Yeah, family I knew nothing about. Family I had no connection with. There was nothing cool about that. "What about you?" After he told me about Dean and WalStock, he got quiet, turned into a master of the fine art of changing the subject. "I've been the topic of conversation all day long. You know I live with my mom. You know I work at her gelato shop…" I held up a finger each time I ticked off a personal item we'd discussed. Then, rolling my eyes, I held up a third finger. "And I even offered up my sexual history, the whole awkward story." My cheeks flushed with heat. I still couldn't believe I'd told him the gory details of that awful night. I wanted to erase that conversation from existence, not to mention the whole terrible five minutes with Scotty. Yet, there was something about Lucas that made me want to open up to him…to tell him all my secrets…save one.

Lucas smiled devilishly, his eyes shining like bright blue stars. He shook his head. "Tragic." Shifting in his seat, Lucas turned his body toward mine and scooped my hand between his. His eyes searched my face, leaving trails of heat in their wake. "All right, I'll tell you a story, but I've got to warn you, you might find it sad."

I nodded. "Tell me."

Again, he shook his head, closing his eyes for a couple of seconds. I could see the struggle on his face like a war between his mind and his mouth. He didn't like letting people in…just like me. "You're sure?"

"Only if you are. If you don't want to share, you don't have to." His struggle was real. This story was deeply personal.

"When I was ten, my mom and dad divorced. When it came time to divide the belongings, my mother went through the house and handpicked all the things she wanted to keep. Sitting quietly on the living room couch, I watched her, wondering which parent I was staying with that night. When they split, I'd been living with my dad. But I had friends whose parents were divorced and they went back and forth between their parents. I figured at some point I'd do the same.

"As I sat on the couch, I counted the times my mom passed by. Seventeen. She walked by me seventeen times and never once beckoned me to come with her. When she finished picking the house apart, she knelt down in front of me, Mr. Waddles in her hands, and looked me in the eyes. 'Lucas, you're a good boy, but right now, I need to be alone. You're better off with your dad.' She set Mr. Waddles in my lap, stood up, rounded the end of the couch, and walked out the front door. I never saw or heard from her again. Parents divorcing each other was one thing, but I'd never heard of one divorcing the kid, too."

I was speechless. Dear Lord. How could a mother do that to her child? My dad had walked out on me, but at least he remembered to send me birthday and Christmas presents. Not a real dad, but he hadn't disappeared completely.

"I'm sorry," he said. "That story was probably a bit much to unload on a stranger." His arm flexed around me.

"No." I cleared my throat. "No, I'm glad you told me. Misery loves company, right? My parents are divorced, too."

I held his gaze. I was happy to have found a kindred spirit, but reality was a bitch, and this perfect day was an anomaly. As the train pressed toward Stazione di Napoli Piazza Garibaldi so did the end of our time together. In just a few minutes, I'd never see him again. As it should be, I guessed. I had no right to want more time with him. I didn't even know him. Yet, selfishly, I did want more. In spite of my corrupted DNA, med school, and the fact that I knew very little about him, I still wanted more.

"Lucas, if Mr. Waddles is tied to such a sad time in your life, why keep him?"

He relaxed into the seat, his arm still around my shoulder. Looking upward, he blew out a loud breath, his internal war still raging. "It's the only thing I remember her ever giving me. Aren't gifts usually given to people you love?"

I nodded but stayed quiet. A heavy tension settled over us like a wool blanket on a summer's day.

The train slowed, pulling into the station. It was the end of the line. Time for us to go our separate ways.

I wasn't ready. I wanted more time.

In these last few weeks, time was the one thing that had become most precious to me. It didn't seem I had enough time to do anything anymore. How much life could I cram into the little moments I had left? I was twenty-two; I wasn't supposed to worry about how much time I had left. But as the train screeched to a halt, the clack of the wheels on the tracks resembled the slowing of a ticking clock.

The wool blanket threatened to suffocate me.

Once the train came to a stop, Lucas rose and I followed. His hand slid down my back as he ushered me toward the open doors.

The train station was still bustling with life despite the late hour. We navigated through crowds of tourists and locals, finally making our way outside the station. This was it, the inevitable good-bye. Today had been a beautiful distraction…just what I'd needed. I was silly to think anything more would come from today.

Lucas wrapped his strong hand around my elbow and pulled me to a stop. Facing each other, I looked up into his eyes. *Damn those eyes.* Even in the darkness they burned so brightly. "Where are you staying?" he asked.

I glanced to the southwest and pointed. "That way, I think. I'm at the Hotel Suite Esedra."

"Can we walk from here, or should I flag down a taxi?"

I shook my head. "No, it's close."

"Good." He looked up at the sky, then back at me, a bemused smile on his lips. "I'll walk you back."

Yes, please! I wanted to shout. "That isn't necessary, if it's out of your way." I shook my head.

Waving away my comment, he continued. "I kind of kidnapped you today. The least I can do is make sure you get back to your hotel in one piece."

"Kidnapped me, huh?" I huffed, a tiny smile tugging at the corners of my lips. "So the truth finally comes out. You are a criminal. I'm in trouble, aren't I?" I was sure to keep my tone light, joking. But when I saw the split-second flash in his eyes, my stomach tightened. I knew I wasn't in danger, but trouble, yes. The kind of trouble that involved my heart. A kind of trouble I had no business welcoming into my life.

* * *

The walk back to my hotel was slow, deliberately so. I was in no hurry to put an end to the day, and by Lucas's leisurely gait, I assumed he felt the same way. Where my feet would have welcomed the five-minute cab ride, I ignored their cries of pain and concentrated on the energy between my body and Lucas's. That energy had grown to combustible limits, and our pace and the silence only added fuel to the fire. I'd never kissed a stranger before, but damn, I wanted to now.

Though we weren't holding hands, we walked close enough that our arms brushed occasionally. Pressure built inside me like charged air right before a lightning strike.

I slowed and turned the corner, leading us down a narrow street that resembled a back alley more than an actual roadway.

"This is me." I stopped in front of the small yellow-and-gray-sided hotel. There was an extraterrestrial glow on the sidewalk courtesy of the huge, green backlit letters spelling out the hotel's name on the building's façade. Sandwiched between two drab-looking apartment buildings, the Hotel Suite Esedra resembled a single ray of sunshine peeking through gloomy clouds. It was very quaint. Not five-star quality, but nice all the same.

"It was a pleasure to meet you, Sophia." Lucas held out his hand. After the intimacy of the day, it felt oddly formal that he'd want to depart with such an arbitrary good-bye.

Ask him to come inside, a tiny voice echoed in my head. It sounded like mine, but with a hint of mischief, wanting, and confidence. The words were on the tip of my tongue.

I brought my hand to his, willing myself to speak as our palms touched. There it was again, the zing of electricity…an opened circuit…free-flowing energy.

Lucas pumped my hand gently up and down.

I felt like a battery; the energy of our touching hands recharged my courage and I opened my mouth to speak. "Would you—"

"What are you—"

We both paused, smiling, having spoken at the same time, then promptly apologized in unison. "Sorry."

I dropped my hand from his and laughed. Lucas continued to smile, the dimple in his left cheek making it hard to concentrate.

Kiss him. Kiss him. Kiss him, the voice in my head chanted.

He ran a hand through his hair and blew out a breath. "What are you doing tomorrow?"

I was in Naples until Saturday; then I was headed to Sorrento. I knew which cities I wanted to visit, but had no formal itinerary, thanks to my mother and her insistence on me absorbing Italy at leisure, "off the clock," as she had put it. I shrugged, fidgeting with the flap of my messenger bag. "I don't know yet. Haven't decided."

Lucas stepped closer. "I thought you weren't the fly-by-the-seat-of-your-pants kind of girl." A light breeze whistled in the alley, blowing a few escaped strands of my messy bun across my face.

"Usually I'm not." My voice caught in my throat.

Lucas trailed his fingers over my cheeks…my temples, brushing my hair back into place. "You're pretty good at it. Glad you bumped into me today, Linebacker." He winked.

Kiss him, dammit!

"Thanks." The lightning was about to strike any second, especially if he kept touching me.

He put his hands on my shoulders. "So, we tackled Pompeii today. Why don't we hit the Naples National Archaeological Museum tomorrow? Oh, and have you had the pizza here yet? We need to get pizza."

My heart paused midbeat. "I thought today was your last day in Naples. Aren't you leaving?" He'd just said that on the train, but I prayed he'd changed his mind.

"Oh," he drawled, "I think I can stick around another day."

And my heart resumed beating, double time. Inside, a *woohoo* fought to be unleashed, but I swallowed it, biting down on my smile. "Great. That sounds great."

I wanted to sing. I felt like a different girl. Post-Penley-Sophia was adverse to spontaneity, always shackled to a textbook or worrying about everything and anything. An über control freak. And in the last few weeks, she had every right to be a control-freak-worrywart of the most obnoxious kind. But right now…this trip…that Sophia was willing to take a backseat so *Sophia Italia* could have some fun…while the clock was still ticking.

The effervescing tingle in my veins was exhilarating. I could have gotten high on the feeling.

"Awesome. I'll pick you up in"—Lucas smoothed his hands down my arms and examined his clunky gold wristwatch—"seven and a half hours?"

The wind picked up and the three flags above our heads waved, snapping mightily. "Perfect," I said, grinning like an idiot.

"Until tomorrow, then." Lucas reached for my hand and pulled me closer. Even though our bodies didn't touch, he was still close enough to kiss me.

Please kiss me. I don't care that you're a stranger. Sophia Italia wants to feel…wants to be alive.

For what seemed like an eternity, Lucas searched my eyes. What was he looking for? Permission? Reciprocation of feelings? *I feel it, too!* I wanted to shout…but I didn't.

Then he leaned in and put his lips to my…

Cheek. A European handshake.

His lips burned against my skin like a live wire. My thoughts ran wild, imagining those lips on other parts of my body, leaving me drunk with desire.

Lucas pulled away and flashed his dimple. "Get some sleep. We'll hit the town in the morning."

I nodded, my voice lost inside me.

"Well, go," he demanded with a chuckle, shooing me toward the door.

I stumbled backward, refusing to turn my back on him, afraid he'd disappear. Lucas shuffled backward, off the sidewalk, and onto the street.

A scooter darted around him. Lucas waved to me, ignoring the motorist who nearly hit him. "*Ciao*, Sophia."

"*Ciao,*" I replied, grasping the handle. I gave the door a shove.

"Oh, Sophia," Lucas shouted, right before I went inside.

I froze. *A second chance. I should invite him upstairs.* "Yeah?" I breathed.

"I didn't get your number." He pulled his phone out of his pocket.

I backed away from the door, joining him on the sidewalk again. "Let me have your phone." I held out my hand. Laying his phone on my palm, I scooped it up and opened his contact list. Quickly typing my number, I added "Linebacker" to his favorites, handing it back to him with a smirk. "Now you do." And I still hadn't invited him upstairs. What's wrong with me?

"*Grazie.*" He dipped his chin. "See you in the morning, then."

"I'll be here." I smiled, kicking myself for not having the courage to ask him to stay. Old Sophia was still holding on, but tomorrow was a new day, a chance to silence her for a while. A chance to forget about things I couldn't control.

Once I made it back to my room, I knew sleeping was out of the question. Butterflies fluttered in my stomach and electricity buzzed through my veins. I kicked my shoes off at the end of the bed and dropped my bag on the floor. Falling onto my back, I sank into the mattress with a sigh. "Holy shit. Did today really happen?" I shook my head in disbelief.

At the foot of the bed, a muffled chime sounded. My phone. Sitting up, I drew in a deep breath and blew it out again, ruffling the wisps of hair around my face. I inched toward the end of the bed and reached for my bag, pulling out my phone.

Across the screen was a text message from Lucas: *I told you so.*

Hmm, what was that supposed to mean? I typed my response: *What?*

Staring at the screen, I awaited his reply.

I knew I'd get your number before the end of the day, he texted back.

I read the text, hearing his deep, cocky voice in my head while a wide smile pulled at the corners of my lips. My thumbs flew over the keyboard. *Yeah, I planned on giving it to you. I just liked seeing you work for it!*

It was the most pleasurable day's work I've had in a long time, even though it started out with me on my ass.

Exhilaration sent the butterflies in my stomach into a tizzy. *Glad I could help with that.*

Night, Linebacker. See you soon.

Good night, Lucas.

And to think I almost threw this trip in the waste can. Italy had just become my favorite place to be.

Chapter Twelve

Outside, the incessant blare of a car horn sounded. I rolled over in bed, blinking away sleepiness, grabbing my phone off the bedside table. Keeping one eye closed, I focused on the brightly lit screen: 5:30 a.m. Lucas would be here in two hours. I threw off the stiff blankets and stared at the decorative makeshift canopy over my head. It was very European and very seventies. I wondered where Lucas was staying. He'd never said. Then a jolt of panic rippled through me. What if yesterday was it? What if he'd changed his mind…or worse yet, never planned to meet with me today at all? What if everything had been a farce, a cruel joke to play on the naïve American girl traveling alone?

I sat up straight. A thin layer of sweat made my pajamas stick to my skin. "Calm down, Sophia. He'll be here." I hoped that by saying it out loud, I'd convince myself it was the truth. But why would he come? I had no hold over him. Heck, I didn't even know him. I checked to see if he'd texted. Nothing.

Get your ass out of bed, Sophia, Sophia Italia's voice commanded.

He'll be here soon and you don't want to look like…this. I looked down at my sensible pj's: a gray Wash U School of Medicine short-sleeve T-shirt and black capri-length yoga pants. Sophia Italia did not approve of my sleeping attire.

It goes well with your stark white cotton panties, too, she chided.

It was probably a good idea to do some shopping while I was in one of the leading fashion meccas on earth.

I sucked in a deep breath, lowered my legs to the dark hardwood floor, and went to the bathroom to shower and get cleaned up.

I took extra time on my hair, twisting the sides into a French braid that circled my head and leaving the back to air-dry into dark waves. I usually wore a little makeup—mascara and lip gloss—but today I broke out the eye shadow, blush, and powder, trying to cover up the new crop of freckles across the bridge of my nose. Spending yesterday in the sun had brought them out in force.

I folded the end of the braid neatly underneath the plastic ponytail holder and secured it with a couple of bobby pins, creating a seamless braid. I admired my handiwork in the mirror and smiled just as my phone went off with a high-pitched trill: Mom's ringtone.

I snatched it off the counter and pressed ACCEPT. "Hey, Mom."

"Sophia!" she shouted. "How is Italy? I haven't heard from you since you got there."

I smoothed down a few flyaway strands of hair. "It's nice, Mom."

"Are you having fun? What have you done?"

Her enthusiasm was contagious. "Yeah, I'm having a good time. Naples is busy. A bit fast paced for my liking and actually pretty dirty. Definitely loud. But it's fun." I gathered up my belongings and threw them in my travel bag. "I went to Pompeii yesterday." The memory brought a smile to my face, but it wasn't the ruins I was re-membering.

"Oh, Soph, that's awesome! I'm so glad you're having a good time," she cooed. "The last time I was in Naples, I was in college. It was loud and dirty," she chuckled. "But even that can't detract from its beauty. I love Naples. How long are you there?"

I set my bathroom products on the floor beside my suitcase. "Un-til Saturday, then I leave for Sorrento."

"Do not leave Sorrento without having a limoncello or two," she commanded.

I laughed. "Are you encouraging me to drink?"

"It's Nonna's favorite." Her voice rose in pitch as she sang the last word. "Have one for her, too."

"Mom, I'm traveling alone. The last thing I should be doing is getting drunk." I recalled the last time I'd gotten drunk and how Penley had died the next day.

"Always Miss Responsible," she clucked.

Yeah right, Mom.

What was with her? Why did she want me to throw all caution to the wind? Granted, she had no idea how much Penley and I partied in high school, but that was a long time ago. I was different now. I was *Miss Responsible*. "Mom, you should be the one telling me to be careful, not supporting a drinking habit."

"Don't be ridiculous. I know you, Soph. You'll have your head in the tourist pamphlets and forget to experience Italy for real. I figure if I give you permission to be wild and crazy, you may opt for slightly less reserved."

I wasn't reserved yesterday, Mom. I picked up a stranger and spent the entire day with him and almost invited him back to my room.

I laughed inwardly, proud of my newfound confidence…I only wished that confidence was strong enough to give a voice to my thoughts.

I pinched the phone between my shoulder and ear while I rummaged through my suitcase. Unfolding a white and tan striped sundress, I shook it out a few times to loosen the wrinkles. "Okay. I'll get my head out of the pamphlets. Listen, Mom, I've got to go. I'm joining a tour at the Naples National Archaeological Museum at seven thirty, and I've got to get dressed." It was only a small lie. But if she knew about Lucas, she'd have us married off within the week. Mom lived to play matchmaker.

"Have a good time. I'll talk to you soon. Love you, *Patatina*."

"Yeah, love you, too, Mom. Bye," I said absently. "Get some sleep. It's late," I scolded.

She groaned. "I'm the parent, remember? Stop bossing me around." Even though she was joking, I could still hear the bite of irritation in her voice. "Bye, Soph."

"Bye, Mom."

And then there was silence on the line. She was gone. But I continued to clutch the phone in my hand, still pressing it to my ear. Thinking about marriage, the word had gotten under my skin. In light of my dad's health revelation and the fact that I could be headed down the same path, was marriage even a possibility? Could I do that to another person? Bring them into a relationship knowing they would have to watch me die? And children? That was definitely out of the question. There was no way in hell I'd want to pass Huntington's on to a child.

I plopped down on the bed, defeated. The promise of a fun day with Lucas was thrown back into perspective. What the hell was I doing? I had no business liking him. Suddenly I hoped he wouldn't show up and that yesterday, and the all-consuming energy I'd felt between us, had been a figment of my repressed and neglected hormones.

I glanced at the time on my phone. I was supposed to be downstairs to meet Lucas in five minutes. Was he here yet?

Standing, I made my way to the window and peeked through a small opening in the curtains. Sure enough, there he was, sitting on one of the large weed-filled planters that divided the street into two lanes. Dressed casually in pastel-colored, mint-green shorts and a lightweight button-down cotton shirt, he looked like he'd walked off the pages of *GQ*. My pulse spiked. What was he doing to me? Sexy didn't even begin to define what Lucas had going on.

With a phone pressed to his ear, I watched his expression fall. Whomever he was talking to, they weren't giving him good news. He didn't look happy.

After a couple minutes, Lucas lowered the phone, punched a button on the screen, and stared at it. Then a second later, he lifted his head in my direction, toward the hotel. I was securely hidden behind the closed curtains, but I swore his eyes, like blue laser beams, landed right on me.

I took a step back and sighed, heart thumping in my chest, having almost been caught spying.

I walked to the bed, grabbed my purse, and slung it over my shoulder before walking over to the small safe in my room. I made sure my belongings inside were securely locked away, gave the room a once-over, and walked out the door. I double-checked that my room was locked and went to the elevator.

As I waited for the door to open, my heart raced as I thought about those blue eyes. I still questioned why I was doing this, why I was willingly spending time with a gorgeous man knowing full well there was no future with him.

He's a fun distraction, Sophia, the voice in my head reminded me. A distraction. I was on vacation. Maybe this was my chance to be on "vacation" from Old Sophia and all her idiosyncrasies as well.

Now you're thinking! Sophia Italia cheered.

The elevator door opened with a chime and I stepped inside. I had two more days in Naples; might as well make the best of it, right? I tapped the button for the ground floor and the doors slid closed. As I descended, I made a pact with myself. I'd have a good time, enjoy Lucas's company, and like he'd said yesterday, live without any expectations…expectations only lead to disappointment.

And damn, was he right.

* * *

Stepping out of the hotel, I was greeted by the sounds of honking car horns, revving engines, and the warm kiss of sunshine on my skin. Naples was awake. The city's heartbeat was loud and pulsated with life. Despite the graffiti and trash that cluttered the sidewalks, Naples was breathtaking.

I filled my lungs with a good dose of Neapolitan air. Infused with the mustiness of ancient buildings and car exhaust, I was ready to hit the town.

"Buongiorno." Lucas waved as he stood from the concrete planter. With three steps in my direction, we stood toe-to-toe. "You look

lovely." His eyes traveled over my body. He didn't hide the fact that he was checking me out.

I smiled, a rush of excitement sweeping through me. "*Grazie*. I'm sure you say that to all the ladies, though."

He winked. "Only when it's true."

Well, I hadn't been expecting that kind of answer. Did he make it a habit of picking up random woman on vacation?

"Ready?" he asked, holding out his elbow.

I slid my arm through and he secured me to his side. "Do you mind walking?" Lucas took a few tentative steps toward the main thoroughfare, leading me beside him.

"No, not at all."

"Good. I was hoping you'd say that." Lucas picked up the pace and we were off, headed in the direction of the Museo Archeologico Nazionale di Napoli.

We walked silently for a while, taking in the bustling city. He led me down each side street with confidence. "You sure know your way around. How long have you been here?" I asked.

"How long have I been in Italy, or how long have I been in Naples? The answers are different."

"Both," I countered.

"I've been in Italy for"—he tilted his head, lifting it toward the sky, mentally calculating—"about a month and a half," he finally answered, locking his eyes back onto mine.

"Wow. And Naples?"

He shook his head. "Just a week. I've worked my way south. I also like maps. My dad's a cartographer. When I was a kid, he'd read me maps instead of bedtime stories. Made me good with directions." He shrugged. "There, now you know everything there is to know about me. Which means I've got two days to find out everything there is about you."

"Uh-uh, *signore*." I tsked, waving my index finger between us. "You don't get off that easy." I wanted to know everything about him. His dreams, hopes, fears. His favorite colors and what side of the bed he preferred. Everything.

He chuckled. "There's nothing more to know about me, I swear." He drew an "X" over his heart with his index finger, then dropped his hand, scooping up mine in the process.

I glared at him while at the same time my heart skipped a beat. "I don't think so, Mr. San Diego. I know you like to stalk unaccompanied American women touring ancient Roman ruins and you play video games."

"Design video games," he corrected.

I dipped my head in apology. "Sorry. Design video games." Lifting my eyes back to his, I couldn't help but stare. The blue of his irises sparkled, almost otherworldly. Lost in them, it took me a moment to remember what I'd been talking about. I shook my head a little, trying to demystify the spell his eyes cast. "Don't you have to play them after you design them?" I asked. I did not speak gamer.

"Well, yes. But what kind of business partner would I be if I left all the work to Dean?"

I had to laugh at the way he said this, all exaggerated and put out. "Taking one for the team, huh?"

"You know it."

"It's been years since I've played a video game," I admitted, the Super Mario theme song echoing in my head.

Lucas came to a screeching halt in the middle of the street, dropping my arm. Clutching the fabric of his shirt over his heart, he put on a pained expression. "Years?"

"Yeah," I answered sheepishly.

"Ah! You're killing me." Lucas threw his head back and winced.

"Video games weren't going to help me pass the MCAT or nail my med school interviews."

"You should give *Surgeon Simulator* a try, then."

"*Surgeon Simulator*? No way that's a thing."

"Honest to God. I have it on my phone. Want to take a stab at it?" He pulled his phone from his pocket, holding it out to me.

"I'll take your word for it. But where was this information a year ago? I could have been having fun and studying at the same time?" I chuckled.

"What do you do for fun?" He started walking again, motioning for me to follow with a tip of his chin.

What did I do for fun? Soccer came to mind. Though, I hadn't played in years. "I used to play soccer," I said solemnly.

"Used to?"

"I played for years but hung up my cleats." I paused, deciding whether I wanted to dive into the real reason I had quit soccer.

He gestured, making a circular pattern with his free hand, urging me to continue. "You hung up your cleats…"

Why not? He'd told me a painful childhood story. I supposed it was my turn. "Sure you want to hear this? It's sad."

"I told you my sad story yesterday. Tell yours today. Two negatives make a positive, right?" he offered.

I smiled. "Right."

"Hit me with it, Linebacker." He swung our intertwined hands and squeezed, giving me some of his courage.

"I played soccer with my best friend, Penley. She was also my cousin. She was only a few months older than me. We were practically sisters. My uncle—Pen's dad—helped my mom run our family's gelato shop. Pen and I were inseparable.

"When we were seven, we decided we wanted to give soccer a try. Our parents signed us up and the rest was history. Year after year, we managed to stay on the same team, and when we got to high school, we both made varsity as freshmen. And along with that came a 'cool factor' we had to uphold. On the field, we kicked ass. Off the field, we partied."

"You partied?"

I glanced up at him. "I used to."

"What happened?"

I thought back to our lunch at McDonald's. "Fucking life."

"Always getting in the way."

I thought about that for a second. Life getting in the way of life. What a profoundly true statement. "Yeah. Anyway." I shook my head, getting on with my story. "Our senior year arrived. Penley, our friend Sasha, and I were the elder statesmen—the leaders—and we had a reputation to uphold. The night before the first practice of the season, we threw a massive party. There was a place in the woods where we usually gathered, away from our parents' prying eyes. We could crank the music and drink to our hearts' content and no one was the wiser. Pen and I were smashed by the end of the night. I still don't know how I made it home and how my mother didn't find out."

"Naughty girl." I didn't miss the smirk that pulled at the corner of his mouth.

"I was bad," I agreed. "So, the team gathered for practice the next day, hiding our hangovers the best we could. Coach thought it would be funny to dedicate the entire two-hour practice to conditioning. I felt like I was going to puke, running suicides down the length of the field. Penley was right beside me, cursing Coach under her breath. I was about to add my two cents, and when I turned my head, she wasn't there. I looked over my shoulder and saw her lying on the ground. I stopped and backtracked, calling her name. She didn't move. Coach tried to resuscitate her before the paramedics came and carted her off to the hospital, but she never regained consciousness. Later we were told Penley had a genetic heart defect, hypertrophic cardiomyopathy."

"God, Sophia," he said, drawing me to his side. "I'm so sorry."

The tightness in the back of my throat was present, but I was a master at holding tears at bay. No amount of crying could bring her back, so what was the point. "Thanks. After that practice, I hung up my cleats, threw myself into school, and haven't partied since. I went from one extreme to the next. I don't handle surprises well, so if I have a plan, I feel more in control."

"Control's only an illusion, though," he huffed.

"Maybe, but that doesn't stop me from trying to grasp on to it with every fiber of my being."

"I'm sorry about Penley," Lucas said, rubbing my shoulder.

I looked up at him. "You know something, I haven't told that story out loud, ever. Now you know another thing no one else knows. But I feel lighter after telling it."

"Glad I could help. Before we go to the museum, there's something I want to show you." Lucas grabbed my elbow and led me to the right, a busy intersection in front of us.

I looked to the left and right multiple times, as did Lucas, waiting for the opportune moment to cross. "Where are we going?"

"Now!" Lucas shouted.

"No, wait!" I yelled, digging in my heels. There wasn't enough time for us to cross, too many vehicles raced toward us.

Lucas grabbed my elbow and pulled me into the busy intersection. A dozen motor scooters barreled straight for us, as well as a tour bus.

Yanking my arm free of his, I broke into a run, leaping onto the sidewalk just as a handful of scooters whizzed by.

"Are you…," I breathed heavily, "trying to get us killed?" I extended my hand, motioning to the ever-flowing traffic.

"Nah," he laughed, trying to catch his breath, too. "We just needed to cross the street, and now you can say you crossed the street like a true Neapolitan. "You've got to cross when you can, or you'll spend your whole vacation on the wrong side of the street. What fun would that be?"

I'd memorized a few Italian swear words before coming here, all of which resounded in my head at the moment. "Getting hit by a tour bus doesn't sound fun." I glared at him.

"Oh, come on, Sophia, there were at least twelve feet between you and that bus."

"That's way too close!"

He continued to grin at me, his eyes thin slits against the bright sun. "Are you going to be mad at me all day? Should we end our friendship here and part ways?" He held out his right hand as an offering to shake, bringing his left hand up to his forehead, creating a sun shield for his eyes.

Hell no, I wasn't leaving. I didn't want to be alone today. The prospect of spending my last couple of days in Naples, with him, made me giddy with delight. "No." I shook my head.

"Good. I didn't want to say good-bye either." Lucas laced his fingers through mine, again, smoothing his thumb over the top of mine.

I looked at our intertwined hands, feeling the same rush of energy, the same connection I had yesterday. I reveled in the fact that the connection grew stronger each time.

"It's not much farther," Lucas said, leading us north.

"Where are we going?"

"You'll see." He winked.

I gave him a wary glance. "Are there more streets to cross?"

"Aw, come on, where's your sense of adventure?"

My sense of adventure? Did I have one anymore? I used to. "I told you, I don't do that anymore. Besides, blowing off med school for a spur-of-the-moment Italian vacation is adventurous enough for me, thanks."

"You said you don't party anymore, but that's not the same as having an adventure. Lighten up, Sophia, live a little."

My heart gave a thump, and I swallowed nervously. *No expectations, Soph. They only lead to disappointment.* But adventure? Where could adventure lead?

I know where I hoped it would lead…but was that expecting too much?

Chapter Thirteen

Lucas smiled widely and squeezed my hand before he turned right, leading us down a street teeming with people. I bet half the city was congregated here. Colorful flowers, vegetables, fruits, artwork, jewelry, and other goods lined the street as vendors set up their shops. People milled down the center, haggling over prices in search of bargains.

"This is incredible," I said in awe.

"It is cool. We'll check it out in a minute, but first I want to show you something over here." He ticked his head to the left.

Pressing his fingers gently to my elbow, he led me away from the shouting merchants. We crossed the street again, but this time my life didn't flash before my eyes. The motorist traffic was significantly less at this intersection, due to the huge marketplace behind us.

"Here it is," Lucas said, pointing at a shadow box decoration on the outside wall of a small coffee shop. "The pride and joy of Napoli."

"Oh yeah, I saw this in a few travel guides. It's the shrine to Diego Maradona."

"Arguably the best footballer who's ever played the game."

I took in the contents of the shrine: Diego Maradona's picture, a lock of his hair, a letter to the city of Naples, and what was presumably a vial of Neapolitan tears, shed when Diego left Naples to play for Argentina.

Flipping open my purse, I pulled my phone out to take a picture.

"When you said you played soccer, this came to mind," Lucas said. "I thought you might like to see it. It's sort of a thing in Naples."

I snapped a couple shots and then zoomed in on each of the individual relics, taking close-ups.

"Yeah, this is cool. Thanks for showing me." I crooked my finger, motioning for him to come closer. Stretching up on my tiptoes, I met him halfway. I put my lips close to his ear, cupped a hand around my mouth, and whispered, "I've always been more of an Arsenal fan." I lowered my feet to the ground and put my index finger to my lips, grinning wider. "Shhh."

Lucas winked. "Your secret is safe with me." He held his hands over his heart.

"Good." I blew out an exaggerated breath. "With my Italian heritage, I'm pretty much a traitor."

A rich, low rumble of laughter bubbled from his chest. "I don't follow soccer." He shook his head. "But maybe I should give Arsenal a chance." He winked.

"You're not a soccer fan? Ugh, you're killing me!" I mimicked his earlier reaction to my video game confession.

"Then I should keep you close by. Your expertise may come in handy should I ever design a soccer game."

My heart clenched around his words. *Keep me close?* I wanted that more than I realized.

"Want to see what the street vendors are pushing?" He nodded to the chaos.

I looked at the crowd, larger than before. "Yeah," I said, turning back to him. "But first, I would love to see what is on the menu in there." I pointed to the coffee shop entrance. The smells drifting out of the open door were mouthwatering.

"I like the way you think, Sophia." He tapped the side of his forehead, then pointed, smiling at me.

The quaint café was nothing like the commercial coffee shops back home. Soccer memorabilia adorned the walls and a plethora of liquor bottles lined the shelf behind the bar.

An old man came around the corner. *"Cosa avrai?"*

I looked to Lucas, hoping he understood what the man had said and order first.

"Un caffè," Lucas answered, then turned to me. "It's espresso."

I wrinkled my nose. I preferred my coffee with more cream and sugar than actual coffee, but from the serious-looking espresso machine behind the counter, I didn't think I would find that here.

Lucas leaned down and whispered in my ear, "Be adventurous."

His breath tickled, sending shivers down my back.

Pulling away, he looked into my eyes. "You've got to try it. You'll be missing out on a Neapolitan treasure."

I still wasn't convinced, but I didn't want to keep the old barista waiting. "Okay. I'll have the same."

Without any pleasantries, the old man went to work, pulling levers that made the machine whir and hiss. It began to spit a dark, steaming liquid into ceramic coffee cups.

When the machine emptied, the man withdrew the cups and brought them over to the counter. I reached into my bag for my wallet, but Lucas already had his money in hand, paying for his and mine.

"You didn't have to do that," I said, putting my wallet back in my purse. "This isn't a date."

Lucas pocketed his change, scooped the cups from the bar, and flashed me a quick smile. "Says who?" He handed me a cup. "Besides, I wanted to."

I took his offering. "Thank you. But I get the next round."

"Always pushing me around. Whatever you say, Linebacker."

We made our way to the back of the café and sat down. Lucas took a sip of his and closed his eyes, seeming to enjoy the infusion of caffeine to his system.

"Fuck, that's good," he moaned. "Try it."

I held the cup to my nose and took a whiff. A strong, earthy aroma rose on the steam, filling my nostrils. Pressing my lips to the rim of the cup, I took a tentative sip. When the espresso first hit my tongue, it was unassuming but gave way to a bold, bitter aftertaste the moment I swallowed. I scrunched my eyes together and stuck out my tongue. "That's disgusting!" I choked, setting the cup down.

Lucas burst out laughing. "Not a fan, huh?"

"Blech, no!" I peered at the revolting liquid in my cup and then at him. "You actually like this stuff?"

"I do. Working the early shift at Starbucks, I would power down a couple shots and be good to go."

"You work at Starbucks? I thought you designed video games."

"Used to work at Starbucks. While I was in college." Lucas took another sip of espresso. "And, yes, I do design video games."

I slid my cup across the table. "Well, then, here you go. Enjoy." I wrinkled my nose in disgust.

Lucas opened his mouth to say something but was interrupted when his phone pulsed with a high-pitched tone. Reaching into his pocket, he pulled it out and connected the call.

"Hey, Deano, what's up?" he answered.

Holding my gaze, he mouthed, *Sorry, I have to take this.* He shook his head apologetically.

"Oh, no problem. Go right ahead," I whispered, waving for him to continue his conversation.

He gave me a tight-lipped smile and went back to his call, leaning back in his seat. "Yeah, Dean, I'm still here."

Should I give him some privacy?

"No," Lucas said with a chuckle.

Yes, I should. I stood, shouldered by purse, and took a step toward the counter when I felt a hand circle around my wrist.

"Hold on a sec, Dean," Lucas said quickly, and then brought the phone away from his ear. "Where are you going?" There was a worried lilt to his voice.

"To get some water." I stuck my tongue out. "Can still taste that god-awful stuff." I pointed to the cups in front of him. "I'll be right back."

"Okay," he said, smiling softly. I liked that smile; it was the one that showcased his dimple the best.

I smiled in return and he let go of my arm, bringing the phone back to his ear. "Yeah, about that. I don't know," he said.

Giving him a chance to speak privately, I made my way to the bar where the grumpy barista was busy unpacking a box.

"Scusami." I cleared my throat, hating the way Italian sounded

coming out of my mouth. It was disgraceful, considering it was my grandmother's native tongue. *"Acqua, per favore."* I hoped that was how to say "water" in Italian; if not, I had no clue what I just ordered.

The old man stood up straight, pulled a glass from behind the bar, and filled it with ice and water. I smiled at the small victory.

"Water," he said, setting the glass down on the bar top.

"Thank you." I shook my head. "*Grazie*, I mean."

With a nod of his head, he pushed the ice water in my direction and made his way back to where he'd been working.

I picked up the glass and turned, taking a large gulp. The lingering taste of bitter coffee still coated my tongue, but the water was refreshing.

From across the room, I watched Lucas. Still relaxed, he sat with his back to the chair and his legs stretched out and crossed in front of him. But the expression on his face said something very different. His sharp jaw was set, pressing his lips into a thin line, the dimple long gone. Then there were his eyes, focused on something far in the distance.

I took another drink. Lucas nodded a few times and then pulled the phone from his ear and disconnected the call. Less than a beat later his eyes landed on me, my cue to join him again.

As I sat down, Lucas smiled and his dimple returned. "You didn't have to leave."

I pointed to the glass sitting in front of me. "I really needed some water after drinking that crap." I gestured to his twin coffee cups.

"I'm sorry we were interrupted. That was Dean."

"No apology necessary." I shooed it away.

"He's getting antsy. He's ready for me to come back."

"Is something wrong?"

His playful demeanor from earlier was gone. He shook his head. "No, everything's chill." He didn't sound too sure of his answer. "Dean's an introvert. Not comfortable putting himself out there. When it comes to pitching ideas to developers, that's where I come in." Lucas's expression shifted, like he was trying to convey something he couldn't articulate. "The thing is, I'm just not sure I'm ready to go back yet."

Why didn't he want to go home? I wanted to ask, but that would have been presumptuous on my part. Whatever the reason, it seemed personal. If he wanted me to know, he would have told me. Then another thought came to mind—maybe he just wasn't ready to leave his present company.

I thought of Aldo and what he'd said about little bumps. Lucas hadn't expected me to bump into him, but maybe that's why he was eager to stay longer, because he was pleased I had.

* * *

After Lucas powered down both cups of *caffè*, we shuffled toward the free-for-all at the other end of the street, joining the throng of tourists and locals bargaining and purchasing goods from the noisy street vendors.

The dingy architecture rose high into the sky, standing in contrast next to the vibrant bouquets of fresh-cut flowers, seasonal fruits and vegetables, and homemade trinkets. The hot moist air carried delicate wafts of lavender, strawberries, and freesia, mingled with the saltiness of the ocean.

Lucas pressed close and wrapped his arm around my waist. The day was shaping up to be stifling hot and the humidity was in the mail. Trickles of moisture ran down my back and between the narrow valley between my breasts. It didn't help matters that I had an insanely hot Californian pressed against me either. But by no means did I want Lucas to move. I'd endure the flames of hell if it meant I could keep his body near mine.

I swiped the back of my hand across my forehead, glad I'd braided the sides back today.

Vendors sang, yelled, screeched, hollered, and wailed, anything that would capture the interest of a potential customer and bring them to the stall. Lucas navigated us through the crowd, keeping his body in a protective stance behind mine as we inched along.

"Crazy, huh?" Lucas said at my ear.

Despite the heat, I shivered, nodding my response.

"Pesce fresco! Polpo, mollusco, vongole veraci!" an old Italian fishmonger cried, trying to be heard over his louder neighbor.

Passing by the stall, he plunged his hands into a tank of water and withdrew an octopus. A real, live octopus. *"Polpo!"* He held the creature out to Lucas and me, an offering.

I hated seafood with a passion. The one time I attempted to cook salmon, Mom, Nonna, and I ended up sick for days. Stomach cramps, puking, the whole nine yards. It was horrible. Mom banned me from the kitchen for months. I wasn't even allowed to put a piece of bread in the toaster, and I'm still not allowed within inches of preparing seafood.

I shook my head and Lucas kept us moving forward. The next few vendors were pushing the same items, with little variations in their menus.

Ugh, is that a vat of eyeballs? My stomach churned as the next vendor we encountered stirred a large barrel full of something round, gooey, and disgusting. I twisted my neck to look over my shoulder. "What is that?" I asked Lucas.

He leaned down again, our faces only a couple inches apart. "Lunch?" he suggested.

"Uh, no." I stuck my tongue out.

He laughed. I could feel the rumbles in his chest vibrate against my back. The musical sound of his laughter was beautiful and the vibrations of his chest provided the perfect accompaniment.

"Oh, look!" I pointed. A few stalls away, a vendor displayed belts, scarves, and other homemade goods. "My nonna would love one of those." I searched for Lucas's hand behind me and clamped down, pulling him along. "Come on."

"Yes, ma'am. I will not stand between a lady and her bargain." He chuckled.

Shouldering past other shoppers, I put on the brakes when I spotted the fuchsia-colored scarf adorned with pale pink peonies. Running my fingers over the silky fabric, I smiled. "Nonna loves peonies."

"Cinquanta euro," a grizzled old woman said from the back of the stall. She didn't make any move to get up, just stared, waiting for us to fork over the cash. By the expression on her face, I could tell she'd seen everything. Probably set up her shop, right here, the same way, for the last fifty years. Lucas and I were as common as the flies to her.

I turned to Lucas. "How much did she say?"

"Fifty, I think."

"Fifty dollars? Holy crap, that's expensive."

Lucas held up his index finger. "Twenty-five," he offered the woman.

"*Trenta,*" she replied.

"Twenty-six."

She batted her hand, an irritated expression wrinkling her face. "Done," she yelled, gripping the sides of her chair. She stood as if each vertebra needed to unlock, one by one.

Lucas patted my back.

"Thank you," I said to him.

I reached for my purse, pulling it into my hands, when a bunch of shouting erupted down the street. Craning my head, I tried to get a look at the commotion, but I couldn't because I was wrenched away from Lucas's side. It took all my strength to stay upright.

In front of me, a boy with mussed hair and a dirty face had his hands around my purse, which was still attached to my body.

"Drop it!" Lucas shouted. With two strides, he was at my side. "Now."

Despite the even tone, Lucas's words were full of rage. If the thief didn't speak a lick of English, I was sure he still understood every word that left Lucas's mouth.

The boy released my purse with a hard yank, sending me falling to the ground. My knees hit, hard. A flash of pain rocketed through my legs on impact, and I bit my tongue.

"*Cazzo!*" the boy screamed, and took off running.

Lucas crouched beside me, holding out his hand. "Are you hurt?" His tone was different now, a mixture of worry and tenderness.

Placing my palm in his, he helped me up. "No, I'm fine." I'd taken harder spills playing soccer. But my heart raced, thumping against my rib cage at breakneck speed. I'd heard all the scaremongers' warnings about thieves and pickpockets, but I'd let my guard down.

"Are you sure?" Lucas breathed, pulling me into a hug. He wrapped his arms around my shoulders and cradled the back of my head in his hands, placing a kiss on my forehead.

My arms went around his waist, welcoming his strong body to balance me. "I'm good," I promised. I still shook from the incident, but Lucas was doing a fabulous job of calming my nerves.

His lips were warm. He kept them there longer than was polite for people who were "just friends," but I didn't mind.

"Hey." He pulled back, looking me in the eyes. "You're safe. I'm right here."

His nearness made it hard to breathe. The connection I felt to him yesterday had multiplied by a million. With our bodies pressed together, each shallow breath I took, I could feel my breasts brushing against his chest. And the fact that I was thinking about my breasts and his body in the same sentence, after just being assaulted, was wrong... so very wrong.

You are not allowed to want him, Sophia.

It scared me how much he saw when he looked at me, how he stripped away all my bullshit and saw straight to my soul. *How could a complete stranger coax this kind of reaction from me?* I felt like I'd known him my whole life, not less than twenty-four hours.

"Soph?"

My nickname on his tongue tied another knot around my heart.

Lifting his hand to my face, he pinched my chin between his thumb and index finger. "What is it?" he asked tenderly. Crinkles fanned across his skin from the corners of his serious eyes. I bit back the urge to touch the delicate skin and smooth away the wrinkles.

His eyes flicked across mine, back and forth, as he read my deepest, darkest secrets. Then his eyes lingered on my mouth. He licked his lips and blew out a slow breath.

Just like yesterday, in the room at the brothel, the world fell away. The noisy, crowded street disappeared, and it was only Lucas and me.

My heart didn't just pump blood, but beat words through my body: *Kiss me. Kiss me. Kiss me. Kiss me.* The words burned through my system, stoking a fire inside, melting away all my fear.

I pinched my legs together, trying to ignore the dull ache growing at my center. Lucas was awakening feelings and reactions I'd worked so hard to repress. *Why did he get to me like this?*

Even in the early days of my relationship with Scotty, I'd never felt an attraction like this. But damn, when Lucas looked at me…touched me…that was hotter than anything I'd ever experienced.

I cleared my throat and placed my palm to the side of his hand. "I'm okay now," I croaked, pulling away. "I let my guard down. Stupid."

His soft expression turned wary. "I don't know what I would have done if he'd hurt you," Lucas muttered under his breath.

"Easy there, tiger. He didn't. I'm fine, really." I smiled in an effort to ease his anxiety. "Thank goodness for cross-body straps, huh?"

"What do you say we get your scarf and get out of here?"

I nodded. "I like that plan."

He kissed my forehead again, pulling in a deep breath before stepping away.

"Thank you."

"Any time, Linebacker." He winked at me and grabbed my hand, lacing his fingers between mine.

Chapter Fourteen

Y ou've got"—Lucas pointed to his cheek—"some sauce right here."

"Oh, geez," I chuckled, freeing my napkin from my lap. "Can't take me anywhere." I was just about to wipe the pizza sauce from my cheek when Lucas leaned across the table and swiped his finger over the smudge.

"Tsk, tsk, tsk." He clicked his tongue. "Whatever will I do with you?" Then he stuck his sauce-covered finger into his mouth, pulling it out with a loud *pop*.

Holy wow. That was hot. What I wouldn't give to be his finger right now.

"First," he continued, "you knock me on my ass in the middle of a world-famous ancient ruin and now you're wearing your lunch."

I shoveled in another forkful of my Margherita pizza with dramatic flare, chewing with a smile on my face before I answered. "Hey, you're the one who wanted to tag along with me. My charm school diploma got lost in the mail. Besides, the jury's still out on whether you're planning on selling me as a sex slave. If I make a big enough mess, my stock will go down, right?"

"Shit!" Lucas pounded a light fist on the table. "You foiled my plan!"

"Ah, see, I knew it. Your intentions are less than chivalrous."

Like a hunter to its prey, a devilish grin flashed across his face, and he took another bite of his pizza, washing it down with his Mediterranean beer. "What'd you like best at the museum?"

I wiped my face on a napkin, thinking about all the different pieces of artwork we'd seen. "I'm not sure. There was so much. The *Farnese Bull* sculpture was impressive. I also really liked the miniature Pompeii exhibit. That was cool."

"Yeah, I liked those, too," Lucas said, an impish grin on his face. With his fork, he pushed around the last few pieces of pizza on his plate. "But what about that secret room?"

"What about it?" I turned the question back on him. I knew he was baiting me, purposefully trying to make my cheeks match Rudolph's nose.

The secret room had been filled with a plethora of erotic pieces of art. Frescoes, sculptures, trinkets, paintings, mosaics, most of them depicting a well-endowed man putting it to a ready and waiting woman…or creature. Apparently, the Romans didn't discriminate when it came to pleasure—if a goat was up for a roll in the hay, then the god Pan made sure she wasn't left wanting.

"What was your favorite piece in there?"

I shook my head. "A lot of them were similar to what we saw in the brothel yesterday. Although, the phallic-adorned streetlamps were interesting." I cocked an eyebrow. "They looked like obscene crib mobiles."

"Crib mobiles?" Lucas laughed, taking a sip of his beer.

"What's so funny? They did." Dammit, he made me blush anyway. I could feel my skin growing warmer, the heat creeping up my neck and pooling in my cheeks.

Lucas took a calming breath and set his cup back down. Staring at me, his expression softened. "Can I tell you something?"

I wanted to tease him back, make light of the situation, but he almost looked scared, like the information he was about to divulge was some dark confession he wasn't sure he should share. He was opening the door to his internal safe room and peeking out to see if the danger had cleared. I didn't want to scare him back inside. I wanted him to open up. I craved his stories like air.

I pushed my plate to the side and reached across the table, wrapping my hands around his. With a gentle nod, I begged him to continue. "Lucas, you can tell me anything." *You're safe with me.*

"Today was the first time in months I haven't questioned the direction my life has taken." His blue eyes bore into mine.

Wow. That was unexpected. But I knew exactly how he felt. Ever since I'd talked to my dad, it felt like I was tumbling down the side of a snowy mountain, wrapped in a cold, lonely layer of snow that was only getting bigger and picking up speed.

"What do you mean?"

Slowly, he withdrew his hands from beneath mine and sat back in his seat. I leaned back, too, waiting for him to continue. Lifting his napkin off his lap, he tossed it onto his mostly empty plate with a heavy sigh. "I wasted six years of my life thinking it would go a certain way. Then, four months ago, a very significant person in my life decided to fuck everything up."

His words were heavy. Whatever had happened left a deep scar on his soul.

"Being with you today was the first time I hadn't replayed the last six years in my head, trying to figure out what I'd done wrong…what I could have done better. It was a nice vacation from reality." There was a slight upturn to the corners of his mouth; his smile wanted to make an appearance, but whatever had happened in the last six years still weighed it down.

How could it be that I wanted more than anything to ease the weight that anchored his smile? I didn't even know him. Yet, I wanted to give him a reason to smile, be the reason he smiled…the reason he forgot about his past.

"What happened?"

Lucas shook his head and straightened his shoulders, as if to brush off the ghosts haunting his memories. His smile lifted, brightened. "I'd rather not ruin today with that shit." He pushed his chair back, sending it screeching across the linoleum. Standing, he held his hand out to me. "Ready to go?"

There was a sinking feeling in my chest, a small pang of disappointment. I wanted to keep him talking, an exotic, foreign need to know everything about him. Yes, Lucas and I were strangers, and I had no right to demand more information than he was willing to give, but I couldn't explain the way I felt. Ever since I ran into him at the Forum yesterday, it was like a steel cable had wound around my heart and tied me to him. I wasn't alone anymore.

Stupid, stupid, stupid, Old Sophia chastised. *DO NOT get attached to this guy.*

Sophia Italia responded in kind, *Sorry,* she drawled, like a know-it-all teenager. *Too late.*

"Yeah," I conceded, not pushing the questioning any farther. The last thing I wanted was for him to shut down completely. But I couldn't hide the disappointment; my voice was laden with it. I was sure Lucas picked up on it, too. Though, he didn't let on, always keeping his personal life on lockdown.

I pushed my chair back and took his hand. Heading toward the door, Lucas and I stepped out onto the sidewalk. Although it was late, it seemed Naples never went to bed. It was high on life. If I didn't know better, I would have thought there were more people on the streets at night than during the day.

The warm salty air helped to lift my spirits. I loved Naples in the evening. The energy of the city shifted once the sun dipped below the horizon. Where daytime is all business and fast-paced chaos, the evening sparked alive with magic, blowing the worries of the day away on the bay breeze. It seemed anything was possible at night.

Music drifted out of the clubs and floated along the streets. Lucas was quiet at my side as we headed in the direction of my hotel. We rounded the corner, pulling off a main thoroughfare, and walked down a deserted alleyway. The streetlamps threw a honeyed glow onto the old sidewalk. Two motorists whizzed by on scooters, the hem of my skirt ruffling in their wake.

The quiet was filled with so much longing. I wanted to say something, anything that would bring us back to the light easiness we'd shared all day. But I didn't know what to say, so we pressed onward in silence. I was reticent, a slave to my unknown future, and Lucas remained silent, a prisoner to his past, I assumed.

The less you know about him, the better, Old Sophia reminded.

In the distance I saw the silhouettes of two people holding hands. Occasionally, the couple would pause, steal a kiss, and move forward. But then passion overtook them. With each step toward them, their affection for one another became more evident.

The man walked the woman backward, pressing her into a brick wall. His hands roamed her body as if trying to memorize every hill and valley, while the woman pushed her hands through his hair, holding their faces together.

I wanted to stop. If we kept walking, we were going to infringe upon their moment.

Yet we kept walking.

Did Lucas see them? He had to; the couple obviously wasn't worried about discretion. I wanted to peek at Lucas, get his take on what we should do, but embarrassment sent my heart racing and my cheeks burning with envy. I couldn't look at him, knowing secretly I wanted him to do the same to me.

Each slow stride was agonizing. I could hear muffled groans now. *Oh, dear Lord, we really need to get off this street.* I didn't want to interrupt them. Yet I couldn't pull my eyes away.

The man's hand disappeared beneath the lady's skirt, and she leaned her head back against the wall, inviting his lips to sweep across her neck.

Pressure built between my legs. This trip, meeting Lucas, witnessing public displays of affection, all of these events had stirred something inside me. I craved intimacy in the worst way, especially now that I wouldn't allow myself the pleasure. What was the point in getting caught up with someone when the future only promised pain and suffering?

Lucas cleared his throat.

Startled out of my voyeurism, I sucked in a breath and looked up at him. He grinned knowingly and captured my hand with his. Bending down, his lips brushed against my ear. "You like to watch?" he asked, slowing to a stop less than ten feet from the enamored couple. They were too busy to notice us, thank goodness.

My throat pinched closed, making it hard to speak, but I powered through, stuttering. "Um…no. God, no!" I whisper-shouted, careful not to draw unwanted attention in our direction. The air was stifling and hot. The cool breeze had disappeared. A thin layer of sweat beaded across my skin.

Lucas whispered in my ear again. "I've wanted to do that to you since I walked you back last night."

I took an infinitesimal step backward and stared into the blue flames of his eyes. *What? Brain malfunction. Words…gone. Can't think.* His statement reduced me to a series of involuntary reactions: accelerated heart rate, dilating blood vessels, shallow breathing, a flood of endorphins.

Lucas countered my retreat with a larger step of his own, closing the distance between our bodies. Hooking his left hand around my waist, he brushed the knuckles of his right hand across my cheekbone.

I sucked in a breath, my eyes still locked on his.

Opening his hand, he smoothed his fingertips across the space behind my ear and slowly down my neck…my collarbone…across my shoulder.

Breaking his gaze from mine, he dipped his head, pressing his lips against the skin of my shoulder.

Oh, sweet Jesus!

Like the man at the end of the alley had done to his companion, Lucas walked me backward until I was pressed against the brick wall. Lucas kissed his way up the path his hand had trailed down. Each time his lips touched my skin, it burned in the most exquisite way possible.

My collarbone scorched. I tilted my head, giving him better access. My neck flamed. My blood pressure rose. Lucas kissed my jaw, his tongue tasting as he made his way to my cheek.

Our eyes locked again, and my knees wobbled, threatening to give out beneath me. If he kept looking at me like that, eyes heavy with lust, I wouldn't be able to stand.

Moving his mouth against the corner of mine, he watched me, gauging my reaction to his nearness. "Tell me you wanted that, too." His voice was husky and deep, vibrating in his chest, and I felt the tremors in my body.

In a swift motion, he brought his hands to the sides of my face, holding me in a strong grip. The heels of his palms at my chin, his fingers splayed over my jaw and behind my ears. With our foreheads pressed together, our lips barely touched…right there…but not fully *there*.

With a slow, deliberate, side-to-side motion of his head, he dragged his mouth over mine, yet refusing to seal our lips together.

We stared at each other, shoulders heaving. Our mingled breaths swirled between us, hot and heavy.

"Yes," I muttered. *I did want it.* I wanted to feel alive while I still had the chance. It was selfish and irresponsible, but dammit, I wanted it. I wanted him.

He smiled against my lips.

My first instinct was to close my eyes and kiss the shit out of him. But I resisted. The magnetic pull of his gemstone eyes was a force to be reckoned with, and I couldn't look away.

I felt the weight of him against my body and still pulled him closer. The bulge in his pants pressed hard against my belly.

I sighed, parting my lips. An invitation.

Lucas still held my face in his unflinching grip. Neither of us dared to blink.

Leaning in closer, he angled his mouth against mine. I sucked in a breath, anticipation reaching a fever pitch.

Lucas dragged his tongue across my bottom lip. Slow, sweet torture.

The ache between my legs grew heavier.

Once his tongue made it across the length of my mouth, he pressed closer yet and tugged my lip between his teeth and moaned.

I came undone.

I pushed my tongue past the seam of his mouth, sealing our lips together. My eyes slid closed, and I gave in to my senses, ignoring all the warnings uttered in my brain.

Lucas responded to my urgency, pressing hard against me. His tongue swept over mine and pushed into my mouth, exploring. He raked his left hand down my neck and over the curve of my chest in a furious rush. Cupping my breast firmly, he rubbed his thumb over my nipple. It hardened beneath the fabric of my bra and dress, sending waves of pleasure through my body. He kneaded my breast, matching the rhythm of his tongue as it delved deeper into my mouth.

I tightened my grip around his waist, begging to be closer.

"Fuck," he growled against my mouth. This time, both his hands went to my side, traveled down my back, smoothing over my ass. I unlatched my arms to better accommodate his roaming fingers, throwing them around his neck, kissing him harder.

Lucas gripped my bottom, pushing me up. Already on my tiptoes, he continued pulling me upward, coaxing my body onto his. Still devouring each other's mouths, I lifted one leg, wrapping it around the top of his hip. Lucas dipped, gripping my upper thigh, right under my butt, and hiking me upward with a thrust of his body. I threw my other leg around him and he caught it easily. He hitched me up again, and the air left my lungs in a *whoosh*. Straddling him, I squeezed my legs, securing our bodies together.

Pinning me against his muscled torso and the building, he set his hands on the wall, caging me inside his strong arms. He ground against me, his hardness pressed deliciously close to where I wanted him most.

In high school, I'd kissed a fair share of boys, had sex once, but none of those experiences held a candle to this. I wanted to climb inside him and never come out. In his arms, I felt safe, precious, like nothing bad could ever touch me, because if it tried, it would have to go through him to get to me.

Increasing the pressure on his mouth, I sucked his bottom lip past mine and took it between my teeth with a teasing bite. His hands went to my ass, squeezing, while he pushed and pulled me against his hard-on.

Bing. Bing. Bing.

Lucas stilled the blissful thrusts of his hips and broke our kiss.

Bing. Bing. Bing.

"What is that?" I asked breathlessly.

All at once, Lucas placed his hands at my waist and backed away from the wall. I slid down his body, feeling *all* of him on the way down. My feet touched the ground, but I wasn't sure I had the strength to stand. Lucas kept one arm around me. "My phone," he replied, running the other hand through his hair. "Sorry."

"No"—I cleared my throat—"don't be." I pulled in a deep breath, trying to regain some semblance of composure, and looked away, brushing my skirt back down where it belonged.

Lucas took his phone out of his pocket and looked at the screen. "It's Dean again," he said, a hint of exasperation in his voice. With a couple button clicks, the phone went dark and he slid it back into his pocket.

"He really wants you to come home." I looked up at him. He stared back.

Every time our gazes locked, it felt like two puzzle pieces snapping together after an endless series of wrong pieces.

Lucas coughed, placing his hand in front of his mouth. "I realize this is way out of line, and I'm going to sound like a total creeper whatever way I phrase this, so I'm just going to ask." He paused and swallowed, his prominent Adam's apple bobbing in his throat. "You mentioned that you're leaving for Sorrento in a couple days. Would you mind if I joined you?"

"What about Dean?" He'd called twice today; shouldn't Lucas be thinking about going home? Why didn't he want to go back?

Shaking his head, his eyes turned sad. The fire our kiss ignited had been suffocated by whatever awaited him at home. "Dean and I can work from anywhere. He's fine."

I was elated by the prospect of prolonging our time together. I wasn't ready to say good-bye either. "How much of a creeper would I be if I said I'd love for you to come with me?"

The corner of his mouth pulled up, the same side that brought out his dimple. That crooked smile could get me to do things I would never consider. He tugged me to his side, keeping his arm securely fastened around my waist. "If I'm a creeper and you're a creeper, then this trip just got a whole lot more interesting." He winked as we continued our way down the dark alley.

The other couple was long gone. I wondered if we had chased them off. *How loud had I been? Had they seen us?* Images of crawling onto Lucas, my legs spread around him, sent chills down my back and goose bumps prickling my skin.

"Cold?" Lucas asked, squeezing me close. He ran his hand up and down my arm, shoulder to wrist.

I pressed my lips into a thin smile and shook my head, looking up at him. "Not in the slightest." For once, it felt nice to shut off my brain and just *feel*.

Chapter Fifteen

My trip was flying by faster than I wanted it to. Instead of looking forward to all the amazing things I had yet to see, I was dreading the inevitable good-bye I had coming. I'd been in Italy for almost two weeks, and because of Lucas, it had been the best two weeks of my life.

We'd eaten our fill of pizza—real pizza, not the sad Americanized version. He'd consumed a gross amount of *un caffè* (how he slept at night, I'd never know), and my affinity for mint chocolate chip gelato was revealed every time we passed a *gelateria*. I couldn't remember a time I'd ever been so gluttonous.

But despite all the exquisite food, my mind focused on other things—specifically, Lucas and his glorious mouth. Since he'd kissed me in Naples, a week ago, there hadn't been an encore, not even a prelude. Which was interesting, considering we shared a hotel room (Lucas gave me the bed and he took the hideaway). Despite the friends-only, no-touch policy he'd adopted with me, I couldn't ignore the tension between us. If something didn't happen soon,

Sorrento was going to suffer a wildfire of epic proportions, because the heat between Lucas and I was bordering on incendiary.

Each night, after a day of roaming the city with "tourist" stamped on our foreheads, Lucas and I would walk back to the hotel, get ready for bed, say good night, and stare at the ceiling for an hour or more, the screams of our hormones ignored.

His demeanor had shifted from exothermic to endothermic in a matter of a week. I didn't understand what brought about the change when there was a definite attraction between us…at least I thought there was.

Most mornings I'd lie awake, pretending to be asleep, as Lucas milled around the room. He worked during the early hours. While he waited for his laptop to power up, sometimes he'd do a set of crunches or push-ups (which, in my opinion, was better entertainment than books and TV combined, and a beautiful reason to give up on sleep.)

When he finished, he'd take a quick shower and log on to his computer. His fingers would click over the keyboard, responding to e-mails, I assumed. Sometimes he'd even call Dean to discuss facts, figures, and game concepts. But occasionally, their conversation would take on a different tone, something hushed and personal; the name Julia was often uttered like a swear word.

Hearing him say her name while he was awake was different, too. Lucas talked in his sleep, and Julia was the name he muttered most often.

Julia. Who was she? What was her connection to Lucas, and why did he say her name like it left a nasty taste in his mouth? Which also begged the question, why did she star in his dreams almost every night?

All these questions bombarded my thoughts, and then there was the stupid voice in my head that reminded me of all the reasons I needed to stay away from Lucas and mind my own business. Lucas would only complicate things and it was important to keep him at a safe distance, because allowing my heart to voice its opinion would only result in suffering.

When my dad left, my seven-year-old heart shattered. When Penley died, it was too much and a part of me died with her. I'd come to realize that being close to people only led to pain and disappointment, similar to Lucas's ideas about expectations.

I had Mom and Nonna. I didn't need anyone else. The wall I built around my heart was the perfect way to hide my emotions and pretend I didn't feel hopeless inside, and school served as the perfect distraction from life.

Chemical equations, chemical bonds, statics, diseases and disorders with long, complicated Latin names were my bricks, and fear was my mortar. I had built a strong wall. If no one came inside, I'd remain safe from ever feeling the kind of loss and sadness I felt when Dad left and Pen died.

It was best that Lucas kept his distance. Accepting that he was my friend already put my wall on shaky ground. I couldn't risk it falling down and exposing the remains of my scared heart, leaving it vulnerable for someone to wreck completely.

Then, like peering into a crystal ball, my brain reminded me of something else…

A handsome, distinguished, gray-haired man bearing a gorgeous dimple in his left cheek sat at the bedside of a sleeping, withered, white-haired lady with sallow, olive-colored skin. He wiped the woman's chin with a napkin, whispered something into her ear, and clasped his hands over hers. He looked on her with love like the ocean, endless and crystal blue, as salt water trailed down his cheeks.

Fear shocked my heart like a cattle prod. A painful reminder of what my future could hold and how much I wanted to spare anyone from witnessing my demise.

I wouldn't let myself fall for him. I had no business letting him inside, not after what my dad had told me. After Italy, he'd go back to California, and I'd leave for St. Louis. We'd take our memories and move forward. He'd live a long, happy life, have a slew of gorgeous children, and grow old with an exotic beauty at his side.

Me, I'd stay the course I charted for myself, because I didn't know what else to do. I'd poured my heart and soul into school, all my hopes and dreams into becoming a doctor. I'd carry on until my body put on the brakes. But no matter what, I'd continue on alone. That was safest for everyone.

* * *

Lucas opened the door of the hotel, and I stepped onto the sidewalk, plopping my new fedora on my head.

"Cute," he said, flicking the brim of the hat. "I like it."

I sported a toothy grin and slid my sunglasses up my nose. "Thanks."

"What's the plan, Linebacker?" he asked, putting his hand on the small of my back.

I shrugged. "For once, I am without a plan." I took in the busy, sun-drenched street, looking left and right. Boutiques and dozens of eateries lined the road, but I wasn't really in the mood to shop or eat.

"What? No plan? I am bringing you over to the dark side."

I turned to look at him just as three motor scooters flew by, observing no speed limit. "Geez, the people who drive those things are crazy."

Lucas raised an eyebrow and smiled crookedly. "Why don't we give crazy a try, then?"

"Huh?"

He nodded in the direction of the long-gone Vespas. "Let's rent a bike for the day and go sightseeing."

"Uh-uh." I shook my head. "You are crazy if you think I'm getting on one of those things."

Lucas nudged me with his elbow. "Oh, come on. Where's your sense of adventure?"

"Drinking gross espresso is about as adventurous as I get."

Leaning down, he whispered in my ear, "Please." His voice was low and sexy. "I've already got the mental image of you straddling me from behind in my head, and I can't think of a better way to spend the day."

Umm… words? Gone.

The combination of his hot breath, deep voice, and the image of being pressed against Lucas's back, him sitting between my legs, had me ready to give in to the crazy. "Okay," I muttered. *God, why can't I function like a normal human being around this guy?*

"Awesome, let's make it happen."

We headed down the street in search of a place to rent a scooter, which I was sure wouldn't be difficult—rental places were as plentiful as lemons in Sorrento.

"Do you even know how to drive a motorcycle?" I asked, getting more nervous by the minute.

"Look at you, all worried." He slung his arm around my shoulders. "Yes, I have a bike at home. Living along the PCH, it's kind of a must. You're safe with me. I promise." A throaty laugh rumbled in his chest. "This place looks good," he said, coming to a stop.

"If you say so." I knew nothing about renting a vehicle. I hoped he knew what he was doing. I took in the bright, modern-looking building with a showroom full of high-end motorcycles.

Walking inside, I took off my sunglasses just in time to see a gorgeous Italian salesman coming to meet us. "How may I help you?" he asked in a thick, panty-dropping accent. I was sure he could sell ghost peppers to the devil.

"We'd like to rent a bike for the day," Lucas answered.

"Ah, yes. Right this way." The salesman led us to a tall counter on the side of the room.

Shuffling some papers to the side, he smiled at us. "I have a few Yamahas left." He pointed to vehicles on display behind us. "Similar to those."

Lucas glanced over his shoulder, then back to the man. "Perfect."

"Excellent."

The gentleman brought out a stack of papers and he and Lucas went to work filling them out. Fifteen minutes later, the man was dropping a set of keys into Lucas's hand. "Enjoy, Mr. Walsh."

"Grazie," Lucas replied. He glanced at me, a big smile on his face. "Ready?"

No! my inner voice screamed. "I guess so." My heart kicked into high gear.

"You're going to love it," Lucas said, grabbing my hand.

"Want to follow me outside? We'll get you on your way." The man came from behind the counter, leading us toward the door.

Outside, a sleek black bike was parked at the curb. "Here she is. The Yamaha X-Max 250."

Lucas's face lit up like a kid in a candy shop as he ran his fingers over the handgrips. "Wow." He whistled. "Nice." Kicking a leg over the seat, he put the key in the ignition. "Hop on, Soph." Twisting his torso around, he patted the seat behind him.

Why did I let him talk me into this? Slipping on my sunglasses, I cringed as I straddled the bike. Hesitantly, I wrapped my arms around his waist. Lucas helped me out, gripping my hands in his, making sure they were secured against his taut stomach. "Hold on tight!" he shouted, firing the engine. He was far too excited about this idea.

The machine rumbled to life beneath us. My stomach was in my throat.

Lucas waved to the salesman, revved the engine a few times, and looked over his shoulder before pulling onto the road.

Merging into the flow of traffic, Lucas took it slow, getting used to the feel of the machine. Weaving in and out of cars and buses, we were forced to stop at a red light.

Glancing over his shoulder, Lucas shouted, "See, it's not so bad."

I pulled off my hat and nodded. "Yeah, as long as you keep it under thirty miles per hour."

"Uh-uh." He shook his head. "We're going to open this baby up as soon as we get out of town."

Shit. What had I gotten myself into?

* * *

The sun hung low on the horizon, kissing the sea as it slowly disappeared. Warm Mediterranean air blew my hair backward as I hugged myself to Lucas, resting my head on his shoulder. Today had been wonderful. He'd been right. I loved this. Our sun-drenched, windy drive along the Amalfi Coast Road was exactly what I needed.

The view from the back of the scooter was breathtaking. The sea was a giant, gleaming sapphire, sparkling in the sun. Italy rose majestically out of the water, the towering cliffs dotted with centuries old buildings painting a rainbow on the landscape. The engine hummed in my ears but didn't mask the howl of the wind. This was freedom.

For the several hours we'd been gone, I'd been able to let go of everything weighing me down. Soaring down the road at seventy, sometimes eighty miles per hour, I was flying…rising up to meet the clouds. And for just a moment, I almost convinced myself that everything was going to be all right. With my lungs full of crisp salt air, adrenaline coursing through my veins, I let myself believe I'd live a full, long, happy life.

I drew in another breath, closed my eyes, and allowed myself to hope.

Lucas steered us back into town as the city's lights twinkled to life. We turned in the direction of the hotel, Lucas weaving in and out of traffic. If there was one thing I learned today, it was that Italian traffic laws were more of a suggestion than a requirement. Even though I'd loved every moment of the day, I still questioned Lucas's sanity for wanting to drive here. I was more than happy being a passenger, even though he'd tried to get me to drive a few times.

With our hotel a block up the street, Lucas pulled the scooter into an open space on the side of the road and killed the engine.

Putting a hand on my leg, he twisted his body around so he could see me, a huge smile on his face. "Well? Was it as bad as you expected? Were you disappointed?"

A smile broke onto my lips, and I shook my head. "It was amazing."

He patted my leg as I kicked off the seat. I shook out my wind-tangled hair and plunked my hat back on my head. Lucas climbed off, too, coming to stand in front of me. I looked up at him, our eyes locked. "I'm glad you had a good time," he said.

"It was perfect."

His big, strong hands gripped my shoulders as he brought me close. Squeezing me in a tight hug, he pressed his lips to my forehead. My hat fell backward, tumbling toward the ground. With lightning-quick reflexes, Lucas caught it between his fingers, resting his hand against my backside.

"Oops," he laughed, his warm breath spreading across the top of my head.

God, his smile was beautiful. His exuberance for life was magnetic. It was impossible to look at him and not feel the same way.

Lucas's hand lingered for a beat longer. Then, slowly, he dragged it upward over my curves…the dip at the small of my back…the length of my spine…never taking his eyes off of mine.

I shivered. I couldn't help it. He made me *want* in a way I'd never wanted before.

"You lost something," his voice rasped as he dropped the hat back on top of my head.

"Glad you found it." I smiled.

He breathed deeply, his chest expanding, as he hugged me tightly again. "Damn, you smell good." He exhaled. "Like sunshine and fresh air."

"Thank you for today."

"Next time, I'm taking you out on the PCH."

Next time. I tried to hold on to my last shreds of hope. I wanted there to be a next time more than I wanted to take my next breath. But was that fair to him?

NO! Old Sophia shouted, guilt boiling away what was left of my hope.

Lucas brushed a few strands of hair off my forehead. "I want to take you out tonight. What do you say we hit up one of the swanky clubs around here?"

"I'm not much of a dancer."

"Neither am I. We'll figure it out together. I've heard it's the 'thing to do' around here." He rocked me in his arms.

It was useless; I couldn't say no to him. "All right," I groaned. "At least we'll look like fools together," I sighed.

"That's the spirit." Releasing me from his muscled arms, he latched on to my hand, threading his fingers between mine.

Heading in the direction of our hotel, once again I felt Lucas's magnetic energy; it rolled off of him in waves. His pull was a force to be reckoned with, and every minute we spent together I grew closer to him, like the tide to the moon. His vitality was a balm numbing the pain and uncertainty that plagued my future.

I knew it was wrong to lead him on, and yet, I couldn't let go even if I wanted to; his gravity drew me right back in.

Chapter Sixteen

The nightclub was crowded and so not my thing. I'd been a soccer player, not a dancer. But Lucas had twisted my arm, said it was the "thing to do." And I had a hard time saying no when he brought out the heavy artillery: his eyes and that dimple. Together they were a lethal combination. It was scary how, with one look, he could short-circuit my brain and give my body the authority to make decisions.

So, here I was, alone, in the middle of a sea of people, most of whom did not speak English, all because my *body* thought dancing was the perfect opportunity to get close to Lucas. I couldn't fault the logic, but it also required Lucas to be here. Dean had called and said it was urgent. Lucas apologized, excusing himself to take the call. That was ten minutes ago.

Scanning the throbbing crowd, I kept an eye out for him. Where the heck was he?

People continued to filter in. Dancing had been reduced to hopping in place to the beat of the music, instead of the dirty variety one would expect. Sensuality died as fast as the nighttime breeze. It was freaking hot in here, and it wasn't because the crowd was getting busy. There were just too many people.

I was so ready to leave.

I fanned myself with a flimsy napkin, bobbing my head to the beat of the music, while I waited for Lucas to return. Then I felt a hand at my waist and a body pressed against my back.

"Whoa!" I shouted, spinning out of the grip of the grabby-handed stranger. Turning around, I saw that it was Lucas.

"Oh, you're back." I sighed, relieved it was him and not an overly affectionate drunk.

The band ended their song and the crowd stilled, but the noise level didn't diminish. I swiped my hands over my neck, lifting my damp hair and twisting it into a knot on top of my head.

Lucas took in the ever-growing mob, rubbing his thumb and forefinger over his stubbly chin. He leaned down, his lips brushing against the shell of my ear. "Want to get out of here?"

His breath tickled. I shivered, letting my hair fall back into place.

He took a step back and our eyes locked. After spending nearly two weeks together, one would think I'd become immune to their sparkle, but that was not the case. If anything, they were more potent than ever. Wide pools of cobalt blue radiance.

My gaze traveled to his mouth, and I ran my tongue over my bottom lip, remembering how they'd tasted…their warmth…how they moved—eager and hesitant all at once. I longed to feel the scratch of the blond scruff on his chin against my cheek.

"Soph?" he said again, snapping me out of our alley-scene replay.

I flicked my eyes to his. "Huh?" I blinked. "Oh, sorry, what did you say?"

I worried my bottom lip between my teeth; a faint citrus tang still lingered. I'd powered down two limoncellos in the span of twenty minutes, knowing I'd need some liquid confidence if this night really did involve dancing. They'd done their job. A zing went through my veins and quieted the part of my brain that chastised me for wanting to live a little.

To hell with what I thought this morning. If I don't kiss him soon, I'm going to go out of my head. Happily-ever-after might not be in the cards for me, but that didn't mean I couldn't have a happily-right-now.

He gestured toward the exit with his thumb. "Want to go?"

I tried my hand at a sultry smile, biting the corner of my lip as I nodded my reply.

"Let's get out of here." His palm trailed over my shoulder, down my arm, and rested at the small of my back.

Pleasure rippled over my skin.

Pressing the front of his body close to my back, he guided us through the throng of intoxicated club-goers.

I elbowed my way through the mob outside, anticipating the warm breeze blowing off the bay.

Once freed from the throng, I sucked in a lungful of sea air. My shoulders slumped, and I relaxed. "Ahh, so much better out here."

"I'll take your word for it," Lucas mumbled, slipping his arm around my waist.

Okay? Since he'd gotten back from taking his phone call, he hadn't said much, and that surly attitude was definitely new. "Is everything all right?"

Ignoring my question, he led us down the busy street, toward the hotel. We turned down another smaller street and he quickened his pace.

"Lucas, is something wrong?" I tried to slow down, but he was too strong. "Lucas?"

Nothing.

"Lucas, stop!" I shouted, digging my heels into the pavement.

That got his attention. He screeched to a halt.

"What is going on?" I pulled away from him. I'd never seen him like this. The muscle in his jaw ticked and his eyes were like solid pieces of ice, hard and unyielding.

He blinked a few times. "Sorry," he said, his voice low and gravelly. "I just had to get out of there."

"Why? What's the matter? Is Dean okay?"

He shoved his hands in his pockets and paced a few steps back and forth. "Yes, he's fine."

"Then what's going on? Talk to me."

He spun on his heel. "I don't want to fucking talk, Sophia!"

Whoa. That came out of nowhere.

Feral, hot anger rolled off of him in waves, puncturing my resolve.

I backed off. Staring wide-eyed, I held my palms up in surrender. "Got it."

This was a first, a side of Lucas I didn't know. The last two weeks had been nothing but longing glances and a well-choreographed getting-to-know-you tango. And he was a *good* dancer. Always careful not to trip and throw us off balance. He'd twirl me in close, turn his bedroom eyes on, whisper into my ear, and just when I thought he was going to dip me—finally let me in—he'd spin me away. His cagey demeanor made it impossible to really get to know him. He was more of a control freak than I was, and that was saying something.

This outburst was different. He wasn't trying to impress me. He wasn't worried about missing a beat in our little dance. In a way, with his loss of control, he was letting me in, trusting me with his anger…or was it hurt? *I wish I knew how to read his facial expressions.*

The name Julia ran through my head. Was this about her? Should I bring her up?

I chewed on my fingernail, contemplating my next move. If I pushed too hard, it could backfire and I'd be finishing this trip alone. I didn't want that. But I didn't want to be a pushover, either. He needed to let his guard down and start talking.

"Lucas," I said, my voice mimicking the lightness of the breeze. "Please tell me what happened. I realize it's none of my business, but I'd still like to help, if I can."

He stopped pacing long enough to glance in my direction. His foot slid across the concrete, crunching gravel beneath his shoe as he stopped in front of me. He stared.

Uh-oh. I'd said too much. He was pissed.

He closed his eyes and blew out a long breath. "I'm sorry."

"I'm here. Talk to me."

"Not here." He clutched my hand, hard, like it was a life preserver in a choppy sea. "At the hotel."

Pulling me along, we made the short walk in record time. Lucas unlocked the door and pushed it open, allowing me to go in first.

I walked across the room and kicked my shoes into the corner, dropping my purse there, too. Turning around, Lucas stood near the door, staring down at the keycard in his hand. Whatever Dean had said, it sure weighed heavy on Lucas's heart. Mine broke for him. For once, it was nice to be there for someone else…to help someone with their problems. I just hoped he'd let me.

Padding across the carpet, I stood in front of him. Grazing his fingers, I took the keycard from his hand. He lifted his head. The wild, skittish glare in his eyes was gone, replaced with something much more devastating...heartache?

"I need to sit." He sidestepped me on his way to the bed.

Plopping down, he sat with his back against the headboard. I left the keycard on the table by the TV and walked to the other side. Regarding me, he patted the mattress. "Keep me company?"

I crawled across the queen bed and sank beside him, folding my hands in my lap, matching his stance.

Without looking at me, he dived into his story. "Ever done something stupid?"

"Haven't we all?" I said with a puff of laughter. Scotty Hendrickson came to mind...partying the night before Pen died...I've regretted those moments of stupidity my whole life.

"Six years ago, I did something I shouldn't have. I was a fucking idiot."

"Whatever it was, I'm sure it's not as bad as you think," I offered in consolation.

He bumped his shoulder against mine. "Ever been in love, Linebacker?"

I rocked my head against the headboard. "Not even close." My heart rapped two staccato thumps, the number of syllables in Lucas's name. A whispered note from deep within me, letting me know I was still alive...still capable of feeling, and love was still visible on the horizon.

"That's what I did wrong. Six years ago, I met a girl, and I fell in love with her." Acid. It was in the way he said "fell in love," all corroded with negativity and hatred. Not the way love is supposed to sound.

Was that where the illusive *Julia* fit into Lucas's puzzle?

A twinge of jealousy flared in my chest, ridiculous, yes, but it was there nonetheless. Of course Lucas would have been involved with someone. He was gorgeous, funny, considerate; it wasn't at all surprising that it had been a serious relationship. Logic aside, I wasn't a fan of this girl.

"And falling in love was bad?"

"The worst fucking thing I could have done."

My jealousy morphed into disappointment…sadness. Was this his stance on love, period? He'd never risk his heart again?

"And then I had to go and ask her to marry me."

Whoa. Marriage? Seriously? This conversation just made a left turn into What-the-Hellville. The word "marriage" lodged in my throat. This was huge. "What happened?"

"She said yes. We planned a wedding. She bought a dress. I got a tux. I went to the church on what was supposed to be our wedding day. And she left me."

His words hung between us for a minute. A stony silence. What did etiquette call for in this situation? I went with the standard. "Lucas, I'm so—"

"No," he interrupted. "Don't say you're sorry. There's only one person who owes me an apology."

"Jesus," I muttered, bewildered.

"Nope, isn't him either." Though diminished by time, his hurt was still real, palpable. This had to be about Julia. Why else would his subconscious call out her name? What was her motivation? The Lucas I knew wasn't a jerk. He'd been nothing but a gentleman over the last couple weeks. I didn't get it.

I wanted to do something, reach out to him, let him know he

wasn't alone in his sadness. Though our stories were very different, I knew what heartbreak was, too. I understood how it felt to have the future you planned for ripped away. I clasped my hand over his, lacing our fingers together. He didn't want apologies or sympathy; the least I could offer was comfort.

"What did Dean want?"

"Up until tonight, I didn't know why Julia left me. I thought things were great between us. In a million years, I did not see it coming." He let out a long, measured breath. "I met her my freshman year at the University of Southern California. We dated for three years before I proposed at the start of our senior year." Lucas stared at the dark television as if his story were being acted out on the screen.

"Julia insisted on a long engagement, wanting to make sure she had enough time to pull off the wedding of her dreams." Lifting his hands, he made air quotes at the end of his sentence. "The long engagement didn't bother me. It actually worked in my favor, giving Dean and me time to make our name in the gaming industry.

"After three and a half years, Julia finally chose a date. When she'd gotten news that her mother's cancer wasn't responding to treatments. Julia got scared her mom wouldn't see her walk down the aisle. February twenty-eighth was supposed to have been our wedding day." He sighed and kept going.

"It didn't matter that I was in the middle of my second year of grad school; I was ready to marry that girl the second I got down on one knee. She was it for me. I loved everything about her. Every freckle that dotted her face, her brilliant green eyes…She was beautiful inside and out. Her fiery spirit, her perpetual optimism, her dedication to social work and the foster kids she took under her wing. Julia wore her heart on her sleeve, especially for those kids."

The jealousy monster stirred inside me. Maybe I didn't want to hear this story. I liked it better when Lucas spiced Julia's name with a dash of contempt.

"We were happy. Our wedding day came. I took a shit-ton of pictures with my buddies and went to wait in the back room of the church until it was time to watch my bride walk down the aisle."

I wanted to hold his hand again, but it felt weird given the way he spoke of Julia, with a hint of desperate longing. Did he want her back?

My heart sank. I couldn't compete with her ghost.

"She sent one of her bridesmaids back to the room. Chrissy. She was a mutual friend of ours, and I could tell she was holding back tears when she told me Julia wouldn't be walking down the aisle. I pleaded with Chrissy. If I could just talk to Julia, everything would be all right. But she wouldn't see me. She wouldn't accept my calls, return text messages, respond to my e-mails. Hell, I'm sure she deleted my voice mails without listening to them. Radio silence." Lucas picked up my hand and squeezed.

"No one knew her reasons, or they weren't talking if they did. Dean called tonight to warn me to stay off Facebook. Apparently, the answer to my only question was on there."

"Did you look?"

He nodded. "I unfriended Julia before coming here. I didn't want her posts showing up in my feed. But after being together for so long, my friends were her friends, and vice versa. Not seeing her is pretty unavoidable. That's why I stay away from Facebook. If I didn't use it for promo, I'd delete my damn account.

"Against Dean's advisement, I looked while we were at the club.

One of Julia's sorority sisters had changed her relationship status from 'single' to 'in a relationship with Julia Conner.' From what Dean had found out, Julia and Courtney had been messing around well before February."

"Oh, Lucas," I said with a rueful sigh.

"Yeah. I was such an idiot. Didn't even fucking know. It was bad enough that she left me for someone else and didn't bother to tell me, but to find out she'd been cheating?" Letting go of my hand again, he scrubbed his face. "You know, it isn't even that I care about her anymore; it's just the principle. You don't fucking cheat. That's what pissed me off."

He fixed his stormy, bleak gaze on me. "Want to know the real reason I came to Italy?"

"Mmm-hmm." The look in his eyes worried me, like a threatening storm gathering on the horizon. As he delved into his story, I braced for impact, sure I was about to be pummeled with truths I didn't want to hear.

"After the non-wedding-from-hell, I tried to pick up where I'd left off, but it wasn't working. I needed to get away. From everybody. At home, people pretended to act normal around me, but I saw the accusation in their eyes: 'What did *you* do to send Julia running?'" he huffed. "I asked myself that same question, every day.

"Italy had always been a place that interested me. I'd always wanted to go. And the women...they have the sexiest damn accent. My goal was to put as many miles—and women—between Julia and myself as I could. Anything to make me forget the sound of her laughter, the whisper of her breath in my ear."

And the storm breaks loose. Women? Laughter? Her breath? I ingested his acrid words. So he wasn't in the sex slave industry, but one-night stands were a thing. He sure traveled a long way to sleep around. What the hell was he doing with me? How many other solo vacations had he hijacked?

"You didn't really come here to do research on one of your games?" That was the story he'd given me the day we met. I liked that version better. His words hit my stomach with a punch, their nauseating poison filling my insides. If I were smart, I'd get off this bed and leave. No way was I going to be a stand-in for someone else.

I turned away, staring at the busy lights outside the window. Lucas continued anyway. "I've been miserable, Sophia." Hearing my name, I turned around. "With each encounter, I thought I'd find some sort of peace, or resolution, find the courage to give Julia the big 'fuck you.' It never came. I still felt like shit. Up until two weeks ago."

"What happened then?"

"A beautiful girl knocked some sense into me." He winked.

Ugh! Please. He wielded his damn charm like a fishing pole. How many other girls had been lured in by that wink? Embarrassment flared on my cheeks. Why hadn't I declined his lunch invitation and carried on with my vacation as planned? There was a reason I was a loner, found solace in academia…It was safe. All mind, no heart. No risk of getting hurt.

But dammit, somewhere along the way he'd reeled me in.

Chapter Seventeen

So, why are you telling me this? I'm just a distraction from reality? What do we have here?" The question was directed at him, but in all fairness, I should have asked myself, too. Wasn't I doing the same thing—using him as a distraction, a reason to hide from my real problems? Granted, I wasn't sleeping with every Prince Charming who flashed his dimple, but I had put miles and a man between a profound, life-altering decision waiting for me at home. I had no right to be angry with him, but yet I was. It hurt to be used.

"I don't know what this"—he waved a hand between us—"is. What I do know…I haven't thought about Julia once since I met you."

I guessed he wasn't counting his unconscious thoughts into that equation. Did he even know that he talked in his sleep?

"I'm not going to lie—the second I laid eyes on you, I wanted to take you back to my room and forget Julia existed."

I stuck out my tongue. No girl wanted to hear that. "And that line works for you?" I was sympathetic to his plight, but with all his talk of one-night stands, it was quickly boiling away, leaving a toxic by-product. Meaningless sex? Yeah, that's what Scotty had been. Been there, done that. Not a fan.

"No. Sitting on my ass in the middle of Pompeii, I shielded my eyes from the sun but looked up and saw something much brighter. I watched your eyes widen in shock as you realized you'd knocked me over. You clapped a hand over your mouth, and *two* seconds after I saw you, I knew you were different. Not the type I wanted to take back to my room and forget about the moment we finished. I wanted to remember your name, the number of freckles across your nose, the sound of your voice. I hadn't breathed in six years, and in that instant, I could."

"So, you didn't want to sleep with me?" I was so confused. First he was saying how much he wanted to get into my pants, and then he changed his tune. I didn't know whether to be insulted, impressed, or thankful. I did know my lady parts had gone into mourning. When it came to Lucas, they were under the assumption that he was not meaningless.

"That's not what I said." Tilting his head to the side, he pinched his eyes halfway closed, studying me. "Give me your hand."

"Why?"

Open palmed, he flapped his fingers back and forth impatiently. "Let me have your hand."

I extended my right hand, palm up. Lucas took my wrist, faced it palm down, and laid it right on his crotch.

Hello, jaw, meet floor. *Holy. Freaking. Shit.* My eyes snapped open wide.

"Does this answer your question? This is pretty much how I am when you're around."

He was so hard. My lady parts threw off their black veils, their clothes, and their lingerie, ready to get busy.

I lifted my hand, slowly, taking note of the lust blazing from his eyes. I settled my hand back onto my lap, unsure of what his expectations were at this point. I knew he tried to avoid those, but with what I just felt in his pants, I was fairly confident he expected us to slip between the sheets. Was I ready for that?

"When I said you were different, I meant it. I don't want you to be another Julia-induced fuck."

Wow. Okay. That was blunt. No sheets, then?

"You know what's funny?"

I shook my head because after having my hand on his…you know…words had fled my brain.

"All those one-night stands were meant to distance Julia from me, but they only kept her close. It was really fucking hard to forget about her when all I kept doing was comparing. Then you came around, and I wasn't comparing. I saw you. I wanted to get to know *you*." He fanned his fingers across my cheek, his eyes searching mine. "That's why I've been so careful." He leaned in closer, our faces a fingerbreadth apart. "I didn't want to mess things up. I want more time."

More time. He picked the wrong girl for that. It's quite possible I already have one foot in the grave. I should tell him. I needed to tell him.

"Sophia, sharing a hotel room with you has been a blessing and a curse. I'm fascinated by the little things you do. The way you loop your hair into a bun and keep it in place with an ink pen." His hand on my cheek swept back, combing through my hair. "When you sit down, you tuck your right foot beneath you." His other hand smoothed over my thigh. "The way you rub lip balm onto your lips with your pinky finger before you go to bed." With the faintest of touches, he moved his mouth over mine, mimicking the back and forth motion of my pinky finger.

His lips continued to brush over mine. "I want to catalogue each and every one of these Sophia quirks."

"Quirks?" I breathed. "Do you think I'm odd?"

Pulling back a little, I saw him smile. "Quite the opposite. I'm captivated by every little thing you do. It's refreshing. At night, when we turn out the lights, it's like I'm in a tug-of-war match with the sun. I lie awake, listening to you breathe, feel the warmth radiating from your side of the room. Every clenched muscle in my body aches, trying to resist your gravitational pull. I've been in a dark place for a while, and all I want to do is step into your light."

My heart was going to beat right out of my chest. Why did he say all the right things? I should still be mad at him, but dammit, I wasn't.

"The first night I walked you back to your hotel, I couldn't get the image of that pretty mouth of yours out of my head. It took all my restraint to kiss only your cheek." He ran his thumb over my bottom lip. I sucked in a breath, my lips parting. "And then, the other night, in the alley, I lost control. I promised myself I wouldn't but…"

He stared at my mouth. *Lose control…lose control,* my heart thumped.

"I'm glad you did." My words were a garbled whisper. He reminded me how bright, how fun life could be…how much I'd been missing. I wanted *more*…with him.

His eyes pulled tight, the two small creases between his brows deepened, and a few wisps of blond hair touched his forehead. "Even after everything I've told you?"

I nodded infinitesimally, our noses brushing. "Even more so." He'd finally let me in. "Most of what you said was hard to take; I didn't want to hear it. But I'm glad you trusted me with the truth."

"I was scared you'd run. I've had enough running to last me a lifetime. I didn't want to give you a reason to leave."

"I'm not running." I said, punctuating my statement by touching the button on his pants.

"Sophia." He swallowed my name and shook his head. His eyes burned with that brightness I craved…I wanted to feel that alive.

Working the button open, I lowered the zipper. My eyes remained locked on his as my fingers pushed beneath the hem of his shirt. Flirting with the waistband of his boxer briefs, I mustered the courage to dip my fingers inside, roaming over the hard V-shaped muscle below his abdomen.

I wasn't sure where my sex-kitten confidence came from, other than the fact that I felt safe with Lucas, but I went with it.

He dropped his forehead against mine and inhaled, his eyelids fluttering closed. "Sophia, this isn't a good idea," he said through clenched teeth. "Not after what I told you."

"Shh, it's okay. I trust you." I did trust him. I knew what we'd shared over the last couple weeks wasn't something fleeting and forgettable.

"You have no idea how badly I want you." He kissed me softly, inhaling my breath.

"Then show me."

The world fell away. It was only Lucas, me, and the agonizing bliss that connected us.

Spurred on by the rush of endorphins, I pulled my fingers away from his lower region long enough to yank the shirt over his head. I'd seen him shirtless before, getting ready in the morning…at night, before bed. He shamelessly walked around the hotel room without a shirt just to torture me, I was sure. I'd pretend not to look; staring was rude…especially openmouthed staring, which I tended to do. But when he was occupied, his attention focused elsewhere, I'd look my fill.

If surfing built bodies like his, I was surfing's newest fan. *Sweet Jesus!*

Now I not only got to look, but also touch. I splayed my fingers over the ridges of his stomach, feeling his muscles ripple under my touch.

Lucas pushed my shoulders back, easing me onto the pillow. Coming to his knees, he brought his leg over my body, straddling me. "I'm only breaking this one rule," he growled, running his hands over my arms. I loved how his round, hard biceps flexed when his fingertips pressed into my skin.

"What rule?"

"I promised myself I wasn't going to touch you." His hands gripped the bottom of my shirt and pulled it off in one, swift motion. "As you can see, that's shot all to hell and then some." A rush of indescribable pleasure reduced me to a quivering mass of rapidly firing nerve endings the moment Lucas put his hands on me. I arched my back, begging for more.

"I won't break anymore." Despite the words, his voice didn't have the same verve, almost like he was thinking out loud, willing himself not to cross any more lines, but I prayed he would.

His thumbs traced over my nipples, through the thin lace of my bra, sending a direct current of electricity right between my legs. Before I could process words, Lucas moved his hands to my stomach and unfastened my button and zipper in record time. Hooking his thumbs beneath the top of my shorts, he eased them down as I lifted my hips. He didn't waste any time with my panties either, pulling them off just as quickly.

Shifting down on the bed, he nestled himself between my legs. He ran his nose along the inside of my thigh, while his tongue teased the sensitive skin. His palms pressed to the inside of my knees, pushing my legs wider; then he kissed me...*there*.

Uh...wha—

Holy. Shit!

Like flipping through radio stations, my brain went from scrambled static to an operatic soprano singing high notes in octaves well out of reach.

His tongue did things a tongue has no business knowing how to do. My body succumbed to the new sensations, quaking each time he moaned against my core. With his hands at my hips, he drew me closer, demanding more. My back arched and my hips begged to move. I'd never felt more alive. The ache low in my belly grew more intense with each flick of his gifted tongue. I knew his mouth was enchanting, but this was on a whole different level. He'd cast a spell and consumed me.

Then, when I didn't think I could take any more, he sent me over the edge. A starburst of white light bloomed across my closed eyes. My arms and legs clenched, and I bucked beneath him as he set every spasm free.

When I came back to earth, he was at my side, tracing lazy circles across my stomach, his hair mussed and a cocky grin plastered on his face. "You're fascinating." His deep bedroom voice rumbled low in his chest.

I cleared my dry, scratchy throat and turned away, my cheeks reddening from what we'd…he'd done. "Yeah, right."

"No, truly, watching you fall apart was sexy as hell." He inched his hand higher, curling it over my breast, across my neck, and onto my cheek. With the slightest bit of pressure, he turned my head in his direction. "When I said I wanted to catalogue all the Sophia quirks, I meant these, too. What makes your body come alive? Where can I touch you and make you scream my name?" He moved his mouth to my ear. "What you feel like on the inside right before you come."

I shivered.

His hand moved southward again, slowly, memorizing all the soft curves of my body. Pressure built in the hollowness between my legs again, demanding to be filled. With only words and a smooth touch, he'd already lit another fire inside me.

Chapter Eighteen

The bathroom door clicked shut and a moment later I heard the shower come on. I let out a long breath and bit my smile, throwing the covers over my head. Inside, I was leaping for joy.

Hidden away in my cocoon, flashes of Lucas and his brilliant tongue cycled through my brain. He went down on me twice but refused to let me do anything to him, insisting last night was about me, a chance to memorize more of my little quirks and a way to prove I was different from the others.

I'd say he proved it…and then some. A giggle bubbled up from my chest, followed by the condescending voice of my responsible side.

God, what are you doing? Yeah, he's sticking around for now. But once you tell him about the Huntington's, he'll leave you, just like he did the others. No one deserves to be burdened with someone who's going to die.

Guilt sliced through my afterglow like a hot knife through butter. It wasn't fair. Lucas deserved to know what he was getting by being involved with me. Not to mention our time together was dwindling. In two weeks, I'd go back to St. Louis, and Lucas wouldn't.

That's right, yet another reason why you shouldn't get attached.

Yeah, another reason. But when it came to matters of the heart, reason took a leave of absence. Lucas had already taken up residence. The hard part would be evicting him before Huntington's took over my body.

"Boo!" he shouted, pulling the covers away from my face.

"Ahhh!" I jumped. "You scared me!"

Laughing, Lucas straddled me, pinned my shoulders to the bed, and started shaking his wet hair in my face.

"Stop!" I yelled, laughing, tossing my head side to side. "Stop it!"

"Oh, come on, I like it when you're wet," he joked, leaning down to kiss the spot right below my ear.

I sighed and relaxed into the pillow, my hands roaming over the hard muscles of his damp chest. "You've got a dirty mind."

"I can't wait to show you how dirty." Nibbling my earlobe, he blew out a hot breath. Pulling the covers away from my body, his fingers slinked their way south.

I put a hand on his. "Nuh-uh, San Diego. I need a shower."

He stopped his thorough study of my neck's geography and popped his head up. "Mind if I join you?"

I cocked my head and smirked. "You already showered."

"Doesn't matter. I told you, I like it when you're wet."

"Ugh! Let me up!" I pushed on his chest and he rolled away with a groan.

Freeing my legs from the blankets, my feet hit the floor. Standing, I stretched, the hem of my shirt riding up over my panties. Lucas watched with shameless lust.

Harnessing my inner vixen, I swayed my hips toward the bathroom, and right before I disappeared around the corner, I crooked my finger in his direction. "Okay, dirty boy, you can keep me company in the shower, but only"—I held up my finger in warning—"if I'm the one doing the washing." Last night, he had all the fun—okay, not *all* the fun—but now it was mine turn to catalogue his quirks.

And faster than a lightning strike, Lucas hurdled the queen-size bed.

* * *

"This is a sorry excuse for a beach," Lucas said, snapping his towel out onto the black volcanic shoreline.

The Mariana Grande wasn't so much a beach as it was a small patch of coast designated for swimming. Sorrento's rocky shoreline didn't make for the best beach getaways. But I was content with plopping my towel down. For me, all a beach needed was sun, salt water, and waves lapping at the shore. I'd take the beach any way I could get it.

"Well, aren't you a beach snob." I made a face and stuck my tongue out.

Lucas got right in my face and sucked my tongue into his mouth, kissing me deeply. "Fuck, yeah," he growled.

"Hmm…," I hummed, taken completely off guard. "What was that for?"

Pulling away slightly, Lucas cocked a devilish grin. "I've wanted to do that since the first time you stuck out your tongue."

"Oh, really? And you remember the first time I did that?"

"The day we had espresso. You took one sip, stuck out that exquisite tongue of yours, and drove me mad."

My jaw dropped. I was utterly gobsmacked. How he remembered something so inconsequential was beyond me.

"I told you"—he tapped his temple—"every little thing you do goes right up here."

I smiled at that thought, but Old Sophia brandished the guilt-knife, slicing open a new cut. All the little things Lucas was storing, his "Sophia quirks," they weren't really me. It was Sophia Italia he was taking note of…the Sophia that pressed pause on the life she didn't want to face at home and picked up a new one in a land far, far away.

I took a deep breath and tried to forget about how wretched it was going to be when I had to set Lucas free. "I drive you mad?"

Tossing his head back, Lucas groaned. "Out of my fucking skull." He pinched my sides, making me squeal. "Now, do I get to see this swimsuit you've kept hidden, or what?"

Grabbing the bottom of my cover-up, I pulled it over my head, revealing the bikini my mom had bought me. The one I had said wouldn't be making an appearance. Well, I lied. Apparently, Mom knew the girls would need to be dressed up at some point.

Lucas's eyes dropped to my chest. His mouth opened and closed a few times, but he uttered no words. Now it was his turn to be speechless.

The girls were showcased well in black and white polka dots. A decorative buckle—at the center of my chest, just below my breasts—held the skimpy top together, while a contrasting strip of alternating black and white stripes ran just underneath the girls, giving them some added lift.

I'd be lying if I said I wasn't pleased with the reaction it got out of Lucas. I dropped my shorts, and now almost nothing was left to the imagination.

I could hear Old Sophia ranting on the inside, but Sophia Italia cheered louder.

I shimmied my hips. "Well?"

"Fuck, Sophia," he half whispered, half groaned. "Are you trying to kill me? How am I supposed to keep my hands off you when you're sporting that?" He moved his hand up and down in reference to my body.

"So you like it?"

Stepping closer, he smoothed his hands over my hips and across my backside. With his body flush against mine, he rasped in my ear, "I'm so fucking hard right now, if I turn around, every person on this beach will know how much I like your suit." To punctuate his statement, he thrust his lower half against me.

Um … hello, sir!

I looked around at all the people milling about. "What are you going to do?" I bit the corner of my lip.

"I thought you might give me a hand." He winked.

"Here? With all these people? I never knew you were an exhibitionist."

The fun-loving Lucas I met in Pompeii had turned into a sex fiend in Sorrento. And we hadn't even had sex yet.

I enjoyed this sexy, playful side. His carefree, easygoing attitude toward the physical turn our relationship had taken made me more relaxed.

Screw plans. I'll take spontaneity for a thousand, Alex!

I waggled my eyebrows. "Care for a swim?"

"I'd love one," he crooned.

With Lucas at my back, we made a mad dash to the water, wading to a semi-secluded spot near one of the platforms that jutted into the bay. The water was tepid, bathlike and glorious; it lapped right at our chests, hiding us from prying eyes.

Lucas put his hand at my shoulders and turned me around to face him, wrapping his arms around my waist. He was still rigid beneath his shorts.

"I take it back," he said, rubbing small circles on my back.

"What?"

"This beach. It's growing on me. But I promise you, I'm going to show you what a real beach looks like one day. I'd love to get you up on a board."

"I'd like that."

Lucas regarded me as if I were the most precious, delicate flower he'd ever seen. Butterflies came alive in my stomach. Tilting his head, he kissed me tenderly, savoring the feel of our lips.

As our mouths tangled together, I looped my arms around his neck and fixed my legs at his waist. The ebb and flow of the ocean rocked our bodies together.

He was *right there*...pressed exactly where I wanted him, and my body trembled with need. I'd always felt connected to him, and I longed to make that connection real.

We were a perfect fit.

I ran my hand down his back, brushing over the elastic of his swim shorts. Working my fingers beneath the waistband, I smoothed my hand over his backside...his outer thigh...

"Fuck, Sophia," he groaned.

My hand skimmed over the top of his leg…then…*him*.

His mouth was demanding, urgent, kissing me like I was all he needed to live. He sucked in a breath as I wrapped my hand around his shaft. "Fuck…"

I moved my hand over him in the rhythmic way I'd done this morning, in the shower. With each stroke, my confidence grew—as did he.

Touching him, kissing him, the call of the ocean, the fact that we were doing something so private in a not-so-private place went to my head. I loved the sounds I coaxed from him with each stroke.

"I'm going to come," he rasped.

I sucked his tongue in my mouth, kissed him harder, and let my hand have some fun.

His arms trembled, struggling to keep a hold of me as he found his release. His head dropped to my shoulder and he ground out a long, gruff, "Jesus."

Withdrawing my hand from his shorts, I wrapped it back around his neck, clasping my hands together to hold myself to him. His shoulders heaved as he came down.

Lifting his head, his eyes were hooded and he had a dreamy, far-off look on his face. "You are entirely too good at that."

I grinned widely, drunk on the power my inner sex kitten possessed. "Why thank you." Unclasping my fingers, I slowly slid down his body, until my feet touched the gravelly bottom. "Now that I've helped you with your problem, it's time to swim, San Diego. Race you to the other side!" I yelled, lifting my hands above my head. With my knees bent, I dove into the sterling blue water, leaving Lucas gaping in my wake.

Chapter Nineteen

Lucas brushed a hand across my shoulders. "You soaked up some rays today, baby."

I glanced down. Sure enough, my shoulders were burned. Not an angry red, but a pink that suggested I hadn't been very smart about reapplying my sunscreen. Usually I didn't burn, but I wasn't ever outside long enough for the sun to do any damage. But today, Lucas and I had spent the whole day in the sun.

As much as I've loved visiting museums, taking in the ancient architecture, and wandering fallen cities, today—the beach—had been my most favorite. I couldn't remember a time when I'd laughed so much. Splashing, swimming, kissing, cuddling on the beach, today was a day I'd never forget.

Holding my hand over my shoulder, I assessed the heat radiating off my skin, gauging the severity of the burn. "It isn't too bad." I shrugged. "I'll be all right."

I finished the last swallow of my white wine and leaned back in my chair. The outdoor café was the perfect ending to our day at the beach. The food was excellent, and the sea breeze rolling in off the bay took my breath away. "I don't know about you," I sighed, "but this is my kind of paradise." I closed my eyes and let the salt air, the warmth of my sun-kissed skin, hushed conversations, and distant music soak into my soul.

Lucas laid his hand on mine. I opened my eyes, and they settled on his. "I'm looking at paradise."

I rolled my eyes. "You and your cheesy-ass lines. You're such a dork."

"I live in an ocean town, sweetheart. The only thing that gets me amped about the beach anymore is my board and some killer waves. But paradise? I'm looking at it. I've experienced paradise at Pompeii, at a McDonald's, in our hotel room, and here. When I get you to San Diego, then I'll have paradise there, too."

My stomach fluttered, his voice setting the butterflies in motion. "You want me to come to San Diego?"

"Hell yeah, I do. When I said you were different, Sophia, I meant it. I know it won't be easy when we leave Italy. You have school starting and Dean and I have a lot to catch up on, but we'll work something out. It doesn't end here for me, Soph."

"Me neither." I clutched his hand, a lifeline.

What have you done, Sophia? You're going to end up hurting him, the ugly voice in my head reprimanded. A gust of wind blew between us, flapping the sides of the umbrella over our table as an icy chill spread over my arms and down my back. Goose bumps prickled my skin, and my paradise suddenly turned cold.

I didn't want to hurt Lucas, but by allowing him to get involved with me, I already had.

"Aiuto! Aiuto!" someone screamed.

A few tables away, a lady stood up from her seat, knocking over her chair, hands raised above her head. *"Ho bisogno di aiuto! Mia bambina!"*

"What's going on over there?" Lucas said, pushing his chair back.

I stood, trying to get a better look at what was happening. "I don't know. What is she saying?"

"I think she needs help."

I moved to the side to see around the table next to me. The frantic woman clutched a child in her hands. "I think something's wrong with her kid." I took off in their direction.

When I came to the lady's table, the little girl in her arms clutched at her throat and was turning very red in the face. She was choking.

Instinct kicked in. My CPR and first-aid training had prepared me well to deal with a situation like this. I tapped the mother on her shoulder. "I can help." I prayed the language barrier wouldn't be a problem.

I patted my chest and said, "Help," again.

"Sì! Sì!" the lady cried.

That was all the permission I needed. I took the little girl from her mother's arms and stood her on the back of the chair, pressing her back against my stomach. "It's okay, I'm going to help," I said reassuringly to the girl.

I made a fist, with my right hand, the lower knuckle of my thumb pressing right above her naval. Wrapping my left hand over my right, I delivered a quick upward thrust to the girl's abdomen.

Nothing happened.

I pushed again. And again. And once more.

Something small, round, and dark green fell from her mouth. An olive. She probably choked on the pit.

The little girl drew in a huge gulp of air.

Crying, her mother scooped her off the chair. The girl wrapped her arms around her mom and bawled. *"Grazie! Grazie!"* The mother bellowed, tears streaming down her face.

As much as I hated to cry, I couldn't help the tears that sprang to my eyes. *"Prego.* I'm glad she's okay."

The mother collapsed into her seat, holding on to the little girl so tightly. I took a few steps backward, letting them have their moment, now that the danger had passed.

As I took in the scene, every diner was up from his or her seat, gawking at what had just happened. Then one by one, the café filled with applause.

An overwhelming sense of satisfaction washed over me. Not because of the gracious crowd, but because of what I'd done for that little girl. She was why I wanted to go into medicine. I wanted to make a difference in people's lives. I wanted to save lives. Save families from being torn apart.

I wanted to make a difference in the world, and holy shit, I just had.

"You. Are. Incredible," Lucas whispered in my ear. His hand swept around my waist, and I relaxed against him.

"You saved that girl's life."

"I'm just glad I was able to help." I let out a long breath, my heartbeat thumping loudly in my ears. Ah, the effects of an adrenaline rush, truly a magnificent hormone.

"Excuse me, sir," Lucas said as a waiter passed by. "Will you please put their check with mine?"

I turned around. Lucas was pointing at the woman and child.

"Sì, signore. I will tell your server," the waiter said.

"*Grazie.*"

As the waiter left and the commotion at the other tables died down, Lucas and I returned to our table. "You're pretty incredible, too. You know that, right?"

My heart swelled. It took a special man, a kind, considerate, and loving man, to help a person in need.

Lucas shrugged, like it was no big deal. "It's the right thing to do. She's had enough to worry about tonight. It was nothing compared to what you did." He took my hand in his and kissed the center of my palm.

I smiled sweetly. "It was the right thing to do."

* * *

"Mint chocolate chip, *per favore*." I watched the vendor scoop the gelato from the tub, his technique identical to the one Nonna taught me so many years ago.

With the gelato spatula in hand, the vendor scraped along the top of the tub, careful not to dig into the tub—that's a no-no. Then, sliding the spatula downward against the side of the cup, my pale green (not bright green, that's bad too) mint chocolate chip gelato was piled high and ready for consumption.

"Mint chocolate chip," the man said, passing it over the counter.

"*Grazie.*" I lifted the cup from his hand.

"And for you, *signore*?" The man turned his attention to Lucas.

"Vanilla, *per favore*."

As I dug through my purse to pay for the gelato, Lucas put his hand on my shoulder and squeezed gently. "What are you doing?"

"Uh, paying?"

"No, you're not." He shook his head.

Giving him a sidelong glance, I replied, "Yes, I am. I don't usually pitch a fit when you offer to pay for something, but tonight's dessert is my treat." Especially after he'd just paid for our meal and the other family's meal, the least I could do was buy a couple dishes of gelato. Besides, this trip was on Daddy's dime; with Lucas around, he was getting off cheap.

"Vanilla, *signore*." Again, he passed the dish over the counter.

Lucas thanked him, took the dish, and wrinkled his nose at me. "You're a pain in the ass, you know that, right?"

"Uh-uh." I shook my head. "I'm a *royal* pain in the ass."

Pulling a handful of euros from my purse, I settled the tab, and Lucas and I headed for the door, gelatos in hand.

Lucas knocked his elbow against my arm. "I didn't know I was in the presence of royalty."

"Oh, yes," I sang. "Wait until you meet my nonna. She refers to me as *Principessa*. My mom usually adds the 'pain in the ass' part."

"Then I offer my deepest apologies. I did not mean to offend, *Principessa* Pain in the Ass."

With a mouthful of gelato, I waved my spoon to object. *"Principessa Patatina,"* I mumbled.

"Okay, my Italian isn't that good, but did you just say 'Princess Potato'?"

I crinkled my nose and plastered on a closed mouth grin. "My mom calls me *Patatina*."

"Why on earth would you mother call you Potato?"

"It's actually a pretty common nickname given to Italian little girls. My mom, with her warped sense of humor, thought it was hysterical, so she stuck me with it."

"So you are 'Her Royal Highness, Princess Potato, Pain in the Ass.'"

"Wrong again." I shook my head and took another bite. "It's 'Her Royal Highness, Princess Potato Linebacker, Pain in the Ass.'"

Lucas nodded. "Yes, how could I forget." Taking a quick bit of gelato, he added, "Your mom and nonna sound awesome. I can't wait to meet them."

"Oh, goodness!" I laughed, nearly choking on the spoonful of ice cream in my mouth. "Be prepared. Knowing my mom, she'll hand you a box of condoms and pat you on the back. And she's a devout Catholic."

"The protective type, huh?" He smirked.

"Yeah. Or thrilled by the prospect that I would be doing something other than schoolwork."

"Sounds like my kind of lady."

"Mmm-hmm. I'm sure." I licked a heap of gelato off my spoon as goose bumps prickled across my skin. The temperature had cooled off, leaving the night air a little chilly. I shivered when a stiff breeze flapped the bottom of my gauzy sundress. My sunburned skin didn't help matters either.

"What about your dad? Are you close?"

"Yeah." He nodded. "My dad's the most stand-up guy I've ever met. I can only hope to be as honorable as him."

I could see the reverence on Lucas's face as he thought about his father. "I can't wait to meet him."

Lucas looked over at me, pointing with his spoon. "He will love you."

My first thought was to ask if his dad had loved Julia, too, but then I didn't want to taint our perfect day by bringing up her name.

Nearing our hotel, Lucas and I walked in silence for a minute, savoring the last few bites of our dessert.

"Thank you for today," I said.

Lucas turned and looked at me, a heart-stopping smile blooming across his face. "Hold up," he said, coming to a halt in the middle of the sidewalk.

"What?"

With a soft touch, Lucas ran a hand through my seawater-tangled, frizzy hair. "I want to record this moment. Store this memory for later."

"A day befitting a romance novel. I understand why."

"No, that's not why." He smiled wider. How was that possible? "Because you've got gelato running down your chin, and it's the most adorable thing I've ever seen."

"What?" I slapped a hand over my mouth. Sure enough, sticky ice cream smeared from my chin to my palm. I elbowed Lucas. "Why didn't you tell me?"

"I just did," he laughed, throwing his hands up as a shield from my pointy elbows.

I flapped my fingers impatiently. "Give me a napkin."

"I don't have any."

"Ugh! You're no help." I wiped the mess from my chin the best I could. Lucas continued to chuckle beside me. "You think this is funny?" *Oh, I'll give you funny, San Diego.*

I dipped my finger into his dish, wrapping it in a nice coating of melted vanilla gelato, then wiped it down the side of his face.

His eyes went wide. "Look out, Princess Potato, I'm the one

who's doing the tackling now." A sinful, panty-dropping smile turned up the left side of his mouth.

"Only if you can catch me!" I yelled, and took off running toward the hotel.

"Game on, sweetheart!" he growled.

Chapter Twenty

"Fuck, Julia, not this time," Lucas shouted.

I was startled awake at the sound of Lucas's angry expletive. Beside me, he was turned the other direction. Had he been snuggled up next to me, he would have shouted in my ear.

The last few nights, his dreams had become shouting matches between him and Julia. I wished I knew what they were fighting about, but the arguments were always one-sided.

I rolled onto my side and faced Lucas's back. He had a marvelous back. I fought the urge to run my fingers over his smooth, tan skin. Anatomy had always been one of my favorite classes in college. I loved memorizing all the bones and muscles of the body and how they moved and worked in conjunction with each other. Lucas's muscle definition was impeccable. Had he lived during the time of the ancient Romans or Greeks, artists would have paid him to be a model for one of their priceless marble statues.

My eyes traced the line of his trapezius, from the top of his shoulder to the middle of his back, where it met the curved teres major, stretching out and arching into his armpit. And then his lower back, the latissimus dorsi. Every part of him was a mesmerizing study of the human body.

Lucas let out a sleepy moan, then muttered, "Sophia."

My ears perked up. This was new. He'd never said my name before.

Hmm, I wondered if Julia and I finally met. Oh, to be privy to his subconscious.

I waited and waited for him to speak again, but he remained silent. After twenty minutes or so, my eyes grew heavy and I drifted off to sleep, excited for tomorrow, Lucas's birthday.

* * *

"Morning, Linebacker," Lucas whispered, crouched at my side of the bed.

"Uhh," I groaned, rolling onto my back. "What time is it?"

"Just after six. We need to get going if you want to go to Capri today." He brushed his fingers along my forehead, sweeping my rat's nest hair onto the pillow.

"Yeah"—I pushed up on my elbows—"I'm up." I yawned. "What are you doing up so early?"

"Dean's pitching a game concept tomorrow, and I had to go over some details with him, help him with slides and screen shots."

"You've been working?"

"Yeah."

Geez, why was he still here? He had so much going on at home, I had no business monopolizing his time. "I'm sorry, Lucas. I hate that

I'm keeping you from your responsibilities at home."

"Hey, you're not keeping me from anything. I'm here by choice. And like I've said before, I can work anywhere. Hell, I could do the damn presentation myself over Skype if Dean wasn't able. You leave in two weeks; that's when I leave."

"You're sure?" I pouted, wretchedness weighing me down. I tried to ignore the voice in my head, the one that reminded me I was screwing with Lucas's life.

"For once, I've never been more sure." He winked. "Now get up, we've got a boat to catch."

"Hey," I said, brightening up. "Happy birthday!"

"Thanks, Linebacker. I have to say, this is already the best birthday I've ever had."

"Yeah, right. You're full of it." I tossed the blanket aside, revealing my bare legs. Lucas smoothed a hand up my thigh.

A fire caught in his eyes. "The best goddamn birthday." He grabbed my hips and yanked me down on the bed, kicking his leg over me. Getting right in my face, he said, "And don't you forget it." Then he planted a kiss on my lips that left the butterflies in my stomach dizzy.

* * *

The sea breeze I'd come to adore on shore was a whipping wind in the middle of the bay. Standing on the deck of the jet boat, my hair blew around wildly, thrashing over my face, no matter how often I tucked it behind my ears. Lucas even tried holding it back. Nothing helped.

Opening my purse, I searched for a hair tie but came up empty. However, I did have an ink pen. Gathering my hair in a ponytail, I looped it around, making a bun at the top of my head. With the ink pen in hand, I weaved it from one side of the bun to the other, holding my hair in place.

Ingenuity at its best.

"I like it," Lucas said, patting the top of my head and tugging on the pen.

"It's the newest fashion trend." I pouted my lips, forming what was probably the most ridiculous duck face in the history of duck faces.

"Hold that pose. Don't move." Lucas pulled out his phone and snapped my picture. The only picture I'd seen him take since we'd met. I, on the other hand, had to set up a second Dropbox account to accommodate my picture-taking fetish. I was determined not to forget a moment of this trip. And I made a mental note to thank my mother for dragging me to the airport...and possibly my dad for arranging the trip. It was the least I could do.

As the boat sped through the bay, we took in the breathtaking view. Behind us, the rainbow-colored buildings of Sorrento lined the rocky hill rising from the water, and off to the right, Vesuvius loomed in the distance like a sleeping, fire-breathing dragon.

Drawing closer to the island, the ferry approached two massive stones rising out of the water. One of the stones had an archway, which the boat was angling to pass through.

Close to my ear, Lucas said, "That's Lover's Arch. Legend says you have to kiss your lover as you pass beneath or you'll be cursed with seven years of bad sex."

I turned around and did my best impersonation of Macaulay

Culkin in *Home Alone*, slapping my hands to my cheeks and dropping my jaw. "Nooooo," I drawled. "I don't think I can endure
another bad sexual encounter."

"Then we'll have to make sure it's a good kiss, then. Wouldn't
want to take any chances." He winked.

Even though Lucas and I had yet to do the deed, I had no doubt
sex with him would be mind-blowing…on the same level as a
Plinian eruption, like Vesuvius.

Pulling beneath Lover's Arch, Lucas bent down and placed a
chaste kiss on my lips, but I wanted more. As I opened my mouth
under his, he took advantage and kissed me deeper.

With all the talk of sex, I had a one-track mind, and the more he
demanded, the more I wanted to give. His hands splayed across my
cheeks, holding me against his greedy mouth. Lucas saw to it that
we would not be cursed for seven years, but blessed beyond all measure.

Pulling away, it took a moment for me to catch my breath.
"Wow," I sighed, thoroughly intoxicated. Who needed alcohol
when Lucas's mouth had the same effect?

"No curse here." He pressed his palm to my chest, right over my
heart.

"I think not." My eyes lingered on his as I trailed a finger down
the golden scruff of his cheek. I liked the way it prickled beneath
the pad of my finger. He blew out a breath and closed his eyes,
soaking in the moment, and that was when I held up my other
hand, snapping a picture. I wanted to remember this moment forever.

Eventually, the boat slowed as it reached the legendary Blue
Grotto. Several dinghies bobbed in the water and people waited

their turn to transfer from the boat that had brought them to the island into a smaller boat that would take them into the cave.

"This is it." I giggled, feeling like a kid on Christmas morning. The day Lucas and I had spent at the beach ranked number one on my list of best days of my life. I wasn't sure, but this had potential of ranking in the top five as well. Visiting the Blue Grotto had been on my "tourist" list since I'd arrived in Italy, and to share this moment with Lucas, it couldn't have been any better.

A dinghy rowed up to the side of our boat, and I, Lucas, and the rest of the passengers got in line to climb aboard.

The dinghies were small, capable of holding no more than four passengers, at most.

I waited in line, with Lucas at my back, while those in front of us climbed in two by two, as new dinghies pulled up to the side.

"You ready for this?" Lucas asked, his breath tickling across the shell of my ear.

"Oh my gosh, yes!" I nodded excitedly.

"Next!" shouted the man at the front of the line.

"That's us," Lucas said, putting his hands at my waist.

I shuffled forward.

Carefully, I hitched my leg over the side of the boat. Lucas kept a strong hand on me as I lowered my body into the rowboat. Next it was Lucas's turn. Lowering his leg over the side, he dropped gracefully beside me.

Getting situated, Lucas sat at the rear, and I climbed between his legs, my back pressed to his front. He took advantage of our seating arrangements, circling me in a tight hug.

The man rowing the boat didn't speak a lick of English and wailed Italian phrases in a pitchy voice. I wished I knew what he was saying, but with his thick accent, even what little Italian I'd picked up didn't help me in deciphering his song.

"Best birthday ever," Lucas whispered, tugging me backward. I knew he wouldn't have been able to hear over the noise, so I nodded in agreement, a giddy smile blooming across my face.

Lying flat, the captain guided us to the mouth of the cave, chanted some unintelligible Italian, and grabbed the rope that protruded from the cave's opening.

We bobbed up and down in the boat, waiting for just the right moment to be squeezed through the tiny opening. The second the tiny swell retreated, the man grabbed the line, and in one swoop, yanked us through the hole.

"Ahh!" I cried, my stomach dropping from the rush.

Wind bellowed in my ears as the rowboat captain crooned in Italian, and we were plunged into darkness. I shuddered, overcome with excitement and the cool, damp mustiness of the cave. This place literally took my breath away.

Staying on the right, as other boats exited on the left, our guide sang his heart out, rowing us toward the back of the cave. A dozen echoes bounced off the cave walls as other boats found their ideal spot at the back of the grotto.

This place overloaded my senses in the most glorious way.

"Turn around," Lucas said.

I turned, understanding why it was called the Blue Grotto. The entire cave was doused in a magnificent electric blue, shining up from the bottom of the ocean floor.

I gasped, speechless. "Oh. My. God."

"Amazing," Lucas said, the same wonder in his voice.

Actually, the cave was so blue, and so beautiful, calling it "the

Blue Grotto" seemed like sacrilege. It should have been called "heaven on earth," or something far more romantic.

The rowboat operator gave up on his song and started speaking, in English, no less. As he described the workings of the cave—how sunlight reflected off the limestone seafloor, giving way to the deep blue color—Lucas put his hand at my cheek. As I strained to see him over my shoulder, he lowered his head to mine and kissed me.

"Thank you for knocking me over," he said against my mouth.

It scared me how quickly Lucas had become a part of me. My heart raced. "Any time," I replied.

The grotto, Lucas's kiss, and all the other memories I'd made in Italy did nothing but remind me that I wasn't allowed to fall for this man. But it was too late.

I already had.

Chapter Twenty-One

Last bite. Sure you don't want it?" I teased, circling the fork in front of his face.

Reclined comfortably in the desk chair, Lucas shook his head, smiling. "Nah, you eat it."

"Oh, thank God," I moaned, sticking the forkful of chocolate cake into my mouth. "I was hoping you'd say that." I savored the rich, dark chocolate frosting as it melted in my mouth. "That," I said, pointing to the empty box, "is the best damn cake I've ever eaten."

"I told you, today's been the best birthday ever."

"You know, I have to agree, and it wasn't even my birthday." I dropped the empty fork into the crumb-filled takeout box with a pang of sadness. The cake was gone.

"When is your birthday?" Lucas asked.

I tossed the box onto the floor and lay back on the mattress, staring up at the ceiling. "December twenty-fifth."

"You were born on Christmas Day?" he asked. Everyone always followed up my birthday with the same question, like I'd lie about the day I was born. Was it that improbable that other people could share the same birthday as Jesus?

"Yep."

"Our birthdays are almost exactly six months apart," Lucas stated almost prayerfully.

I lifted my top half off the bed, propped on my elbows. "Yeah. Something to celebrate every half of the year."

Except, I didn't know how many birthdays I'd get. And was it fair to involve Lucas in that kind of uncertainty?

No. I was being selfish.

My heart sank. I flopped back on the bed, wondering what the hell I was doing.

"What is it, Soph?" The bed dipped, and then I felt Lucas climbing over me, until his body covered mine.

Staring up into his face, I took in his features, brushing my hand across his scratchy cheek. "Your eyes are the same color as the Blue Grotto." I rubbed my thumb at the corner of his eye.

"Now you're talking nonsense. What was in that cake?"

In my mind, I could list an infinite number of reasons Lucas and I shouldn't be together, how it would never work between us. The possibility of my declining health, the fact that we lived half a country apart, and the undeniable truth that Lucas deserved so much better than me. But with him stretched out over me, I only wanted one thing, the worst thing I could possibly want…him.

My desire to make love to him was all consuming, and so, so wrong.

"I got you a present," I said, pushing him away.

His brows pulled tight. "Really?"

"Well, yeah, silly. It *is* your birthday."

Lucas rolled off me, and I stood, walking to my suitcase. One day, while we were out strolling, Lucas ducked into the restroom, and I seized the opportunity to buy him a small gift. When he'd finished, he was none the wiser.

"You didn't need to get me anything. Meeting you and getting to spend time with you has been the best gift I could have asked for."

"Oh, shush! Those cheesy lines only work in romance novels." I waved off his comment. "Everybody loves presents on their birthday."

Plopping back onto the bed, I held out a small black box. Picking it up, he pulled his lips together and shook his head.

Lifting the lid, he peered inside, then withdrew the golden key-chain I'd gotten him.

"I wasn't sure if you used a keychain, but I liked the charm." While he cradled it in his palm, I smoothed my index finger over the cold metal. "It's an Italian horn, said to ward off bad luck. It offers protection."

"Sophia," he breathed, his voice gravelly and pinched. "I love it. Thank you. This is the most thoughtful gift anyone has ever given me." Closing the distance, he put his mouth on mine, his tongue insistent, pushing past my lips. He tasted me hungrily, our kiss growing more urgent.

Pressing me back onto the bed, he dragged his lips across my cheek and down my neck. My whole body came alive at his touch.

He licked over the pulse point in my neck, and I sucked in a breath, arching my back. "I love the reaction I get when I touch you here." He licked again, followed by the dizzying press of teeth. "The way your pulse beats against my mouth is maddening."

"God, Lucas," I panted, tilting my neck so he could work his magic again.

His unshaven jaw scratched against my skin, while his mouth did wonderful things to my neck. Caressing a hand up my thigh, his fingers disappeared beneath my dress.

He danced over my most sensitive parts, and even through the fabric of my panties, my body throbbed, needing more. I lifted my hips, pleading…begging. "Lucas," I sighed, his fingers teasing at my center.

"God, I love it when you're wet." A grunt of lust rumbled in his chest.

He slicked a finger… *oh, God*…two fingers beneath the lacy edge of my panties and started circling them over me.

My hips moved of their own accord, absorbing every ounce of pleasure from his dexterous touch.

"That's it, baby, take what you want," he coached, sliding his tongue into my mouth.

I kissed him feverishly; the friction his hand provided drove my need through the roof. "Lucas, I need more," I clamored. "Please…" My back arched and my hips jerked upward.

Lucas slid a finger inside me, thrusting a rhythm that matched his mouth.

I saw stars. I was sure my skin glowed from their radiance as he drew constellations across my field of vision.

Two fingers inside me.

I was done for. Like a supernova, light burst from my center, burning up everything in its path. Every star in my little heaven exploded at once.

My toes curled, my body shook, and I cried his name. "Lucas!"

He kissed my mouth, drinking his name from my lips.

"Holy. Shit." I blinked a few times, letting his face come back into focus. "Wow. The voodoo magic those fingers possess is scary. Whose birthday is it again?"

Cupping my face, he smiled. "It's mine. Definitely mine."

"So I should be the one giving to you." I tweaked his nose.

"Watching you come undone like that was everything."

"Yeah, but…" My heart sank a little. I wanted to give myself to him in every way, make our connection real. With everything we've done, he hadn't even hinted at taking our relationship to the next level. "Don't you want more?"

"You mean sex?" he asked.

"Well, yeah. What we do is amazing, but…" I trailed off, not knowing what else to say.

"Listen, Sophia." He brushed his hands over my cheeks. "When I got to Italy, I was a dick. Not the nice guy you think I am. I'd have a woman in my bed, have my way with her, and send her packing the minute we finished.

"But with you, I wanted to be the nice guy you saw. There have been so many times when I wanted to lose control with you. If you could see into my head, you'd find out just how badly I want you. But I also want you to know that it isn't just about getting into your pants for me. I want to know you here"—he smoothed his hand over the crown of my head—"and here." He placed his hand over my heart. "I've said it before—I want all of you, Sophia."

I wanted all of him, too. Every little thing he did solidified his place in my heart. The way he held doors open for old ladies when we were out, the reverent look in his eye when he talked about his dad, how he sang off-key in the shower.

But how was I supposed to give him all of me, when I knew it only meant giving him endless years of heartbreak?

Chapter Twenty-Two

My trip to Italy was coming to end. In four days I'd be home. Since Lucas's birthday a week and a half ago, we'd visited Salerno and spent a few days touring the Amalfi Coast.

Six weeks. Who knew it was possible to fall for someone in just six weeks.

Lucas mentioned visiting me in St. Louis, and I could visit him in California when my school schedule allowed. He was pretty adamant about making things work between us, despite the distance. And that was all well and wonderful, but something huge plagued me. The one big thing he didn't know about me. The one thing that would be a deal breaker…as it should be.

I already knew what my test results would say.

If you cared about him, you'd let him go, the voice inside me cautioned.

Yes, Sophia Italia had had her fun, but it was time to ditch her in the Italian countryside. After my visit with my grandfather today, I'd tell Lucas the truth and set him free.

* * *

"Maybe this isn't the right house." I stepped away from the door, bumping into Lucas.

He put his hands on my shoulders and gently pushed me back toward the door. "Yes, it is. You've checked the address at least a hundred times this morning."

"Well, maybe he's not home. We should go." I turned to leave, but Lucas kept a strong grip on my shoulders, anchoring me to the concrete front stoop.

"Sophia," Lucas admonished. "You talked to him last night. He's expecting you."

Now that I was here, I did not want to go through with this meet and greet. How was I supposed to play nice with the father of the man who abandoned me? "Maybe his plans changed unexpectedly." I scowled at him over my shoulder, sticking my tongue out.

Lucas leaned in close, hovering above my ear. "You kill me every time you do that." He put a kiss right below my ear. "Will you do something for me later?" he whispered in a sexy, husky voice.

I leaned back, resting against his strong chest. "What?"

"I want you to stick your tongue out, just like you always do, but when we're alone, I'm going to suck it right into my—"

The front door pulled away from the frame with a loud creak, cutting Lucas's sentence off just when it was getting good.

I stood up straight with a jolt. I had to give Lucas credit; he'd certainly taken my mind off of meeting my grandfather. The sick, nauseous feeling in the pit of my stomach had momentarily been replaced with a beautiful want.

But now that the door was open and a white-haired gentleman stood before me, I felt sick again.

"Sophia?" the man said in a heavy Italian accent. He was friendly-looking, short, not overweight. He had a kind face. My dad looked nothing like him.

I cleared my throat. Lucas massaged my shoulders, his strong fingertips infusing me with courage. "*Sì*." I nodded.

"Come in! Come in!" the old man sang, stepping back to allow our entry.

I crossed the threshold of Martino Belmonte's home. I glanced around the entryway of my father's childhood home. It was strange. I thought I'd feel some sort of cosmic familial connection to this man, to this place…but I didn't. It was as impersonal as entering my neighbors' homes when I was a kid selling Girl Scout cookies.

Martino closed the door behind us with a soft *thunk*. I took in my surroundings. The old brick archway separating the foyer from the living room was breathtaking, and the ceiling was unlike any I'd ever seen. Several mini brick arches ran parallel to one another, creating a scalloped finish. The floors were dark wood, covered with ornate rugs, and many priceless antique tables and bureaus lined with dozens of framed photos—long-ago evidence of a woman's touch.

"Sophia," the old man crooned. He managed to make my name sound like an old-timey Italian love song. "Thank you for coming, my dear." Despite his thick accent, his English was impeccable.

"Thank you for the invitation," I said quietly, not at all comfortable with meeting him. If Lucas hadn't agreed to come with me, I wasn't sure I'd have had the courage to meet him. His son was a stranger to me, so what did that make him?

"And who is this?" Martino asked, gesturing to Lucas.

Before I could open my mouth to speak, Lucas jumped in, holding a hand out in greeting. "Lucas Walsh, Sophia's boyfriend. It's nice to meet you, sir."

Boyfriend? Did he really think that? Or did he have no better way to describe us? "A distraction from reality" didn't have quite the same ring to it.

Julia had really messed him up. There was no way he was ready for anything so formal and declarative. And then there was my health issue. Lucas had no idea what he was signing on for when it came to me. Yeah, this whole trip…us…we were exactly the distraction the other one needed.

But uncertainty weighed heavy on my heart. Each day I spent with Lucas, the more I wanted to know what I had to look forward to. Did I really have a reason to worry? The names and numbers of my dad's genetic counselor and doctor were in my phone. I needed to set up an appointment and find out my fate once and for all.

Martino clapped his hands together, snapping me out of my thoughts. "Oh, how wonderful!" Joy overflowed from his grinning face. "Come in, let's sit." He motioned for us to follow as he led us into the small, museum-like living room.

I fell in line behind my grandfather with Lucas at my back, keeping a reassuring hand at my waist.

The room held a matching plastic-covered floral sofa and love seat, an ancient television (complete with a rabbit-ear antenna), and a large bookshelf lined with a few books, but mostly pictures.

Lucas and I sat down on the larger couch, the plastic crinkling in protest beneath us. My grandfather sat on the small love seat across from us.

"You have a lovely home," I commented, at a loss for what to say.

"Thank you." Martino nodded. "Can I get you two anything? A drink maybe, a snack?"

I shook my head, as did Lucas. "Oh, no thank you. I'm good."

"Nothing for me, thanks," Lucas added politely.

The awkward level in the room was redlining, and I couldn't think of a single thing to say to even it out.

Martino beamed. "I was delighted to hear that you were in the country. I've been very excited to finally meet you."

"Likewise." I smiled with a nod. *Ugh. Where's a sinkhole when you need one?*

"Tell me, what have you been up to? How did you two meet? Tell me about yourself," my grandfather asked.

I glanced at Lucas. Where did I begin? "Well…," I muttered. "Lucas and I met while we were both in Naples, about five weeks ago." Wow, had it really been that long ago? Where had the summer gone? It was odd, though, five weeks wasn't all that long, but there had never been a moment when I didn't feel like I didn't know Lucas. He fit right into my life like he'd been there all along and I hadn't realized.

"Pompeii, actually," Lucas chimed in. "I can honestly say I didn't see her coming."

"We never do," Martino sighed, a dreamy smile on his face.

Lucas nudged me with his shoulder. "She knocked into me, and I fell…hard."

Yes, I had knocked him down, but why did I get the feeling Lucas wasn't talking about falling on the ground?

I narrowed my gaze at him. "I didn't bump into you *that* hard." Lucas put his hand on my thigh and squeezed, flashing a teasing grin.

I looked at my grandfather again, feeling the temperature of the room spiking. The last thing I needed was a full-on blush to turn my face the color of the red stripe on the Italian flag.

Martino regarded us with a happy smile and a definite twinkle in his eye. "You two remind me of when I first met Graziana." He nodded in my direction. "Your grandmother, Sophia."

I didn't want to feel anything for this man. I didn't want a relationship with him or to know any personal stories. Personal stories made people care, and I didn't want to care. I was scared. If I cared about him, and his stories, did that mean I cared about his son, too?

But gosh darn it, my fondness of all things romantic had me opening my big mouth. "How did you meet?" I asked.

"Our families were cordial. Graziana was the eldest daughter of a local olive farmer. I worked in the groves. Our parents thought we were a good match."

"You had an arranged marriage?" I was shocked; it was nothing like Nonna and Pappous's story. Nonna was a bit of a wild child who ran off with the Greek bad boy, then fled to America nearly penniless but very much in love.

The idea of Martino's arranged marriage didn't strike me as romantic at all, only very archaic.

"Yes, but Grazi and I had been eyeing each other for a while." He chuckled. "I worked her daddy's fields, tending to the harvests, and she'd always go for a stroll past my trees. That coy smile of hers got me every time. She was the most beautiful creature I had ever laid eyes on, so when my father told me she and I had been promised to one another, I counted myself as the luckiest man in the world."

Okay. That was a pretty romantic story. I stand corrected.

"There isn't a day I don't miss her." The sadness in his voice stabbed at my heart.

"May I see a picture of her?"

"Oh, yes, of course." He stood with a groan. "Ugh…these old bones don't get around like they used to," he sighed, walking over to the bookcase. He withdrew two small picture frames and returned to the couch. Admiring the photos behind the frames, he passed one to me. "That one was taken when your grandmother and I were probably close to your age. Grazi was pregnant with your father."

I held the heavy, ornately carved wooden frame with both hands while Martino passed the other frame to Lucas.

"And that one was taken on the last birthday Grazi celebrated. She'd just turned sixty-seven."

I was on sensory overload. I couldn't digest Martino's story of young love with the picture Lucas held in his hands. My stomach roiled. The pregnant woman in the black and white photo literally glowed with happiness; there was no way the bedridden woman in the other photo was the same person.

"You look just like her, Soph," Lucas said, tapping his index finger on the picture I held.

"You really do," Martino agreed with a nod. "I thought that the second I opened the door."

I'd always thought I looked like Mom, and I was still holding on to the fact that I did, but there was no denying my resemblance to my dad's side of the family as well. Graziana and I shared the same long, dark brown hair. I was about her height, and despite her pregnant belly, I could imagine we had similar figures.

What else had I inherited from her?

I snatched the frame out of Lucas's hand, stacked it beneath the one I held, and passed them back to Martino. "Here." I couldn't get rid of the pictures fast enough. They were like holding a fistful of stinging bees.

Once Martino took them back, I wrung my hands together.

"You okay, Soph?" Lucas asked, rubbing his hand down my back.

I looked at him, my eyes wide. The room spun like I was on some crazy theme park ride. I couldn't draw in a breath, and I needed air in the worst way.

"Let me get you some water," Martino said, standing again. He walked to the shelf, put the frames back in their place, and disappeared into the kitchen.

"Sophia?" Lucas shifted his body so he could face me. "You're as white as a ghost," he said, brushing his fingers over my cheek. "What's wrong?"

This was turning out to be just like the day I went to visit my dad. "She was only sixty-seven," I managed to choke out.

Lucas nodded, combing his hand through my hair. "Yeah, she was young," he agreed. He didn't understand the significance of her age and what it had to do with me.

I locked my eyes on his, feeling his fingers pull gently at a few tangles. *Oh, Lucas, what am I doing with you?*

Martino cleared his throat, coming back into the room. "You should drink this." He handed me a cold glass of iced water.

Wrapping my hands around the glass, the phantom stings disappeared against the wet coolness. I took a generous sip, hoping it would help open my throat, too.

"Have you spoken to your father lately?" Martino asked. "How is he doing? He doesn't call often."

I shook my head and swallowed. "We don't speak."

"Sophia." Martino leaned forward, resting his elbows on his knees, looking me directly in the eye. "Do me a favor." He cast his eyes to Lucas for a split second, then back to me. "Get tested."

If I had just taken a drink, he would have been wearing it. "Excuse me?" I played dumb.

"Your grandmother didn't know when she had your father. Before you start a family, Sophia, please get tested."

My throat pinched shut again, and I knew water wasn't going to help this time. Tears welled in eyes. I handed the glass back to him and stood. "I'm sorry, I have to go," I said, my voice thick. I hated crying. I needed to get out of there before he said anything else that would push me past the point of losing control.

Lucas and Martino stood, too. "Are you sure, Sophia?" Lucas asked, hooking an arm around my waist.

I sniffled, pulling in a large breath of air through my nose. "Yes. I need to go."

"I'm sorry if I've overstepped my boundaries, Sophia. I only want what's best for you, sweetheart," Martino said apologetically. "I watched my wife die, and now my son is going through the same thing. I know we never had the opportunity to get to know one another, but I've always loved you. My beautiful granddaughter." He set my glass down on the small table beside the love seat and reached for my hands, taking them into his crooked, wrinkled ones. "When Gio told Grazi and me, we cried for days. I don't wish that kind of pain on anyone, especially you, sweetheart."

I had the Hoover Dam of tears ready to break free at any moment. "It was great to meet you, Martino. Thank you." I squeezed his hands and let them go, turning for the door.

"Mr. Belmonte, thank you," Lucas said, offering his hand.

"Take care of her, Lucas."

"Yes, sir," Lucas replied. "You have my word."

The dam broke. Tears streamed down my face. While they finished their good-bye, I walked to the door, trying to get myself under control.

Lucas couldn't make promises like that, especially when he had no idea what his promises entailed.

Dammit, Sophia. What have you done?

Chapter Twenty-Three

I'd made it in time. The second I slammed the rental car door shut, the small trickle of tears leaking from my eyes turned into full-on sobs. Burying my head in my hands, my body convulsed with sadness and anger. A vise wrapped around my guts and squeezed like a boa constrictor. The last time I'd cried like this was the night of Penley's funeral.

I'd held it together all day. Through each hug, every condolence, I'd plastered on a thin-lipped "thank you for coming" smile and pretended to be brave. I didn't cry. Didn't shed one tear. Crying was for the weak, for those who had no control. I could control myself even in the face of tragedy.

I reminisced with school friends, teammates, and relatives while Penley's made-up, plastic-looking, lifeless body was laid out in a casket behind me.

I refused to look at her. Pen hardly ever wore makeup, but the funeral home decided she needed some color. Why did a dead person need color? Penley's color came from life, not makeup...the red flush of her cheeks when she ran down the soccer field…the spray of freckles across the bridge of her nose that darkened in the sun…her smiling hazel eyes that lit up when she got a text from her crush. Life was color…not death.

I'd never see the light in her eyes again. Her freckles were hidden under a permanent layer of flesh-colored spackle, and the flush on her cheeks was painted on. I didn't understand why my uncle and aunt, Mom's brother and Penley's parents, insisted on the artifice, the illusion of a colorful Penley. Maybe it made them feel better? I didn't know.

To me? It made me want to puke…to expel the monstrous, angry beast that had taken up residence inside me.

Everyone prided me on how well I was holding up, how strong I was.

But that strength was a farce. I wasn't strong. I wasn't in control. I had as much control over the things in my life as Penley had, and look where that got her. Every time someone wrapped their arms around my neck and whispered, "I'm sorry for your loss," tears stung my eyes, my stomach twisted in knots, and control slipped through my fingers.

That night, when Mom, Nonna, and I came home, I held on to my dignity a moment longer. I walked stoically to my room. I heard them mutter, questioning whether I should be alone, but they respected me enough to let me go. As soon as I shut my bedroom door, the monster clawed its way out of me. I crumbled to the floor, empty, lifeless, and out of control. My world had turned black and white. Colorless.

Just like Graziana's pictures. Even though she'd been alive in those pictures, Huntington's had stolen her color, robbed her of life.

Would it steal mine? Had it already?

Still blinded by tears, I shifted my hands to the sides on my head, trying to stop the blaring siren of Martino's words. *Get tested...don't start a family...I watched my wife die...now my son...not you, too, Sophia.*

The driver's side door pulled open and the car shifted as Lucas climbed inside. He closed the door with a quiet click. "Sophia," he said somberly. His voice was warm and soft, like a blanket just pulled from a dryer. I wanted to wrap myself in its warmth and hide forever.

"Martino wanted me to give you this." He held his hand out to me.

I looked up from the floor, my eyes tired and bloodshot. I sucked up snot running from my nose. I suppressed the mocking laughter in my chest. If the way I looked right now didn't send Lucas running for the Tuscan hills, then my awful genes were sure to do the trick. He needed to get away from me; I would only end up hurting him, and that was the last thing I wanted. He'd already been through so much.

The confusion and sorrow in his eyes crashed into me, knocking out what little air I had left in my lungs. "What is it?" I croaked, swiping my hand across my eyes, clearing away the tears that hadn't fallen.

He picked up the silver chain with his other hand and stretched it out. Swinging from his fingertips, a beautiful antique pendent twirled at the end. "Martino said it was your grandmother's."

Reaching for the necklace, I scooped the delicate charm into my palm. A figure of the archangel Raphael was etched into the metal. Lucas dropped the chain into my hand.

My eyes flicked back to him. "I can't accept this." I shook my head. "I have to give it back." If this was Graziana's, she'd probably had it for years. It was an heirloom. I didn't deserve something that special. Heirlooms were reserved for loved ones. Graziana hadn't known me. I wasn't a loved one.

I turned toward the door and reached for the handle, ready to march the necklace right back to Martino.

I felt Lucas's strong hand on my shoulder. "Sophia," he said softly. I looked over my shoulder.

Lucas licked his lips and sucked in a breath. "I think it would mean a lot to him if you kept it." With the hand on my shoulder, he guided my body around. He brushed his fingertips across my tearstained cheek and went on. "I don't know what happened in there, but I want you to know that whatever it is, you're not alone."

As he spoke, his eyes never wavered, never flinched. I believed him, every word...and that's what scared the shit out of me.

* * *

I clutched the necklace in my hand as we drove back to the hotel, rubbing my thumb over Raphael's image. The little bumps in the metal massaged my skin. The symbolism behind Martino's gift wasn't lost on me. Even as a non-practicing Catholic, I knew Raphael was a patron saint; I just didn't know when he was to be invoked.

Curious, I pulled my phone from my purse. Tapping the Chrome app, I typed "St. Raphael the Archangel" into the search bar. Scrolling through a dozen hits of various churches and schools by the same name, I found Raphael's Wikipedia page. I touched the link and waited for it to load.

Lucas remained quiet in the driver's seat, never once pressuring me to explain what my grandfather had meant when he'd said I needed to be tested. After my outburst, Lucas was probably looking for a way to ditch the crazy girl. I wouldn't blame him. Heck, if he were smart, he'd go his own way and forget he ever met me…If I were smart, I'd tell him to go.

Wikipedia populated. The information I sought was near the top of the page. Scanning the patronage list, I noticed Raphael was called upon for many different reasons.

For Graziana, I imagined she'd prayed to St. Raphael for healing, as he's the patron saint of bodily ills and sick people. He also warded against nightmares, served as a guardian angel, watched over young people, and guided lovers to one another. A very busy saint.

Martino's gift made sense and was very thoughtful. I didn't think I'd find it comforting, but I did. "I wish I had told him thank you," I mumbled, breaking the silence.

I glanced at Lucas just as he turned in my direction, our puzzle pieces snapping together when our eyes met. It was like that every time. We fit.

"I don't think he'd mind a phone call," Lucas suggested with a soft grin. He put his hand on my leg and squeezed gently.

"You're right. I should call him." Now that I had some distance between the ghostly memories filling Martino and Graziana's home, I realized rushing out like I had was incredibly rude. I owed Martino an apology as well.

I found his name in my recent calls and dialed.

After a couple rings he answered gruffly. *"Pronto?"* I hoped he wasn't angry that I'd left so abruptly.

"Martino?"

"Sì."

"It's Sophia," I clarified, not sure he recognized my voice.

"Oh, Sophia," he sighed in relief, as if the weight of the world had been lifted off his shoulders. "Sweetheart, are you all right? *Mi dispiace*, I called your father. I was worried about you. He may call you soon."

I doubted Gio would call, but I'd bet my last euro he'd call Mom, and she'd be calling me shortly. "That's okay. I'm okay. I'm the one who should be apologizing. I shouldn't have run out like that. I'm sorry."

"I'm just glad you're all right. Did Lucas give you the necklace?"

I nodded, even though he couldn't see me; it was habit. "Yes, he did. I called to say thank you. It's very beautiful."

"Wonderful." I could hear the delight in his voice. "Your grandmother is smiling down from heaven. I know for a fact that she'd want you to have that necklace."

"I love it. *Grazie mille.*" After almost six weeks, my Italian was sounding more authentic.

"Prego, Tesoro. Sweetheart, it was my pleasure."

I smiled for the first time all day and glanced at Lucas. He smiled back.

"Call any time. I'd love to hear from you."

"Ciao, Martino."

"Ciao, Tesoro."

I ended the call and immediately opened my translator app. I didn't know what *Tesoro* meant and I needed to find out.

"What are you doing?" Lucas asked.

I typed the word into the app. "Martino kept calling me *Tesoro*. I don't know what that means, so I'm looking it up." I clicked go, and the translation popped up. "Sweetheart. *Tesoro* means sweetheart."

"Yeah, that's about right," Lucas said, turning into the hotel parking lot.

"Oh really? What about 'Linebacker'?"

"That's definitely right." He glanced at me with a wink.

Lucas found a place to park and killed the engine. During the hour-and-a-half trip back to Sorrento, the sun had dipped below the horizon, and now the city glowed in amber lights. This was when Lucas and I usually got ready to go out (Italy had turned me into a night owl), but tonight I was content with staying in. It had been a long day, and all I wanted to do was collapse into bed.

Unbuckling my seat belt, I pulled the latch on the door and stepped out. My phone buzzed. Looking at the screen, sure enough, it was Mom. My parents had the strangest relationship.

I ignored the call, opting to send her a quick text. I didn't want to hear the panic in her voice, and I wasn't game for a lengthy phone conversation.

My thumbs flew over the keyboard: *I'm fine, Mom, really. I'll call you tomorrow.*

Her response was immediate. *Are you sure? Your dad said Martino was very concerned about you.*

Yes, I'm good. I promise. Just tired. I'll call tomorrow, I typed again.

Love you, Patatina. Call me. Can't wait to see you in a few days.

"You okay?" Lucas had come around to my side of the car and draped his arm around my shoulder.

I looked up at him. "Yeah. Just texting my mom."

While we walked to the hotel's entrance, I sent one last text. *Love you too, Mom. See you soon.*

I slipped my phone into my purse. The events and conversations of the day clinked like heavy armor between Lucas and me. All the unasked questions and silent answers had reached rock concert level decibels, making the ringing in my ears unbearable.

I owed him an explanation. He needed to know what Martino had meant when he pleaded for me to be tested. I could only imagine what had been running through his head this whole time.

Last week, Lucas had confided in me; he'd finally let me in. It was time I put on my big-girl panties and did the same.

Chapter Twenty-Four

Lucas swiped the keycard in the door handle and ushered me inside. He was so quiet. Without a word, he flipped on the light and went straight for the bathroom, shutting the door. I didn't get the vibe he was angry, but he definitely wasn't acting like himself.

I kicked off my sandals and pushed them under the desk before I fell onto the bed. Staring up at the ceiling, I raised my right hand above my face, the one clutching the necklace. Holding on to the end of the chain, I let go of the pendant. It swung freely over my head. When it slowed, I tapped the angel with my left index finger, making him fly again.

I always wondered why people prayed to saints. Didn't it make more sense to go directly to the source? If we could pray to God, why did we need an intercessor? Ultimately, wasn't God the only one who could answer the prayer? The saint had no power to fix things, only God did.

How many prayers had Graziana sent up to Raphael? Would it have made a difference had she prayed to God directly?

I felt Lucas lie down. Glancing his way, I saw we were both on our backs. Lucas lay in the other direction, so we were nearly cheek to cheek, our bodies drawing a horizontal line across the middle of the bed.

St. Raphael watched over us.

Lucas reached for the pendant, catching it between his thumb and two fingers. "Who is it?" he asked.

"Raphael, the archangel."

Lucas rubbed his thumb over the image.

"He's a saint," I said.

"It's pretty." He let go and dropped his hand to his stomach. I lowered my arm, too, the necklace still in hand but resting against my belly. I let my head fall to the side. I watched him.

He stared at the ceiling as my eyes traced the outline of his profile. A few tousled strands of hair brushed against his forehead. His long eyelashes curled in just the right way, barely touching the skin at the top and bottom of his eyes. Most girls would kill to have lashes like that. There was a slight dip at the bridge of his nose before it straightened out, turning up slightly at the end. His full lips were pressed together, surrounded by a shadow of scruff covering his cheeks, chin, and upper lip.

I took in all of him, the way each feature tapered and flowed into the next. How his sun-bleached blond hair darkened to a dirty blond at his sideburn, and in front of his right ear was a tiny birthmark, no bigger than the pad of my pinky finger.

I smiled. It looked like an upside-down outline of Mickey Mouse's head.

God, he is beautiful.

Lucas shifted, looking at me. The tips of our noses touched and my eyes had the perfect view of his heart-shaped mouth.

"Checking me out?" He smirked. Even his laugh lines were gorgeous.

His warm breath spread across my face. I inhaled, my eyes fluttering closed for a second. I wanted to remember this moment, because after I told him what Martino had meant, our good-bye was inevitable. He deserved so much more than me.

"Yeah," I whispered, a hesitant smile at my lips.

Lucas shifted on the bed, moving upward, the crown of his head touching my shoulder. "Soph…"

I loved the way his mouth caressed my name. His lips puckered around the "o" and his bottom lip barely touched his top teeth, making a gentle *ffff* sound.

He searched my face, scooting closer. Bringing his hand up, he put the heel of his palm on my cheek. His fingertips brushed against my neck and under my chin. With a slight part in his lips, he leaned in and closed his mouth over mine.

I shivered and let my eyes fall shut, bathing in the sensation of our lips wrapped in an upside-down embrace.

Lucas pulled at my bottom lip with delicate pressure. Slowly, our mouths moved against each other while his hand massaged my cheek with the same unhurried passion.

I guided the tip of my tongue along the inside of his bottom lip, deliberately slow, its half-moon curve sending hot chills coursing through my veins.

Lucas sucked in a breath and swept his tongue over mine.

Our mouths explored the landscape from this new and exciting angle.

My lips tingled, hungry for more. My body screamed to be close to him…as close as humanly possible. I wanted Lucas to replace the only memory of sex I had.

He moved his hand from my face, sliding it to the bed. He broke away and sat up, turning his body around. I scooted up on the mattress just as Lucas swung his leg over, straddling me.

Both of his hands cupped my face as he tilted his head, crushing his mouth against mine. He kissed me deeply. His right leg pressed back and he used his knee to push my legs apart. Stretching his body out, he planked me, holding his weight in his arms.

Chaos and desire threatened to shatter my control. Circling my arms around his neck, I drew him closer. I wanted to be devoured by him.

Our tongues knotted together, mesmerized by the feel of the other's.

He tasted so good. What was it about him that made him taste so delicious? I couldn't explain it, but I knew it was everything a man should taste like. Raw…tender…bold…sweet…hot. Sex. He was killing me. He made my head spin, dizzy with want.

Carried away, I nipped at the corner of his bottom lip, just as he'd slanted the other direction, changing the angle of our kiss. Lucas growled against my mouth, "Sophia, God"—he rocked his hips against me—"you're driving me insane." I could feel just how insane I'd made him.

His left hand traveled down my body like it was on a mission. Lifting the hem of my shirt, his heavy palm pushed its way up my abdomen, across my rib cage, until he found what he was looking for. Cupping my breast in his hand, he squeezed greedily. His tongue explored my mouth. Our bodies moved in a way that demanded we lose the clothes; they were only in the way.

I wanted him so badly. I loved the way he made my body come alive. How, with a simple smile and a sultry kiss, he could drive away the ghosts that haunted my unknown future. I wanted to bask in his light and forget about the shadows that lurked around the corner.

But what I wanted didn't matter. He did. And more than anything, I wanted him to have a happy future, unblemished by sorrow and tragedy.

His hands moved to the button on my shorts. My breath came up short. "Lucas," I muttered. "Stop. Please."

There. I said it. Albeit, not very authoritatively, but the words passed from my lips and touched his.

He stilled immediately, obeying my command. Pulling back just enough to look me in the eyes, he scanned my face and swept a hand across my cheek. "Baby, what's wrong?" A knife sliced through my heart. For the second time today, I knew I was going to cry. I refused to let the tears fall this time, though. I was stronger than that.

I put my hands against his chest and pushed. He didn't fight me but quickly stood, giving me the space I needed so I could muster up the courage to set him free.

"Soph?" He wiped his thumb and forefinger over the corners of his mouth and down his scratchy chin. The fire in his eyes was still there but was close to being extinguished by confusion. It was written all over his face.

I sat up on the bed, scooted closer to the headboard, and crossed my legs. Lucas sat on the edge, waiting for me to say something.

"Sorry," I mumbled, reaching for Graziana's necklace in the middle of the bed. It had fallen out of my hand. I picked it up and laid it on the bedside table.

"Talk to me, Soph," he demanded, his voice deep with concern.

He caught my chin with his thumb, forcing me to look him in the eye. "I know this has to do with what happened earlier, with Martino. Tell me."

A single tear escaped my right eye. Lucas ran his thumb over my cheek, wiping it away.

"I don't even know where to start," I whispered. If I talked any louder, I wouldn't be able to hold the rest of the tears at bay.

"What made you run out on Martino this afternoon?" he asked.

Okay. This was good. If he asked the questions, I could answer. I'd get through.

I shook my head. "Those pictures of Graziana were too much." I tried to swallow the lump in my throat. "She was so pretty. Brimming with life…" I trailed off, remembering the black and white photo of my grandmother holding her pregnant belly, smiling, infinitely happy.

Lucas pulled his legs onto the bed and sidled up next to me. My shoulder rested against his bicep. Sitting like this would make things easier, too. I could stare off into space and detach myself from the conversation if I didn't have to look into his eyes.

"Here, sit up." He pushed me forward, wrapping his arm around me. "That's better."

Yes, this was better. No soul-searching blue eyes to drive the knife in my heart deeper, not to mention being cradled at his side gave me an extra measure of confidence.

"Graziana died of a genetic disorder." Just pull the Band-Aid off quickly. "The same one my dad is dying of," I added.

"God, Sophia," Lucas said. "I'm so sorry." He flexed, squeezing me closer.

Based on his reaction and the sound of his voice, I was sure he'd missed the implication behind what I'd said, the unspoken truth I was skirting around. I'd hoped he'd be able to jump to conclusions so I wouldn't have to spell it out. It didn't look like that was going to happen.

I pulled in a long, calming breath through my nose and exhaled slowly through my mouth. *Just tell him, Soph.* "There's a chance I might have it, too." My voice was monotone, devoid of any emotion. If I kept it clinical, I wouldn't fall to pieces. I'd told Mom without tears; certainly I could do the same with him.

My heart beat loudly in my ears. I didn't move…didn't breathe. I waited for him to say something, anything. I half expected him to spring off the bed, give me a wave and a hurried *arrivederci*, and get the hell out of Dodge. But he didn't move either. He was as still as me. *Is he breathing?*

I turned to look at him, violating rule number one: Don't look into his eyes. But I had to see. I had to know. What was he thinking?

His eyes were wide. He pierced me with an icy stare. The knife in my heart had been removed, dipped in poison, and reinserted, burning me from the inside out. I couldn't read the expression on his face. Anger? Sadness? Indifference? It could have been any of them. Or all of them. I hated that I couldn't tell, but more so, I loathed the fact that he wasn't talking. I needed him to say something before I went out of my mind.

Then his mouth moved, forming words, quieting my mind just a little. "What is it?" he asked. "What disorder?"

He still had his arm around me, but it was heavy, dead weight.

"Huntington's disease."

There it was, out in the open. The part of me I'd hoped to keep quiet. My Italian summer fling didn't need to care about terminal genetic disorders when there was no future for us. In three days, I'd leave for the States, Lucas would go wherever the wind blew him, and we'd have the memory of our month and a half in Italy. That was it.

Then why does this hurt so much?

My heart bled. Even through the pain of Dad leaving when I was little and missing my best friend every single day, I was always able to move forward, despite the ache their absence left behind.

But this was different.

"Well, what do we do?" Lucas asked. He lifted his arm from my shoulder and climbed across the bed. He sat in front of me, crossed his legs, and stared me down with his blue eyes.

I blinked and shook my head, trying to make sense of his question. "What do you mean?"

"You said 'might have it.' That means there's a possibility that you might not. How do we find out?"

We? Why wasn't he running? Getting as far away from me as possible? "There is no 'we,' Lucas." My eyes flooded. The dam was full and about to be breached.

He pulled his eyebrows tight, creases forming between them. "What the hell does that mean? Of course there's a 'we.'" He grabbed my hands. "You don't think I'm going to let you figure this out alone, do you?"

More damn tears spilled over my bottom lids. "That's really sweet," I choked, "but I can't…I just can't." I cried. My resolve washed away. "You deserve so much better."

He put his hand on my wet cheek. "Sophia, I don't know what scares me more, the fact that you think you're not good enough for me or the reality of being without you."

I brushed his hand away. He did need a dose of reality. "Where's your computer?"

"In the safe. Why?" he answered, confused.

I looked into his eyes, a challenge to myself not to let my guard down just because his eyes could see into my soul. "You need to see what reality will be like if you *do* stay with me. You saw Graziana's picture. At sixty-seven she was already confined to a bed, having lost most, if not all, of her motor function. She was on a feeding tube and oxygen. Is that what you want?" I yelled through my tears. "To wipe drool off my mouth because my body no longer works? To sit by my bedside until my heart gives out and I flatline?"

"Yes," he said with a simple nod. His eyes were a soft, honest, tranquil blue. A placid sea of truth. I believed him.

But I didn't want to. He didn't deserve that sucky reality. "No," I protested. "You are going to find someone who colors your world with life, gives you children, someone to grow old with."

"I've had more color in my life these last six weeks than I've ever had, Sophia." His words were biting but not angry. I knew what he was trying to do; he saw my defenses crumbling and he was prepared to bring them down. "Do I need to spell it out for you?" he asked, gripping my hands so hard between his. "Crimson: the color of your cheeks when you're embarrassed or excited. Espresso: the color of your hair in the lemon-yellow Italian sunshine and a drink that makes you stick your tongue out and cringe with disgust. Almost black: your eyes beneath the white, twinkling stars at night. Mint green: your chin, after you dribbled mint chocolate chip gelato all over. Olive: the night you saved that little girl who was choking. Periwinkle: the color that knocked me on my ass."

He remembered the color of the shirt I was wearing the day I bumped into him. I closed my eyes, bombarded with so many different emotions. Why was he doing this?

"Should I go on? There are about ten million different colors the human eye can see. I see you, Sophia, and you're a fucking rainbow. A promise after a shit storm."

I sniffled and leaned over to the table by the bed, pulling a tissue from the box. Lucas leaned over and grabbed the whole box, plunking it down between us.

"No one is guaranteed tomorrow," he said. "We live the day we're given, enjoy the time we have, and love the people in our life. A damn piano could fall on my head the second I walk out of this hotel."

I wiped my eyes and blew my nose into a tissue, giving him a dirty look. "What, are you a cartoon?"

He shook his head, his mouth curling into a crooked smile. He tugged on my hands and pulled me toward him. With our foreheads resting together, he stared into my almost-black eyes. "You know what?"

"What?"

"The day Julia left me at the altar was the third best day of my life."

Where was this coming from? He made no sense. "The third?"

"*Sí*, because if I had married her, I would've been in Paris on my honeymoon, not Italy. And you would have never had the chance to bump into me. I should call her and say thank you."

"You might have been better off if I hadn't bumped into you." I yanked a pillow onto my lap and hugged it tightly.

"Uh!" He pointed. "Shush! None of that. They're my best days. You don't get to disagree."

"Okay, then, what about the second best day of your life?"

"Pompeii. The day I met you."

I rolled my eyes.

"Soph," he warned. "Are you making fun of the best days of my life?" He spread his legs apart, dragged me across the bed, turned me around, and wrapped his strong arms around me.

I loved this. Being secured in his arms. "No, never," I said. "But I'm curious—what was the best day of your life?"

He paused, then tilted my head to the side, sweeping my hair away. His lips touched the hollow below my ear, and he whispered, low and husky, "Right now."

He didn't move away so quickly this time, kissing me again. "And right now." His mouth opened and closed along my neck. "And now…and now…and now…"

With each kiss, he repeated the same words. I craned my head, looking over my shoulder, a desperate need to look into his eyes.

We stared at each other for a long minute. The connection growing stronger and stronger.

"And now," he whispered, lowering to my lips.

Slow, sweet kisses quickly segued into deep, soul-searching embraces.

Hooking a hand around my waist, he turned me and pushed me back on the mattress. Caged by his arms at the side of my head, I looked into his eyes. "You could have a chance at something normal, Lucas. Why me?"

"Normal's boring. I want the ten million colors in full, gleaming high definition." He lowered his arms and tilted his head, coming in to kiss me again, but I stopped him, pressing my index finger to his lips. He kissed my finger and mumbled, "What?"

"What if I do have it?"

He rolled off me and propped his head up in his hand. Sweeping the fingers of his other hand across my cheek, he asked, "How do we find out?"

I folded my hands on top of my stomach. "A blood test. There's a fifty-fifty chance either way."

"So, this is what we'll do," he said, unlacing my folded hands, one finger at a time. "When you get back to St. Louis, make an appointment to have the test done." With his right hand, he pushed his fingers between mine. "And I'll be right there with you."

I craned my neck to get a better look at him. "You'd come to St. Louis? You'd go with me?"

"In a fucking heartbeat." He lowered his arm and rested his head on top of his bicep.

"I did not see you coming." This time, I was the one who moved in for a kiss.

I felt his lips break into a smile against mine. "Ain't that the truth."

Chapter Twenty-Five

Lucas slowly trailed his hand down my cheek, over my neck, and across my collarbone—the only exposed skin. But my clothing didn't deter his southward pursuit. Even through the thin cotton of my shirt, I was hyperaware of his touch. How his fingertips grazed over the swell of my breast, lingering at the peak…teasing.

With each deliberate, enticing swirl of his thumb, my body came alive. Yet, it wasn't his gifted hand alone that made my breath come quicker and send shivers down my spine. It was his eyes. Always his eyes.

To say they were expressive was an understatement, just the tip of the iceberg. His eyes told a story. One of happiness, desire, intrigue, sadness, warmth, love—it all radiated from their bright cerulean cores, the center and focal points that surrounded his pupils. From the day we met, I wanted to swim in that ocean, be swept away by his gaze and get lost beneath the crushing waves of his stare. To be a part of his story.

I touched his arm, my fingers disappearing under his shirtsleeve.

His skin was smooth over the hard, taut muscle of his bicep. I clenched it, feeling him flex as he moved his hand lower on my belly, lifting the hem of my shirt.

The instant he made contact with my skin, I sucked in a breath. "Are my hands cold?" he asked.

I moved my head side to side. "Very much the opposite." My voice was garbled and shallow. I attempted to clear my throat.

As the branding touch of Lucas's hand moved up my body, he shifted his weight and sat up, lifting my shirt higher. I subtly raised my shoulders and he pulled my shirt over my head, tossing it to the floor.

His eyes slowly roamed my body, landing on every hill and valley. He watched the rise and fall of my chest, not allowing himself to touch until his eyes touched first. Even though this wasn't the first time he had seen me like this, tonight was different.

The night of his birthday, I'd wanted to give him everything I had. I was ready. I needed that last connection to him. But Lucas still thought he had to prove himself to me. He wanted me to know that every part of me was special to him, not a fleeting moment in bed.

But tonight was different. He was right here with me. There were no more secrets between us. He wasn't chasing a ghost from his past, and for once, I wasn't afraid of my shadowed future. I needed this. I wanted him…all of him, everything he was willing to give me. I needed to feel alive while I still had the chance.

Working my hand down to the bend of his elbow, I memorized how my fingertips flowed over his skin and how the hair on his arm bristled at my touch.

"Two more colors I can add to my list." He touched my shoulder, hooking his index finger around my bra strap and sliding it away.

"These are going to be the death of me when I get the rest of your clothes off." He fingered a line from my shoulder to the curve of my breast, dipping into my bra at my cleavage.

I craned my neck to see what he was talking about. "What?"

He leaned over and kissed my shoulder. "I'm going to call this color…mocha."

My head fell back onto the pillow the second his lips touched me. Dragging his mouth and tongue down the line his finger had trailed, he murmured, "And this is ivory." His tongue slid across the contour of my breast, along the hot pink lace of my bra. "Fucking tan lines get me every time. I can't wait to see the outline of that little bikini you wore the other day." He looked up and caught my eye.

I flashed him a teasing smile. "Tan lines? Really?"

He nodded, like a kid in a candy store. Kicking his leg over, he sat up on top of me. I watched as his eyes grazed over my body and his fingers traced the lines down my other shoulder. I loved the unhurriedness, the deliberate, measured pace he'd set…like I was something to savor…to cherish…to remember.

With my hand at his waist, I wanted the same pleasure, to be able to drink in the view of his glorious body. I lifted his shirt, tugging it upward until he reached behind his back and pulled it all the way off.

The musculature of his torso was a thing of beauty, utterly mouthwatering. I wanted to touch every defined muscle—no, it was more like I wanted to *lick* every defined muscle. The urge to run my tongue over every dip and rise of his six-pack nearly consumed me.

I started to run my fingers along the ridges of his stomach, but he stilled my hand. "Uh-uh," he said, shaking his head. "If you get the whole view, then so do I."

Letting go of my hand, he pushed his beneath me, deftly unclasping the hooks of my bra. Not supported any longer, my full breasts spilled from their cups. Lucas dragged the straps down my arms, until I shrugged out of them altogether.

"Better?" I smirked.

"Getting there." He winked, cupping my breasts gently. Inhaling sharply, he breathed, "So much better."

My eyes fluttered closed, soaking up every burst of pleasure from the millions and millions of nerve endings firing on my skin. His thumbs circled over my nipples, drawing them into tight beads, driving a pulsing ache between my legs. Involuntarily, my chest rose, begging for more attention from his clever hands.

Lucas dropped his head to my left breast, taking it into his mouth, while his other hand stayed busy on the right.

His mouth was hot and slick. Incredible. He sucked, drawing in more of me. He varied his pressure, circling his tongue over my nipple before tugging it between his teeth.

"Uhh," I whimpered. My hips bucked, and I could feel him, ready, at my center.

I raked my short fingernails down his back, pushing my hands into the waistband of his shorts, cursing that damn belt he wore. There wasn't enough room for my hands to get very far.

Sliding them along the top edge of his pants, around to the front, I fumbled with the belt buckle. Lucas sat up, abandoning his divine ministrations to my chest. I yanked on a belt loop. "These have to go."

His eyes shined with eagerness. "Reciprocity, my dear."

I giggled. "Yes, sir."

Lucas dropped a leg to the floor and stood, unbuckling his

belt. With a quick flick his button came undone; he lowered the zipper and pushed his shorts and boxer briefs down all at once. With his clothes puddled on the floor around his ankles, he stood naked in front of me. I'd meant to wiggle out of my pants at the same time, but watching him undress had short-circuited my brain.

He stepped out of his discarded shorts and took a half step toward the bed. "Let me help you with these." He put his hands at the waistband of my shorts and tugged. "I have a thing about being the only one naked. I don't like it much."

I heard the words he was saying; I thought I even comprehended them...maybe. I think he was even touching me. But at the moment, my brain was focused on his massive erection. No matter how many times I saw him naked, my jaw still hit the floor. I knew it wasn't possible, but I swore he got bigger every time we took our clothes off.

Fighting with my shorts, Lucas yanked harder, pulling me down the bed.

"Whoa!" I laughed. Raising my hips off the bed, Lucas gave one last tug, and I was just as naked as him.

He tossed my shorts to the floor. "Soph," he breathed, "you are so damn beautiful."

He lifted his leg onto the bed, wedging his knee between mine. With our eyes locked, I opened to him. He drew his other leg up, kneeling. He was right there, on full display, a beautiful temptation I couldn't resist touching.

I put my hands on his waist, running my fingertips across his tan stomach. His abdominal muscles clenched, rippling under my touch. With my right index finger, I traced the trail of golden brown hair leading from his belly button, downward, until I reached his length. I brushed my fingers over him.

"Hhhh," he breathed, letting his head fall back.

I liked that I was able to elicit that kind of reaction from him, not to mention how hot it was.

Exploring his body with my hands, I took note of all the places that made his muscles quake, the spots that made him groan, low and deep. Being a student was second nature; I observed, catalogued, processed, and Lucas just became my new favorite subject. I wanted to find and remember all the places that made him come to life.

Sweeping my hands over the slight curve of his backside, down his thighs, I slowly dragged my fingers to the front, moving toward his inner thighs, teasing. Lucas looked down at me and took my hand, wrapping it solidly around his erection. "You're killing me, Soph."

He was hard in my hand, and when I moved my fist, he got harder. "Fuck," he groaned, his legs shaking.

In a rhythmic motion, I pumped my hand along his length, increasing the pace, until I couldn't take it any longer. I lifted up, balancing my weight on one elbow, and wrapped my mouth around him. My hand always made him convulse with pleasure, so I was eager to use my mouth as well.

"Sophia…" He threaded his fingers through my hair, gripping the back of my head. "Jesus."

He rocked his hips and guided my head with his hand. I took him, deeper and deeper, the ache between my legs growing every time I swirled my tongue around him.

"Mmm," I hummed. I couldn't help it; I was so turned on.

"Soph," Lucas said with a sense of urgency. "I'm so close…" He pulled away. I looked up at him, towering above me. "I don't want to come like this, not tonight."

Caressing my cheek with his knuckles, he leaned down, pushing me back on the pillows, stretching out along my body. "That was fucking amazing," he said, brushing my hair away from my forehead. "That pretty mouth of yours is lethal."

I smoothed my hands across his back, my inner sex kitten smiling unabashedly.

"Sophia, I don't know what the future holds, but I do know that I want to figure it out with you. No matter what. Coming to Italy was the best decision I ever made." He tilted his head and kissed me.

His lips tangled with mine. Moving his hand downward, he skimmed over my breast and kept going…farther…until his hand was between my thighs.

He circled his thumb over my clit, while his fingers inched closer to my center. "You're so wet."

My back arched, and Lucas took complete advantage of the angle, kissing and licking his way up my neck. I rocked my hips against his hand. "Oh…Lucas," I groaned.

I wanted more. I needed it. "Please…"

With him, the lead-up to sex was infinitely better than the act itself, at least from what I knew of it. Lucas made my body sing with just a touch. What was it going to be like when he was inside of me?

Dear God, what is he doing with his thumb? It felt like lightning or fireworks were going to burst through my skin.

"Talk to me, baby. Tell me what you want." His lips moved at my ear, nibbling my earlobe, pulling it between his teeth.

Caught up in him and his skillful hands, he made it hard to talk, but I managed a breathy reply. "You…I want you."

He slipped a finger inside me. In and out. In and out. My hips bucked.

"How do you want me?" he whispered, sliding another finger inside. His thumb continued the torturously delicious circular motion over my clit.

I was ready. I wanted the orgasm…craved it…*needed* it.

So close…almost there…

I was about to come undone. Pressure built in my core and between my legs. My fuse was burning away fast and detonation was inevitable…if I could just get him where I needed him. I grit my teeth together and whimpered. "I want you inside me."

"I am inside you, baby. Do you feel me?" He crooked his fingers and rubbed a sweet spot even he had never touched.

Goddamn, yes, I feel you! I shook my head. As much as I loved his magic fingers, I needed more. I looked him right in the eyes, my hand wrapping around his length. "I need *you* inside me. *Please*! I want to feel connected to you in every way possible."

Lucas stilled his hands and pulled away with a low growl. "Fuck. I need a condom. Now." He was off the bed and across the room in a hurry.

Breathlessly, I sat up, supporting my weight with my arms. I watched as he bent over his suitcase, fumbling with the zipper.

He cursed, yanking on the pull tab. It wouldn't budge. "Shit!"

I stifled a laugh. Naked and squatting in front of uncooperative luggage wasn't an image of Lucas I'd ever thought I'd see. It was damn cute and really freaking sexy. I could stare at the dimple on his left ass cheek all night.

"Finally!" The zipper gave way and he flipped open the top. Tossing a few articles of clothing aside, he stood and turned around, a foil packet between his fingers. "Sorry." He grimaced, walking back to the bed.

Grinning, I lay back. "That was highly entertaining, and the view wasn't too bad, either."

He climbed on top of me. "I'm sure the view I have right now is better." His eyes skimmed over me while he opened the packet and slid the condom on.

I watched his nimble fingers, captivated. *Yeah, he's right. This view is infinitely better.*

"Sophia? You all right?"

At the sound of his voice, I jerked my eyes up to his face. "Uh…yeah…"

He lengthened his body over mine, positioning himself at my opening. He was so close to where I needed him. "You sure?" he asked again.

Despite the jumble of emotions crashing through my head, I nodded in affirmation. I was ready to be in the moment for once. Spontaneous. Adventurous. I needed this to remind me I was still alive…that it was okay to live, to hope, to dream. That is was okay to not have all the answers, because sometimes, it's the unexpected bumps in life that make life worth living.

My heart beat loudly in my ears, and if I concentrated, I could feel Lucas's elevated pulse against my chest.

"Baby, what's wrong?" His bedroom eyes darkened with concern.

"Thank you, Lucas. Thank you for this…for reminding me what it's like to feel alive."

"I could say the same to you, Sophia."

I lifted my head, yearning to taste him, and he met me halfway, locking our lips together. I let my head fall back on the pillow, opening to him. *Make me feel alive, Lucas.*

Our kiss was sweet and seductive. His body pressed along the length of mine, stealing away my breath. Lucas seated himself at my center and slowly pushed inside me. I gasped and arched my back, overcome with a storm of sensations. I may not have been a virgin, but I didn't remember it feeling like this...so full...so...perfect.

Now we were connected. Anchored. A perfect fit.

"Don't worry, we'll take it slow," Lucas breathed in my ear. He pulled out just a little and slid back in again, farther this time.

I exhaled loudly. Tiny beads of sweat coated my flushed skin. "Hhhh..." My hips rose, begging for more of him.

He repeated the same, steady motion a few more times, sliding in a little farther with each exquisite push and pull, until he sank into me fully, burying his head against my neck. "Sophia." His hot breath zinged across my skin. "You're so tight. You feel so damn amazing," he groaned.

We fell into a natural rhythm as I loosened up. I never imagined it could feel this way. It was special, rare, and mind-blowing, and it erased all the terrible memories of my first time. I deemed this my first time...This was what it was all about. We were synced. I'd found my other half, and now I was whole. We moved together as one.

Lucas kissed along my neck, running his hands down my sides and around the curve of my ass. He pushed me up, crashing deeper into me as he flipped us around, my legs astride him.

"Whoa!" I gasped. "Dear God, that was awesome," I laughed breathlessly. "I thought that only happened in books and movies."

He smiled full-on, dimple and all. "What kind of books are you reading?" He raised an eyebrow curiously.

"Wouldn't you like to know." I wiggled my hips and sucked in a breath, feeling him deeper inside me. He'd given me all the control with this new angle. A girl could get used to this.

He hummed. "Damn, I thought having you beneath me was a great view, but this one is fucking glorious." He grinned, smoothing his hands across my hips, guiding my tentative movements. "That's it, baby, do what feels good."

I splayed my hands across his pecs, getting comfortable with my movements, letting the pressure build with each dip and rise of my hips.

"Fuck… Sophia!" Lucas palmed my breasts and I rode him faster, harder.

"Lucas," I yelled.

"I love it when you say my name like that."

He sat up and I wrapped my legs around his waist. He circled his hands at my middle and hitched me up onto his lap, holding me so close and so tight. I squeezed my legs, pulling him into me as far as he could go. I ground my hips down as he pulled up, our rhythm fevered and out of control.

"Lucas! I'm going to…," I cried out, unable to finish the sentence before my world exploded.

Every muscle clenched. I squeezed my eyes shut. Colors burst behind my lids. I was sure there were ten million, if not more. Lucas kept moving, coaxing more spasms from my body. They ricocheted off one another, lighting more sparks, spreading a wildfire, and sending up fireworks all at once. I was aflame.

Lucas thrust into me, his panting breaths hot against my neck. I forced my eyes open; I wanted to see him come to life.

He squeezed my middle, impossibly tight, and slammed into me two more times before throwing his head back with a deep, satisfied groan.

Slowly, he brought his head back up. His eyes were hooded as he stared back at me. "That was incredible." He pulled his thumb over my kiss-swollen bottom lip and across my cheek.

I nodded, leaning my forehead against his. "Thank you."

"I should be the one thanking you." His shoulders heaved, as did mine, as we tried to catch our breath. "It's like the sun has finally broken through the rain clouds that have drenched my life the six years."

I held on to him with everything I had, my arms tight around his neck, refusing to let go. I feared that the minute we parted, real life would come crashing between us. "Will you just hold me for a minute longer?" My voice shook.

He hugged me close, binding me in his arms. "Baby, I'll hold you forever if you'll let me."

Chapter Twenty-Six

Startled awake by the sound of a voice, I opened my eyes but lay still. Lucas was pressed against my back, his arm draped over my waist, while one of his legs was tangled with mine beneath the covers. His breathing was heavy and even; he was sound asleep.

But I could have sworn I heard a voice...

Now, wide awake, I lay there, staring across the dark room. Outside, lights still glowed brightly, despite the late hour. I was physically exhausted and a little sore, but I smiled, my mind blissfully content at the moment. Quiet for once.

Lucas stirred, stretching his leg out. "Soph," he mumbled, my name garbled with sleep.

"Yeah," I whispered. I listened for a reply, but none came. "Lucas?"

He remained quiet, breathing deeply.

Sleep talking again.

Lucas was a noisy sleeper. Actually, tonight had been the quietest he'd slept since we'd teamed up on this vacation. Most nights, I heard him tossing and turning, the pullout bed whining in protest. He'd mumble random things, most of which made no sense. But the one word he did say repeatedly was "Julia." He'd uttered her name at least a dozen times over the last month.

I wondered what he dreamed about when he called out her name. And a small pang of jealousy pinched my heart each time.

But tonight he'd said *my* name. Only my name.

I gloried in that, a thrill sending goose bumps over my skin. I wiggled my backside, snuggling closer to him. Now I was desperate to know what he was dreaming about.

"Two days," he said.

Two days?

I was due to return to the States in two days. Is that what he meant?

What would happen in two days? Lucas mentioned coming back to St. Louis with me, but how feasible was that, really? He had a life and a business waiting for him in California. It's one thing for him to take a vacation, get his life straightened out, but it was certainly another to disrupt his life for a girl he hardly knew. Besides, I had med school starting in a month. Once I left Italy, I'd have to pick up my real life from where I'd dropped it before I came.

And then there was the issue of a blood test.

Lucas sighed heavily. "Sophia, wait."

"Wait for what, Lucas?" I whispered.

No reply.

For the longest time, I listened to him breathe. Enjoyed his body's warmth.

I waited, like he'd asked.

My eyelids drooped. I pushed my hands beneath the pillow and waited for sleep to cover me.

"I love you, Sophia," he exhaled.

My eyes sprang open, no longer heavy. *What? He loved me? Did he really say that?*

"Lucas?" I said, wondering if he had woken up. He didn't move, didn't speak.

He *loved* me?

No. No, no, no. He couldn't love me. Only pain and suffering would result from loving me. He was breaking his own rule: no expectations. Well, love came with expectation, and with expectation came disappointment. Lucas didn't expect things. He lived in the moment. Thrived on adventure. Took risks. Saw color and beauty in the world on the grayest days. Helped those in need without a second thought.

And he challenged me to do all those things. During our time together, he'd grabbed me by the hand and refused to let go. He showed me there could be beauty in mayhem, just like the day Lucas and I drove through the streets of Sorrento and along the Amalfi Coast. I hadn't wanted to, but he pushed me to see things in different ways and to try new things.

He showed me the color in life, and I broke my own rules: no guys, no distractions, keep everyone out.

I let him in, and I fell in love.

My heart beat faster at this revelation. *Oh, dear sweet, Jesus. I love him.*

Feeling him beside me, my heart swelled like it had when he'd been inside me. He was a part of me now, our puzzle pieces snapped and locked together.

Panic bloomed in my chest. Loving me came with the possibility of uncertainty, anguish, sadness, worry, grief—the list went on and on. I wouldn't do that to him. I loved him far too much for any of my baggage to touch him, ruin his chance at a future. I had to save him from me.

Slowly, I pulled my leg from beneath his, sliding it off the bed. My foot touched the floor. I paused…held my breath…waited for him to wake up….

Lucas stayed still.

Carrying on with my plan, all I needed to do was lift his arm up; then I could slip off the bed. I took his fingers in my hand with a whisper's touch. At the same time I pulled his arm upward, I rolled away, my knees hitting the floor with a quiet thud.

Lucas stirred, grasping the pillow I'd been using. He hugged it to his body and muttered my name. "Sophia?"

I froze.

He squeezed the pillow a few times and fumbled the blanket with his feet, but his eyes never opened.

I kneeled at the bedside for a long time, afraid if I moved, he'd wake up. He looked so peaceful. The faint lines that creased his forehead were smoothed away. His cheeks were a little flushed; I had to fight the urge to run my fingers over them.

A door slammed down the hall. I flinched, holding my breath. I had to leave now, before he woke up. I stood, tears trickling down my face. I didn't want to go, but I had to. For him.

Quietly, I dressed and haphazardly threw my belongings into my suitcase. The pinch in my heart was more like a stab wound by the time I slipped on my shoes. With my bags ready at the door, I went to the desk drawer and pulled out a pen and pad of paper.

Lucas,

When I flew into Italy six weeks ago I met a sweet old man on the plane. There was some turbulence during our landing and he held my hand and told me not to worry about little bumps, they're nothing. It sounded like good advice at the time. It got me through the bumpy landing.

But he's wrong. If there's one thing I've learned on this trip, it's that the little bumps are everything. They're what wake you up, force you to take notice of the world around you. A reminder that you're still alive.

Bumping into you at Pompeii woke me up. Your smile, the light in your eyes, your sense of adventure, your kind, compassionate heart, you forced me to take notice of the beauty I was missing in the world. And last night, wrapped in your arms, I was alive.

But I also know that love comes with expectation, and the last thing I want is to disappoint you. Martino's story ended in disappointment, my mother's story ended in disappointment. Each of them expected their loves to last, but illness robbed them of it, in one way or another. The odds are not in my favor. Being with me will only end in disappointment.

Did you know you talk in your sleep? You said you love me. I love you, too, Lucas. I love you so much that I have to say goodbye before I become a disappointment.

Maybe one day we'll bump into each other again and look back on the Italian adventure we shared. I hope you find your unexpected, because you deserve ten million colors and more.

Ti Amo, Lucas,
Soph

I tore the paper from the pad and folded it in half. I wrote Lucas's name on the outside and walked over to the bed. Laying the note on the pillow he wasn't using, I whispered, "*Ciao*, Lucas."

* * *

My flight home wasn't scheduled until tomorrow, which gave me another day to be angry, sad, and mopey in my hotel room. Early yesterday morning, I checked into a hotel close to the Naples airport. I didn't want to go back to the Hotel Suite Esedra, fearing Lucas might track me down there. Thankfully, Naples was a big city, easy to get lost in.

Hiding under the covers in my room, my plan for the day was the exact same one from yesterday: stay in bed, cry, and eat copious amounts of gelato.

But no matter how much ice cream I packed away, how many tears I shed, nothing filled the hollowness inside me.

I'd lost count of the times Lucas called and texted; to say a lot would have been an understatement. I had at least ten voice mail messages from him, which I couldn't bring myself to listen to.

I thought once I'd left, put some distance between us, I'd feel better. I wasn't sure leaving had been the right answer. My head was foggy and clouded with so many "what ifs." Each minute that ticked by, it became harder to breathe. All the unknown variables and unanswered questions were a growing cloud of suffocating toxic gas, and I was lost inside.

I needed help. I didn't know what to do.

I sat up in bed and set my dish of mint chocolate chip gelato on the bedside table. Patting the blankets, I searched for my phone. Even at twenty-two, I still needed my mom. I needed to hear her voice and have her tell me everything was going to be all right. Maybe even Nonna would be home and I could talk to her, too.

Untangling my cell from the sheets, I swiped the screen, flipped through my contacts, and tapped on "Mom."

It rang a few times and then she answered, her voice thick with sleep. "Sophia? What is it? Is everything okay?"

"Hi, Mamma." I hadn't called her that since I was in junior high.

"Now I know something's wrong. Spill it, Sophia," Mom commanded, her voice no longer burdened with sleep.

My throat closed up tight as I tried not to cry. I'd done so much freaking crying in the last day, I was surprised I had any tears left to shed.

"I miss you, Mamma. I'm just ready to come home."

"I miss you, too, *Patatina*. But I know there's something more here than just homesickness. I can hear it in your voice. And the whole time you've been gone, you've never once called me at one in the morning. You have always been mindful of the time difference, so tell me what's really going on."

Dammit. I didn't remember the time difference. "Sorry, Mom. I didn't mean to wake you."

"I'm glad you did. It's good to hear your voice," she comforted. "Now talk, Sophia."

I took a calming breath. *Just rip the Band-Aid off.* "I met someone."

For a moment, there was silence on the line.

"Mom? You still there?"

She cleared her throat. "Um, yeah. You met someone?"

"Yeah."

"So, is this the phone call where you tell me you're not coming home? That you're renting a little flat and moving in with some Italian man who barely knows English but knows you perfectly well in other ways?"

A smile broke through my sadness. "Not exactly, Mom," I chuckled. "But I did meet someone. An American. He's from California. And, no, I am coming home tomorrow. No flat. No Italian guy who knows me in *other* ways."

Nope. None of that. Just an American man who knows me in every way.

I heard Mom's sigh of relief come through the phone. "So you're moving to California, then?"

"No, Mom! Will you stop making stuff up? Lay off the romance novels, will you? Does that even sound like something I'd do?"

"Then talk to me, *Patatina*. What's his name?"

"Lucas. Lucas Walsh. He owns his own software company in San Diego."

"Oh, I get it now." Mom's voice was calm and soothing, knitted together with understanding. "Tomorrow, you part ways."

"Yeah. But that's not all."

"What do you mean?"

I grabbed one of the pillows, hugged it to my chest, and got comfortable with my back against the headboard. "He was willing to come to St. Louis with me."

"Just like that? Pick up his life in California and move? I'd say that boy has it bad for you as well." She laughed.

"He went with me when I met Martino. He knows about Graziana and Dad. He knows that it could happen to me, too. He said he wants to go with me when I get tested."

"Sounds like a pretty awesome guy."

You have no idea. "I love him, Mom."

"I can tell." Even though I couldn't see her, I knew there was a smile on her face. I could feel it. "So what's the problem?"

"I love him so much, Mom, that I had to set him free. He deserved so much more than I could ever give him." I could feel the monster that had clawed its way out of my chest after Pen's funeral stirring again. "I can't put his future at risk. He needs to find someone who can promise him a lifetime of happiness, not pain and suffering."

"I don't know where I went wrong."

"What?" I snapped. Was she even listening to me?

"You chastise me for having romanticized ideals of love, but you're right there with me."

I shook my head. No, I wasn't. I did what had to be done. Love meant sacrifice. In order for Lucas to be happy, I had to take myself out of the equation. I was no longer a variable that could wreck his life. "If I'm sick, Mom, he can't have a normal life with me."

"But what if the test tells you something different?"

Claws scraped against my insides. "It's too late," I choked.

"I'm sorry, *Patatina*. I wish I could wave a magic wand and show you the future. But I'm only your mom, not a fairy godmother. I've always wondered why godmothers were given the wands when a mom is on call night and day. Do you know how many times I've wanted a goddamn wand? Every scraped knee, every nightmare, every time you were scared of a storm, every temper tantrum—"

"I never threw temper tantrums," I interrupted.

"Okay, that one was for Nonna. But my wand would work on her, too."

Laughter, deep in my belly, stilled the angry monster clawing at my throat. "Leave my Nonna alone."

"Yeah, yeah. Whatever." She paused for a minute; then her voice changed from joking to somber. "I know this hurts, Soph, but the pain will fade. Sadly, though, I can tell you it will never disappear. Your first love leaves a deep mark on your soul, and when that person's gone, the ache is permanent. You just grow to accept it as a part of who you are, because they're a part of you. Always."

I held back my tears with every ounce of strength I could muster. "I know why moms don't get magic wands. Because you're real. You have words, and arms, and lips, and a heart. Words to speak the truth in love, arms to hug and protect, lips to kiss away sadness, and a heart with the capacity to love endlessly. Moms don't need magic wands with that kind of arsenal."

"I love you, Soph. You're going to be all right. And when you get off that plane tomorrow, I'll have my arms and lips ready."

"I love you, too, Mom."

Chapter Twenty-Seven

Wheeling my carry-on behind me, I pulled up to the end of the security line. I wouldn't be going anywhere quick. One would think the city was being evacuated with the number of people flying out today. This place was packed.

With a sigh, I dug through my bag, pulling out my travel documents so I'd be ready when I needed them. I was antsy to get home. The more distance I put between Lucas and me, the easier it would be to get back to reality. With all of Mom's talk of fairy godmothers and magic wands last night, I realized my summer in Italy had been the fairy tale. I'd lost sight of what was real and let myself get carried away. I needed to go home; then everything would be fine.

I shuffled forward.

With each step I took, my legs grew heavier. My heartbeat pounded in my ears the closer I got to the front of the line. I might as well have been standing in quicksand, because I was sinking.

Instead of focusing on the excitement of going home—getting

to see Mom and Nonna—my mind replayed the time Lucas and I spent together.

I inched forward despite the bog of memories. *It had only been six weeks. How can six weeks' worth of memories weigh this much?*

Lucas's dimple and smiling eyes ran through my head, as did other things I loved about him: the way he slept with one foot poking out of the covers…the way his not-awake voice broke through the silence late at night…his exuberance to try new things without any fear…his deep, throaty laugh that segued into a cough when he got excited…his gentle, yet firm touch…the way he kissed me, like I was something precious to behold, and with the simple act of our lips touching, the planet would continue to orbit.

I flipped open my messenger bag again and yanked out my phone. Memories were often subject to tricks of the mind. Our brains had a unique way of distorting the truth, especially when our hearts decided to get involved. Maybe it would help shift things into perspective if I looked at a picture of him; I'd see the Lucas in the photograph, not the idealized, flawless creation my brain had conjured in his absence.

I scrolled through some landscapes of Capri, a picture Lucas took of me sticking my tongue out after sampling some terrible gelato, a photogenic dish of lemon shrimp cream pasta Lucas and I shared, and the selfie we'd taken as we passed through Lovers Arch on the way to the Blue Grotto.

My heart sank. Staring at the photo didn't reset my opinion of "the real Lucas." My brain hadn't raised maudlin notions of the time we'd shared.

It was real. Everything.

The warmth of his hand on my cheek, the whisper of his breath at my ear, the brush of his smile against mine, the gravitational pull of his eyes, and the anchoring of my heart with his.

There was a tap on my shoulder and I gasped, looking up from the photo. An older woman started at me, irritation bleeding from her eyes. "Move ahead," she commanded, gesturing to the large gap in front of me.

Move ahead. Yes. That's what I should do. I took a tentative step forward and stopped.

Move ahead? Is that what I want to do?

Behind me, the lady groaned.

I'm having a crisis of conscience here. Didn't she understand that?

What had I done?

"*Spostarsi!*" she shouted. "Move!"

I glanced at her, taking another step forward in line. As I closed the gap, little truths echoed in my head, voices…Mom, Nonna, and Dad's nurse Lydia, all of them intertwined with Lucas's.

I will always love your father, Mom said.

Your dad loves you, Sophia, Nonna affirmed.

He left because he didn't want you to watch him die, Lydia confided.

I love you, Lucas dreamed out loud.

But Lydia's words were the punch to my gut. Dad had walked out on me all those years ago, and I'd just done the exact same thing to Lucas. *For* the same reason.

I was my dad. I finally understood him.

Sometimes, in order to move ahead, you have to go backward.

"Excuse me!" I shouted, whipping my head around. Staring at the annoyed lady behind me, she cocked her head, clearly exasperated. "I have to leave." Gripping the handle of my suitcase, I squeezed past her. "Excuse me. Thank you."

She stepped aside but grumbled something in Italian. If I had to guess, it probably wasn't very nice.

Once I got beyond her, I continued to the back of the line, elbowing my way through a throng of travelers, trying not to roll my suitcase over anyone's feet. "*Scusi*…pardon me…," I apologized.

Clearing the bustle, I took a deep breath and gathered my thoughts. I had no clue what I was doing, but I did know I needed to call Lucas.

With my suitcase in one hand, I started walking while I searched my phone for Lucas's number. I walked with purpose, in a hurry to get somewhere quiet.

I alighted on Lucas's name and tapped it just as I ran full steam ahead into something solid and unmoving.

"*Umph—*" I groaned, my breath rushing out of my lungs from the impact. Large, strong hands gripped my shoulders, absorbing some of the impact.

I looked up and saw two cobalt eyes boring into mine.

His ringtone sounded, a high-pitched staccato.

"Oh, sweet Jesus!" I gasped. "Lucas!" How was he here? How did he find me? I just ran into him, again. How is that possible?

Beep. Beep. Beep.

"Sophia." He let go of me and stepped back, putting a polite distance between us. His tone was cold, detached. Hurt.

Beep. Beep. Beep.

He lifted his hand and glanced at the incoming call. I caught a glimpse of my name at the top of the screen.

Oh, shit! I'd called him. I fumbled with my phone and stabbed my thumb at the bottom, ending the call. "Sorry."

His expression softened slightly. "You were calling me?"

"Uh…yeah." My reply came out sounding more like a question, but I couldn't help it. I'd just been knocked for a loop. I was reeling. Coherent thought was impossible at the moment. "How did you find me?"

"It wasn't that hard, Sophia. I knew when you were flying out; we'd talked about it."

Oh. Right. "Um…"

Now's your chance, Sophia. Spill your guts, tell him how stupid you were, what an idiot you are. Tell him you love him, the voice in my head demanded.

"Why are you here?"

"Why were you calling me?" he countered.

So many reasons ran through my head, but I couldn't verbalize one. "Uh…" I just stuttered.

Lucas clutched my elbow and tugged, leading us out of the middle of a busy thoroughfare. "Let's get out of the way." Dozens of people filtered around us, hurrying in all directions.

"You forgot something," he said, holding up a necklace.

St. Raphael dangled between us.

"Oh my goodness, thank you." My heart swelled. I put my palm at the bottom of the pendant. Lucas dropped the chain, and it pooled in my hand.

"When I woke up the other day, I expected to see you but had a nice view of the night table instead. That was lying on it." He nodded, regarding the contents of my hand. "Then I rolled over, thinking maybe you were on the other side of me, and I found this." He dug in his back pocket and pulled out the note I had left him.

"You know what sucks about this whole situation?" he asked with a humorless chuckle. "I broke my own damn rule. I expected.

I expected to wake up with you next to me and when you weren't there…" He trailed off.

"You were disappointed," I finished.

He blinked a couple times, his eyes a furious blue. "Damn fucking right I was disappointed. Against my better judgment, I let myself hope for something, and once again, all I got was disappointment."

So much hurt bled from his eyes. I wanted to erase the last forty-eight hours, go back and make it so he'd wake up to my face instead of a cold, empty pillow and a piece of paper. Sickness boiled in my belly. He was the last person on earth I ever wanted to hurt. What I had done, I'd done out of love, because I didn't want him to feel any pain.

He rubbed a hand over his stubbled chin. "I don't know what it is about the women in my life, but they all have this deep-seated urge to leave me at some point."

A knife plunged right between my ribs, piercing my heart. My face contorted into a grimace. I was no better than his mom or Julia.

"Lucas—"

"Nuh-uh." He shook his head, glaring at me. "I get to talk now. You had your chance right here." He held my folded note between his thumb and forefinger.

I bit back tears. He had every right to be angry with me. *God, what did I do?*

"This"—he flicked the paper—"is bullshit. Well, some of it isn't, but most of it is." Ripping open the letter, he scanned my words, his eyes flicking from me to the paper, then back again. "Should we start with the bullshit first? 'Love comes with expectation.' 'Love is like a bump that wakes you up,'" he read.

"Here's where you're wrong, sweetheart." He turned the full force

of his blue eyes on me. "Love is unexpected. It slams into you with
the force of a damn bullet train, crashing into you at speeds greater
than two hundred miles per hour. There's risk in love, adventure,
peace, happiness, and the thrill of figuring out the future with the
person you're in love with. Love isn't a momentary bump in the
road, something you get over and forget about. It's a high-speed
journey of shared unknowns. Unexpecteds."

Tears filled my ears.

"When my mom left," he continued, "it hurt, but I didn't have
the energy to go after her, no desire. I had my dad. He was cool. I
carried on. When Julia left, I had the energy but no desire to win
her back. I opted to use that energy to run as far away from her
as possible." He regarded me with steely eyes. "Then you left. I
was fucking pissed. I wanted to write you off as an inconsequential one-night stand, forget your name, and pick up where I'd left
off."

My heart beat like a jackhammer, ripping me open violently and
all at once. His words, salt water on my wounds.

"Believe me, I tried. For two days, I stared at your necklace and
tried to talk myself into hating you. I lost count of how many times
I threw the fucking thing in the trash."

I looked down at St. Raphael in my hand. A tear plopped onto
the pendant.

"But dammit, every time I said I was going to leave it in there, I
was already walking over to pull it out. That's how I knew this was
different than all the other times. I kept going back to the trash, to
salvage what was there. Time after time after time. No matter how
tired I was, how little energy I had, I bent down, picked it up, and
brushed it off. Always coming back."

He put his fingers on my chin, gently forcing me to look at him. I didn't want to. I didn't want to see the pain in his eyes…the pain I'd caused.

"Sophia," he said calmly. If this had been a fairy tale, I'd say he'd said my name lovingly. "Look at me, please."

I shook my head but looked anyway. He shoved his phone into the back pocket of his jeans and wrapped his hands around mine, running his thumb over the necklace, wiping away my fallen tear. "I couldn't throw something this beautiful away." He squeezed my hands. "Two nights with no sleep, I figured out what makes you different from my mom and Julia."

"What?"

"They left for selfish reasons. They had to do what they felt was right for them, I guess. But you…you ran because you thought I'd be better off without you, that you weren't good enough for me—which by the way, is more bullshit. What you did was selfless. That's what made you different from them."

"Lucas," I choked, "I'm sorry."

"Shh…" He lifted his hand to my cheek. "Want to hear the parts that aren't bullshit?"

I smiled. "Yeah."

"One line you wrote really got to me. You said, 'Maybe one day we'll bump into each other again and look back on the Italian adventure we shared.' For starters, you have a bad habit of running into me, and it's a habit I hope you never break." His lips broke into a crooked smile. "One day's here, baby, but I'm not looking back. I'm looking forward, to a future with you."

I nodded, a dopy grin on my face. "When I ran into you, I'd just gotten out of the security line to call you. I had to tell you how stupid I was. That I was wrong. I couldn't leave without you knowing how much I love you."

The blue of his eyes sparkled. "You're my unexpected. And there will never be any disappointment in that." He kissed me softly, whispering against my lips, "I love you, Sophia."

I kissed him back, with everything I had to give. No matter what the future promised, I knew I didn't want to face it alone. And with Lucas by my side, I knew I wouldn't have to.

"Silver," he said, pulling away.

"What?"

"Another color. The necklace."

Lucas peeled my fingers back, pulling it free. "May I?" He unhooked the clasp, and I lifted my hair. Looping his hands behind my neck, he fastened the necklace.

He admired the pendant. "I get more than ten million colors, Soph. I get you."

Epilogue

Once again, I was seated in Ms. Turner's homey office. When I began the testing process four months ago, right after I'd gotten back from Italy, I thought it would be a simple blood test and I'd find out the results. That was not the case.

Ms. Turner, my father's genetic counselor (and now mine), had seen me on two other occasions, preparing me for the test and today, results day.

For the last four months, I'd been a nervous wreck. I knew why my dad had given me that trip to Italy. It was the calm before the storm. A chance to forget about life for a while and just live. Dad knew that once I got home, uncertainty would gnaw away at my sanity and the only way to satiate its hunger would be to get tested.

I liked Ms. Turner's office. It was devoid of the obligatory human anatomy posters and cheap dollar-store prints of flowers and lighthouses that usually lined the walls of a doctor's office. Instead, she filled her space with personal photos. Trips to third world countries, her arms wrapped around smiling children. I'd like to do that one day, travel to an underprivileged nation and offer free medical care. Maybe Doctors Without Borders?

But before I started making travel plans, I needed to find out if I was going to have the opportunity to pursue a career in medicine in the first place.

The nervous beast ate at my insides, feasting on the last morsels of my bravery. Lucas held my hand tightly, grounding me, keeping my thoughts in the light and away from the shadows.

The window shades were open, allowing sunlight to filter through. Had Ms. Turner done that on purpose? With the room drenched in light, buttery sunshine, would her news come across less devastating?

"Sophia!" Ms. Turner said cheerily, sweeping into her office. Was her attitude a sign? Was she so pleased with the results she couldn't contain her joy? Or was she overcompensating, dipping the terrible news into the buttery sunshine to make it more palatable. I knew a spoonful of sugar helped the medicine go down, but I didn't think the same applied to finding out if I'd won or lost the genetic lottery.

"Thanks for coming in." She shut the door behind her.

Turning around, she held her hand out for me to shake. "Yes. Absolutely." I reluctantly let go of Lucas's hand to return the pleasantry.

I'd wanted to have the test done before I started med school but hadn't known the process was so detailed. I had two preliminary meetings with Ms. Turner, which Mom and Nonna accompanied me to because Lucas was in California. He'd promised to be here for the test (which he had been) and now, for the results. He'd wanted to be by my side for everything, but I understood he had a life in California. We were grown adults, and we were committed to making our long-distance relationship work. Which meant making sacrifices and compromises. I loved him, so that was the easy part.

Sitting here in this room was the hard part. Finding out if all my hopes and dreams ended today.

"Hi, Lucas," she said, extending her hand to him. "Nice to see you again."

Lucas stood, putting his palm to hers. "Likewise, Ms. Turner."

"How long are you in town?"

Why did she ask him that? What does it mean? Will I need him to stay longer?

Dr. Turner rounded her desk and took a seat. She shuffled some paperwork off to the side, save one manila folder. "How are you, Sophia?" she asked, clasping her hands on top the file.

"I've been better." I grabbed for Lucas's hand again.

"Yeah, this part is never easy," she said, her smile sinking a little. "Well, let me tell you where we go from here. We've looked at your DNA—your chromosomal makeup—from the blood sample you provided. With HD, we specifically concentrate on what is called a 'CAG repeat' to confirm a diagnosis."

We'd been over this before, and I'd done so much homework on HD these last four months, I could write my graduate thesis on the CAG repeat. "Less than twenty-seven repeats is ideal." I nodded.

Ms. Turner bit the corner of her thin smile. "Yes, anything below twenty-seven is considered a negative result." She withdrew a white 8.5 x 11-inch sheet of paper from my folder. Passing it across the desk, she flipped it around so I could read it.

I latched on to the necklace my grandfather had given me, dragging it side to side over the chain. "Wait!" I hollered, louder than I'd meant.

"Soph?" Lucas said, squeezing my hand. "What's wrong?"

Panic rose in my chest, blooming like a field overrun with dande-lions. My throat pinched closed. "I…I just…," I stuttered.

Ms. Turner got up from her cushy chair and went to the water dispenser. She stuck a cone-shaped paper cup under the spigot and lifted the lever. Water flowed from the spout and bubbles rumbled in the deep blue tank.

She handed me the damp cup.

I took a sip. It was cold and smooth running down the back of my throat. Lucas rubbed circles on my back.

"I think I've changed my mind."

"Baby, are you sure?" Lucas asked.

No, I wasn't sure. I wanted so much…to know the answer…but only if the answer was the one I wanted to hear. But then again, I wanted to know if the result wasn't favorable, too…but then…I didn't want to know. It was a vicious, eye-clawing battle in my soul.

"Okay," Ms. Turner said, coming to stand in front of me. "Listen, Sophia." She sat on the edge of her pretty polished desk. "Until you're certain, without a shadow of a doubt, that you want to know what's on that paper, I will seal it up."

"Seal it up?"

"No one's forcing this decision on you. It's one you have to make on your own. If you're not ready, then we wait until you are." She grabbed the paper from her desk and walked around to the other side. Pulling open a drawer, she took out a white envelope. Meticu-lously, she folded the paper and slipped it inside, licked the flap, and pressed it closed.

She held it out.

"When you're ready, you can open this. For many people, being at home, surrounded by loved ones, seems to do the trick. Others prefer to be alone, finding comfort in solitude. No matter what you choose, though, if you open it, call me. I want to follow up with you, regardless of the outcome. I don't care if you open it fifteen years from now. I will still be expecting a phone call, Sophia." She smiled warmly; it matched the glow of the room.

I couldn't bring myself to touch the envelope. When I didn't take it, Lucas did for me, lifting it from Ms. Turner's fingers.

"Take care of her, Lucas," she said, coming back to the side of the desk where we stood.

Lucas got up from the chair and pulled me up with him. "I plan to."

"Sophia, call me."

"I will."

The three of us walked to the door, my future sealed away in an unassuming white envelope.

* * *

We'd left Ms. Turner's office hours ago. It was late, but I still had no desire to go home. I was, however, in need of gelato, despite the freezing temperature outside. Sadness was best drowned in ice cream, no matter the season. I'd called Mom and told her Lucas and I were headed to the shop so she wouldn't worry. I knew she was worried about me; I'd heard the anxiety in her voice. But she understood and respected my decisions, giving me the time and space I needed to figure things out. Again, another reason why my mom didn't need a magic wand; she knew me, no magic required.

Lucas and I spent the day visiting tourist destinations around the city, anything to serve as a distraction from the contents of that damn envelope—really, the same thing I'd done in Italy. When he'd come into town for my blood test, it had been a short visit—just two days. We'd spent most of it in his hotel room. We hadn't seen each other in over a month and didn't waste any time getting reacquainted.

This trip was different. I was different. A sad mixture of Sophia, Atlas, Pandora, and Chaos. Controlled, burdened, addled, and unnerved.

Even though I hadn't opened the envelope, somehow I still knew what the paper inside would say. When I'd talked to my dad six months ago, I knew. In my mind, I was still Sophia, but my body had committed an act of treason, and the sentence was death.

I glanced at Lucas in the driver's seat. He'd been quiet most of the day. With my thoughts trapped in darkness, I never once thought about what he was feeling. He was amazing and selfless, and I still hadn't figured out what I'd done to deserve him.

"I'm sorry, Lucas."

He turned his head. "For what?" His brows pulled together.

I shrugged. "For everything? For being self-absorbed and whiny, inconsiderate, mopey, indecisive…" I paused, trying to think of more adjectives to describe my current attitude. Lucas took my silence as the perfect opportunity to interject.

He lifted his hand from the steering wheel and held it up. "Whoa, stop right there, Linebacker. First of all, I don't like the way you're talking about my girlfriend." He shot me a sidelong glance. "Second, you have every right to be all of those things. I'm not going to minimize what you're going through. It's scary shit, and if you want to be self-absorbed, mopey, and inconsiderate, then go ahead, sweetheart. I'll be right here." He grabbed my hand. "No matter how whiny you get, I still won't let go."

"Make the next left turn." I pointed, changing the subject.

He turned the car into the narrow alley that ran behind the shop. "It's right there, on the left, the green and white awning."

Lucas came to a stop and we got out. Rounding the car, I untangled my keys from the bottom of my purse, sending the envelope drifting to the ground. Quickly, Lucas bent to retrieve it from the dirty, icy slush.

With the envelope in his fingers, he stood back up, holding his arms out wide. "Will you get over here and keep me warm? How you people live like this, I'll never know."

I tried hard to suppress a smile, but I couldn't. My golden California guy didn't fit in with the dreary grayness of winter. "Not a fan of snow?" I sidled up next to him.

"Give me sand, surf, and sun any day. You can keep this shit." Salt crunched beneath our feet.

I unlocked the door and went inside, Lucas right behind me. I flipped on a few light switches in the back, knowing it would be enough to penetrate the darkness at the front of the shop.

Shrugging my coat off, I tossed it onto a chair along with my purse. Lucas laid his on top of mine, along with the envelope. "So this is the famous Andrea's Gelateria." He wound through the tables, brushing his hand across their tops.

"I don't know about famous, but it's pretty popular among the locals." I went behind the counter, pulled on my apron, and dug out some bowls. "What will you have, sir?"

For the first time today, I relaxed. I'd thought gallivanting all over the city would keep my mind off the envelope, but it hadn't. It weighed heavy in my purse…at the Arch…while we ate Gus's pretzels…walking through the botanical garden…it was all I'd thought about. But this—the simple act of slipping on my apron, holding a gelato spatula in my hand—settled me. Finding comfort in the little things. My muscles unclenched and I could breathe. *This* was me, not the results of some blood test.

Lucas walked up to the freezer. "Hmm…" He considered the choices. Tapping a finger on the glass, he said, "Pumpkin salted caramel swirl."

"A fine choice." I smiled. Reaching into the freezer, I scooped the gelato from the serving dish and passed it over the counter.

He took the dish, lifting the spoon from the center. "Thank you, ma'am," he mumbled, licking the spoon. I shivered. I couldn't help it. I knew what that tongue was capable of.

"Holy shit," he groaned, "this is amazing."

Chuckling, I scooped some mint chocolate chip into my dish.

"I bet all those other flavors cry when you're around."

I put the scoop down and licked my fingers before joining him on the other side of the counter. Hoisting myself up, I sat in front of the cash register. "Why would they cry?"

"From neglect. You give them no love. It's always mint chocolate chip with you." He turned his spoon upside down and shoved another bite into his mouth.

I pulled my spoon from my mouth with a pop. "It is the best."

"Uh-uh, I disagree." He took another bite. "Pumpkin caramel is the best."

I shook my head. "Nope. Mint chocolate will always reign supreme in the land of Princess Potato. I'm an expert. I know these things."

He cocked his head. "Let me taste."

I dug my spoon into my dish, offering him a heaping bite.

"Huh-uh." Shaking his head, he leaned in and put his mouth to mine, opening my lips with his tongue.

He tasted like autumn. The earthy sweet fusion of pumpkins and caramel flooded my senses. His warm mouth coupled with his ice-cream-cooled tongue reminded me of a glorious fall breeze, of hoodies, and campfires, and home.

I parted my legs so he could settle between them. Lucas crooked an arm around my waist and slid me forward on the counter, pressing our bodies together.

Pumpkin salted caramel was my new favorite.

His lips were firm yet soft as they worked over mine. He kissed me deeper, holding me close as he pressed his hand against the curve of my backside. With a slow lick across the seam of my lips, he pulled away, but only a little. "Mint chocolate, Your Highness," he breathed heavily, "reigns supreme."

Kiss-drunk, I stared into his blue eyes. "I disagree."

Looking back at me with an intensity I'd never seen before, he whispered, "You're it for me, Sophia." He took my gelato in his hand and reached behind me, setting both our dishes on the counter; then he cradled my head between his hands. "No matter what's in that envelope over there? Whether we get five years, ten years, or a hundred years, there will never be another person I want to spend this life with. And I guarantee that whatever time we do get, it won't be enough, but it will have been everything."

I sucked in a breath, my heart clenching. He ran his thumbs over my cheeks.

"So many people have bucket lists, things they want to accomplish before they die. Mine isn't a list; it's one thing…to hold your hand." He dropped his hands to my lap, lacing our fingers. "Kiss your mouth," he continued, leaning close, our lips brushing together. "Touch your skin," he said, unclasping his left hand from mine to run it under my sweater. His right trailed through my hair. "To look into your charcoal eyes and wonder what you're thinking." He stared.

"That's more than one thing," I muttered.

With an imperceptible shake of his head, he held up one finger. "One. They're all pieces of the same thing…all the colors that make up the same rainbow…I want to love you."

"I want that, too. More than anything. But I'm scared, Lucas. The rest of my life hinges on what's inside that envelope. I'm not ready to lose pieces of myself." Tears streamed down my face. "I'm not ready to die." I choked on the last word.

He backtracked a few steps and snatched the envelope off his coat. "I'm dying, Sophia," he said matter-of-factly, standing between my legs again. "You're dying, my dad's dying, your mom, Dean, anyone with a pulse. The only difference between you and the rest of us? You get a life meter. You get to know when yours will start to run out." He held up the envelope. "If your number is higher than twenty-seven, what are you going to do with the time you have left?"

"I don't know!" I shouted. "What can I do?"

He pulled at my chin, forcing me to look at him. "Live. Just like the rest of us."

I yanked the envelope from his fingers. "And you're really signing on for this? All the heartache and devastation? You saw the ache in Martino's eyes when he looked at pictures of Grazi, the longing in his voice when he spoke of her. That will be you. Is this what you want?" I waved my hands up and down, gesturing to my body.

"I wasted six years of my life with the wrong person. I'll be damned if I spend the rest of my life without the right one. I want all of you, Sophia. I want to love you. I'm going to love, no matter what."

I put my finger under the seal and tore through the envelope, like ripping off a Band-Aid. My fingers shook as I pulled out the test results. "Ms. Turner was right about one thing," I said. "This is how I want to find out. In the shadowed light of a comfortable place, in your arms."

Thoughts of Penley raced through my head. If she'd had the chance to know, would she have looked? Would she have given up soccer, something she loved, in order to save her life? Probably not. Penley was soccer. She adored it. It gave her life meaning and purpose.

Despite what number was on my paper, could I give Lucas up?

Absolutely-freaking-not. He helped me remember what it meant to be passionate and alive. He was the sunshine to my rainy day, and together we were the rainbow. We'd weather the shit storm together.

He ran his hands up and down my arms, like he always did.

I held my breath. This was the turning point. There was no going back, no unknowing.

All I have to do is open it. One look and I'll know for sure….

Pulling the flaps apart, I stared at the words. So. Many. Words. Numbers. I couldn't focus on any in particular but scanned for one phrase, anything that would tell me where my CAG expansion levels fell.

"What is it, Soph?" Lucas asked, his voice a low, quiet rumble, like distant thunder.

My eyes locked on his. Tears cascaded down my face. "Twenty."

Lucas exhaled. "Twenty?"

Crying, my lips broke into a wide smile, and I collapsed against him. "It's twenty."

"That's less than twenty-seven. Oh my God, Soph!" Lucas cried, throwing his arms around me.

"I've spent half the year thinking I had one foot in the grave." My shoulders shook. "I was convinced I had it." I hiccupped, lifting my head from his shoulder. "I thought you were going to have to watch me die," I sobbed.

"Baby," he whispered in my ear. "I've done nothing but watch you live."

I hugged him to me, refusing to let go. My heartbeat thumped in my chest…

Bump. Bump. Bump.

Bump. Bump. Bump.

It didn't matter what that paper said…when I remembered how to love, I truly started to live.

See the next page for an excerpt from Marie Meyer's *Across the Distance*!

Chapter One

The tape screeched when I pulled it over the top of another box. I was down to the last one; all I had left to pack were the contents of my dresser, but that was going to have to wait. Outside, I heard my best friend, Griffin, pull into the driveway. Before he shut off the ignition, he revved the throttle of his Triumph a few times for my sister's sake. Jennifer hated his noisy motorcycle.

Griffin's effort to piss Jennifer off made me smile. I stood up and walked to the door. Heading downstairs, I slammed the bedroom door a little too hard and the glass figurine cabinet at the end of the hall shook. I froze and watched as an angel statuette teetered back and forth on its pedestal. *Shit. Please, don't break.*

"Jillian? What are you doing?" Jennifer yelled from the kitchen. "You better not break anything!"

As soon as the angel righted itself, I sighed in relief. But a small part of me wished it had broken. It would have felt good to break something that was special to her. Lord knew she'd done her best to break me. I shook off that depressing thought and raced down the steps to see Griffin.

When I opened the front door, he was walking up the sidewalk with two little boys attached to each of his legs: my twin nephews and Griffin's kindergarten fan club presidents, Michael and Mitchell.

Every time I saw Griffin interact with the boys, I couldn't help but smile. The boys adored him.

I watched as they continued their slow migration toward the porch. Michael's and Mitchell's messy, white-blond curls bounced wildly with each step, as did Griffin's coal black waves, falling across his forehead. He stood in stark contrast to the little boys dangling at his feet. Their tiny bodies seemed to shrink next to Griffin's six-foot-four muscled frame.

"I see that your adoring fans have found you," I laughed, watching Griffin walk like a giant, stomping as hard as he could, the twins giggling hysterically and hanging on for dear life.

"Hey, Jillibean, you lose your helpers?" he asked, unfazed by the ambush.

"Yeah, right," I said, walking out front to join him. I wrapped my arms around his neck and squeezed. I took a deep breath, filling my lungs with the familiar scents of leather and wind. A combination that would always be uniquely *him*. "I'm so glad you're here," I sighed, relaxing into his embrace. I felt safe, like nothing could hurt me when I was in his arms.

Griffin's arms circled my waist. "That bad, huh?"

I slackened my grip and stepped back, giving him and the squirming boys at his feet more room. "My sister's been especially vile today."

"When isn't she?" Griffin replied.

"Giddy up, Giff-in," Mitchell wailed, bouncing up and down.

"You about ready?" Griffin asked me, trying to remain upright while the boys pulled and tugged his legs in opposite directions.

"Not really. I've got one more box to pack and a bunch to load into my car. They're up in my room."

"Hear that, boys? Aunt Jillian needs help loading her boxes. Are you men ready to help?" he asked.

"Yeah!" they shouted in unison.

"Hang on tight!" Griffin yelled, and started running the rest of the way up the sidewalk and onto the porch. "All right, guys, this is where the ride ends. Time to get to work." Griffin shook Michael off his left leg before he started shaking Mitchell off his right. The boys rolled around on the porch and Griffin playfully stepped on their bellies with his ginormous boots. The boys were laughing so hard I wouldn't have been surprised to see their faces turning blue from oxygen deprivation.

Following them to the porch, I shook my head and smiled. Griffin held his hand out and I laced my fingers through his, thankful he was here.

"I'll get the trailer hitched up to your car, and the stuff you have ready, I'll put in the backseat. You finish up that last box; we've got a long trip ahead of us." Griffin leaned in close and whispered the last part in my ear. "Plus, it'll be nice to say adios to Queen Bitch," he said, referring to my sister.

"Sounds like a plan." I winked. "Come on, boys." I held the door open and waved them inside. "If you're outside without a grown-up, your mom will kill me." They both shot up from the porch and ran inside.

"Giff-in," Michael said, coming to a stop in the doorway. "Can we still help?"

Griffin tousled his hair. "You bet, little man. Let's go find those boxes." He winked back at me and the three of them ran up the stairs.

I trailed behind the boys, knowing that I couldn't put off packing that "last box" any longer. When I got to my room, Griffin held a box in his hands, but it was low enough so that the boys thought they were helping to bear some of its weight. "Hey, slacker," I said to Griffin, bumping his shoulder with my fist. "You letting a couple of five-year-olds show you up?"

"These are not normal five-year-olds," Griffin said in a deep commercial-announcer voice. "These boys are the Amazing Barrett Brothers, able to lift boxes equal to their own body weight with the help of the Amazing Griffin."

I rolled my eyes at his ridiculousness and smiled. "You better watch it there, Amazing Griffin, or I'll have to butter the doorway to get your ego to fit through."

Still speaking in a cheesy commercial voice, Griffin continued. "As swift as lightning, we will transport this box to the vehicle waiting downstairs. Do not fear, kind lady, the Amazing Barrett Brothers and the Amazing Griffin are here to help."

"Oh, Lord. I'm in trouble," I mumbled. And as swift as lightning (but really not), Griffin shuffled the boys out of the room and down the stairs.

I grabbed my last empty box and walked across the room to my dresser. I pulled open a drawer and removed a folded stack of yoga pants, tees, and dozens of clothing projects I'd made over the years. Shuffling on my knees from one drawer to the next, I emptied each of them until I came to the drawer I'd been dreading. The one on the top right-hand side.

The contents of this drawer had remained buried in darkness for almost five years. I was scared to open it, to shed light on the objects that reminded me of my past. I stared at the unassuming rectangular compartment, knowing what I had to do. I said a silent prayer for courage and pulled open the drawer.

Inside, the 5 x 7 picture frame still lay upside down on top of several other snapshots. I reached for the stack. The second my fingers touched the dusty frame, I winced, as if expecting it to burst into flames and reduce me to a heap of ashes. Biting my lip, I grabbed the frame and forced myself to look.

There we were. Mom, Dad, and a miniature version of me. Tears burned my eyes. My lungs clenched in my chest and I forced myself to breathe as I threw the frame into the box with my yoga pants. I pulled out the rest of the photos and tossed them in before they had a chance to stab me through the heart as well.

Downstairs, I could hear the boys coming back inside and then footsteps on the stairs. Quickly, I folded the flaps of the box and pulled the packing tape off the dresser. With another screech, I sealed away all the bad memories of my childhood.

"Well, my help dumped me," Griffin said, coming back into my room alone. "Apparently, I'm not as cool as a toy car."

Before he could see my tears, I wiped my wet eyes with the back of my hand, sniffled, and plastered on a brave smile, then turned around. "There. Done," I proclaimed, standing up and kicking the box over to where the others sat.

"You okay?" Griffin asked, knowing me all too well.

"Yeah." I dusted my hands off on my jean shorts. "Let's get this show on the road." I bent down to grab a box, standing back up with a huge smile on my face. "I'm ready to get to college."

* * *

Griffin took the last box from my hand and shoved it into the backseat of my car. "I'll get my bike on the trailer, and then we'll be ready to hit the road." He wiped his upper arm across his sweaty forehead.

I looked into his dark eyes and smiled. "Thanks," I sighed.

"For what?" With a toss of his head, he pushed a few errant curls out of his eyes.

"For putting up with me." He could have easily gotten a plane ticket home, but he knew how much I hated airplanes. The thought of him getting on a plane made me physically ill.

He swung his arm around my neck, squeezing me with his strong arm. "Put up with you? I'd like to see you try to get rid of me."

With my head trapped in his viselike grip and my face pressed to his chest, I couldn't escape his intoxicating scent. Even though it was too hot for his beloved leather riding jacket, the faint smell still clung to him. That, coupled with the heady musk clinging to his sweat-dampened T-shirt, made my head swim with thoughts that were well beyond the realm of friendship.

I needed to refocus my thoughts, and I couldn't do that pressed up against him. I shivered and pulled away. Taking a step back, I cleared my throat. "I'm going to tell Jennifer we're leaving." I thumbed toward the house.

He scrutinized my face for a minute, then smirked. "Enjoy that. You've earned it."

I turned on my heel and let out a deep breath, trying desperately to rein in my inappropriate fantasies.

Months ago, our easygoing friendship had morphed into an awkward dance of fleeting glances, lingering touches, and an unspeakable amount of tension. I thought he'd felt it, too. The night of my high school graduation party, I went out on a limb and kissed him. When our lips met, every nerve ending in my body fired at once. Embers of lust burned deep inside me. I'd never felt anything like that before. The thought of being intimate with someone made me want to run to the nearest convent. But not with Griffin. When our bodies connected, I felt whole and alive in a way I'd never felt before.

Then he'd done what I'd least expected…he'd pushed me away. I'd searched his face for an explanation. He, more than anyone, knew what it had taken for me to put myself out there, and he'd pushed me away. Touting some bullshit about our timing being all wrong, that a long-distance relationship wouldn't work, he insisted that I was nothing more than his friend. His rejection hurt worse than any of the cuts I'd inflicted upon myself in past years. But he was my best friend; I needed him far too much to have our relationship end badly and lose him forever. Regardless of his excuses, in retrospect, I was glad I wouldn't fall victim to his usual love-'em-and-leave-'em pattern. Griffin was never with one girl for more than a couple of months; then he was on to the next. That would have killed me. So I picked up what was left of my pride, buried my feelings, and vowed not to blur the lines of our friendship again.

Climbing the steps to the porch, I looked back at him before going into the house. Griffin had gone to work wheeling his bike onto the trailer. His biceps strained beneath the plain white tee he wore. I bit my bottom lip and cursed. "Damn it, Jillian. Stop torturing yourself." Groaning, I reached for the doorknob.

"Hey, Jennifer, we're leaving," I said, grabbing my car keys from the island in the middle of the kitchen. She sat at the kitchen table poring over cookbooks that helped her sneak vegetables into the twins' meals. Poor boys, they didn't stand a chance. Jennifer fought dirty…she always had.

"It's about time." She turned the page of her cookbook, not even bothering to lift her eyes from the page.

"What? No good-bye? This is it, the day you've been waiting for since I moved in. I thought you'd be at the door cheering."

Usually I was more reserved with my comments, but today I felt brave. Maybe moving to Rhode Island and going to design school gave me the extra backbone I'd lacked for the last twelve years. Or maybe it was just the fact that I didn't have to face her any longer. By the look on Jennifer's face, my mouthy comments surprised her as well. She stood up from the table, tucked a piece of her shoulder-length blond hair behind her ear, and took a small step in my direction. Her mannerisms and the way she carried herself sparked a memory of our mother. As Jennifer got older, that happened more often, and a pang of sadness clenched my heart. Where I'd gotten Dad's lighter hair and pale complexion, Jennifer had Mom's coloring: dark blond hair, olive skin. But neither of us had got Mom's gorgeous blue eyes. The twins ended up with those.

Beyond the couple of features Jennifer shared with Mom, though, their similarities ended. When Mom smiled, it was kind and inviting. Jennifer never smiled. She was rigid, harsh, and distant. Nothing like Mom.

Jennifer curled her spray-tanned arms around my back. I braced for the impact. Jennifer wasn't affectionate, especially with me, so I knew something hurtful was in store. I held perfectly still as she drew me close to her chest. The sweet, fruity scent of sweet pea blossoms—Jennifer's favorite perfume—invaded my senses. For such a light, cheery fragrance, it always managed to weigh heavy, giving me a headache.

Jennifer pressed her lips to my ear and whispered, "Such a shame Mom and Dad aren't here to see you off. I'm sure *they* would have told you good-bye." She slid her hands to my shoulders and placed a small kiss on my cheek.

And there it was. The dagger through my heart. Mom and Dad. She knew they were my kryptonite. For the second time in less than an hour, I felt acidic drops of guilt leaking from my heart and circulating through my body. But what burned more than the guilt was the fact that she was right. It *was* a shame they weren't here. And I had no one to blame but myself.

I held my breath while my eyes welled up with tears. *Not today, Jillian. You will not cry.* I refused to give her the satisfaction. I stood up taller, giving myself a good two inches on her, and swallowed the lump forming in my throat. She was not going to ruin this day. The day I'd worked so hard to achieve.

"Ready to go?" Griffin said, coming around the corner. "The boys are waiting by the door to say good-bye."

Jennifer stepped away from me and gave Griffin a disgusted once-over. "And yet another reason why I'm glad Jillian decided to go away to school," she said. "At least I get a respite from the white trash walking through my front door." Piercing me with an icy stare, she continued. "With the endless parade of women he flaunts in front of you, the tattoos, the music"—she scowled—"I've never understood the hold he has on you, Jillian." She stifled a laugh. "Pathetic, if you ask me."

Griffin took a step in her direction. "Excuse me?" he growled, his expression darkening. I knew he wouldn't hurt her, but he was damn good at intimidating her. He wasn't the little boy who lived next door anymore. He'd grown up. With his deep voice and considerable size, he towered over her, the muscles in his arms flexing.

She shuffled backward. "Just go." With a dismissive flick of her wrist, she sat back down at the table.

"Yeah, that's what I thought, all bark and no bite." Griffin pulled on my arm. "Come on, Bean. You don't have to put up with her shit anymore."

I glanced at Jennifer; she'd already gone back to her broccoli-laced brownie recipe. Griffin was right; I wouldn't have to put up with her shit while I was away. But he was wrong about her bite. When he wasn't around to back her down, she relished the chance to sink her teeth into me. It hurt like hell when she latched on and wouldn't let go.

We walked down the hallway. Michael and Mitchell were waiting by the door. "I need a big hugs, boys," I said, bending down and opening my arms wide. "This hug has to last me until December, so make it a good one." Both of them stepped into my embrace and I held on to them tightly. "You two be good for your mommy and daddy," I said.

"We will," they replied.

I let go and they smiled. "I love you both."

"Love you, Aunt Jillian," they said.

"Now, go find your mom. She's in the kitchen." Knowing the boys' penchant for sneaking out of the house, I wanted to be sure their mother had them corralled before Griffin and I left.

I stood back up and looked into Griffin's dark eyes. "I'm ready." I tossed him the keys.

"I'm the chauffeur, huh?" Griffin smirked, pulling his eyebrow up. He opened the door for me and I stepped out onto the porch.

"You get the first nine hours; I'll take the back side." This time he gave me a full smile. *What would I do without him?* On the porch, I froze. It finally hit me. What *would* I do without him? Sure, I wanted out of Jennifer's house, but at what expense? Couldn't I just go to the junior college like Griff and get my own apartment? Why had I made the decision to go to school eleven hundred miles away? How could I leave him—my best friend?

The lump in my throat came back but I forced the words out anyway. "Griff…" I sounded like a damn croaking frog.

Griffin wrapped his arms around me. "Yeah?"

"Why am I doing this?"

"What do you mean? This is all you've talked about since you got the scholarship."

"I know." I sniffled. "But I don't know if I can do this. We'll be so far apart."

"Uh-uh. Stop that right now. I am not about to let you throw away the opportunity of a lifetime just because we won't see each other as often. You're too talented for Glen Carbon, Illinois, and you know it. Now go, get your ass in the car." With his hand, he popped me on the backside, just to get his point across.

I jumped, not expecting his hand on my ass. My heart skipped and my cheeks flushed. "Hey!" I swatted his hand away.

"Get in the car, Jillian."

Damn, I already miss him.

Acknowledgments

One would think this part would get easier to write with each new book, but that is not the case. Writing hundreds of pages, breathing life into characters, none of that would be possible without the people named here. I am humbled and so very thankful for all their love, guidance, and support.

My agent, Louise Fury: I've had so many memorable moments in the last two years, and meeting you at RWA15 was yet another! The energy and devotion you give to your clients is awe-inspiring. Your advice, attention to detail, and enthusiasm make me a better storyteller, and for that I am grateful. I am blessed to have you in my corner. Thank you for guiding me on this journey!

Lady Lioness: RWA15! It was so wonderful to finally have met you! I'm so thankful to have you and Louise to edit and mold my writing into something presentable. Now, three years after Pitch Wars (Wow! Has it really been that long? Crazy!), I still love opening your edit letters!!

My editor, Megha Parekh, of Grand Central Publishing: The summer of 2015 contained so much awesome, and meeting you at RWA15 only made it that much more awesome! From having lunch together to the Forever Romance party, the whole experience was surreal and wonderful! Thank you for your patience and insightful edits with *The Turning Point*. I'd also like to thank Dana Hamilton, whose edits and enthusiasm for my work helped make *The Turning Point* what it is today (I also loved meeting you at RWA as well)! Working with everyone—Megha, Dana, and the Forever Yours team—this last year has been an amazing journey and a dream come true!

To the Grand Central Publishing/Forever Yours Production Team: my publicist, Fareeda Bullert, thank you for helping readers encounter *The Turning Point* (and AtD & CGB)! From blog tours to teasers, thank you for everything! Also, it was so lovely meeting you at RWA15! My cover designer, Brian Lemus, thank you for giving TTP such a beautiful cover! You captured Sophia and Lucas perfectly! And to everyone else at GCP/Forever Yours, thank you for helping transform *The Turning Point* into a book and getting my words into the hands of readers!

A special thank you to Rachel Van Dyken, for graciously reading *The Turning Point* and writing a lovely blurb. Thank you so much, Rachel!

My Darlings: Guess what? I love you! There are not enough thank-yous to shower upon you, but I do pay in hugs and kisses... and Mini Reese's Peanut Butter Cups! The two of you are the lights of my life and the reason I work so hard.

Tex, thanks for escorting me to the big city! There isn't a person in the world I would rather see the world with. Here's to many more vacations together (and not waiting fifteen years in between them). I've got a good one mapped out here (hint, hint)!

My family: Thank you for all your love and support, for watching the kids while I write or head to New York City! Without your help and encouragement, I wouldn't be where I am today. Love you all!

To my Internet family—NAC! You are all the best, the most talented people I know! I love our group!! Once again, I'm going to reflect on my time at RWA15, because meeting so many of you was a dream come true (and I cannot wait to meet those of you I haven't yet…RWA16?)! Thank you for everything, all the tweets, posts, and our chats about things that are pink! ;) You all make me smile and keep me sane! And I cannot forget my Pitch Wars pal, Annie Rains! I love getting your e-mails and chatting with you! Thank you for all your help with everything!

A big thank you to Ed Sheeran for writing songs that fueled my imagination with countless scenes. Your music is my muse.

My local Starbucks and barista friends who kept me well caffeinated so I could subsist on four hours of sleep and continue to write coherent scenes. I'm cheers-ing you with my usual—green tea in one hand and a flat white in the other.

My readers, the greatest part of being an author is having the opportunity to share my stories with you. I'm humbled by your love and support. Thank you for taking the time to read my stories, embrace my characters, and write such lovely reviews. I am so appreciative! Thank you from the bottom of my heart!

All praise and thanks to my Savior, Jesus Christ.

About the Author

Marie Meyer was a language arts teacher for fourteen years. She spends her days in the classroom and her nights writing heartfelt new adult romances that will leave readers clamoring for more. She is a member of RWA and the St. Louis Writers Guild. Marie's short fiction won honorable mentions from the St. Louis Writers Guild in 2010 and 2011. She is a proud mommy and enjoys helping her oldest daughter train for the Special Olympics, making up silly stories with her youngest daughter, and bingeing on weeks of DVR'd television shows with her husband. Marie is represented by Louise Fury.

Learn more at:

MarieMeyerBooks.com

Twitter, @MarieMwrites

Facebook.com/MarieMeyerBooks

Instagram.com/mariemwrites

Subscribe to Marie Meyer's newsletter: http://bit.ly/1hoCwlC